July in September

by Felicia Mabuza Nixon

RoseDog Books
PITTSBURGH, PENNSYLVANIA 15238

RoseDog Books
585 Alpha Drive, Suite 103
Pittsburgh, PA 15238
Visit our website at *www.rosedogbookstore.com*

ISBN: 978-1-64957-907-2
eISBN: 978-1-64957-928-7

July in September

Chapter One

"Name?"

"Dorian."

"Last Name?"

"Benson."

"B. E. D. S. O. N?" She licks the word as she spells it, and I can hear her tasting each letter.

"Not D. Benson with an N." I patiently correct her.

"Sex? You are definitely male." She smiles as she scribbles without looking up.

"Height?"

"Six two."

"Weight?"

"One hundred and seventy-five pounds."

"Date of birth?"

"Why doesn't she just give me the form so I can fill it out myself?" I whisper to my best friend and business partner Enoch Fink, who is silently filling out the same piece of paper beside me.

"You look about 28. Am I right?" I nod, although she is off by a year.

"Maybe because she likes you, and she plans on hiding your application for herself," he states without looking up.

I turn back to the tall red-head, whose lips are ruby-red as she purses them in wait for my response. I give her my date of birth before Enoch rudely interrupts her.

"Do you do this for everyone? Cause if so, I'd like you to *do me* next."

Her face sours as she hands me my application and points to it.

"You don't have to worry about questions 9 and 11. My name is Greer if you need anything else." She disappears into the back room right after giving me a smile and Enoch an evil look.

"You are such a jerk," I state to Enoch as we make our way to an empty table to finish the paperwork. "I can't even believe you convinced me to do this."

"How else am I supposed to meet a good wholesome girl? The girls we meet aren't exactly the kind that you bring home to Mama. I need a girl that I can bring to my sister's wedding and so do you. You know how my mother is."

"And you think you'll meet a girl like that at speed dating?"

"Do you have a better idea?" he raises an eyebrow.

I shrug and continue scribbling.

"I mean we're both approaching 30. My mom thinks it's time we think about settling down."

"You and I both know that's not going to happen. There is no way you are ready to commit to one person for the rest of your life."

"Maybe I am. Don't judge me." His tone admits that I'm right.

"I'm not judging you; I'm being realistic."

The voice on the intercom announces that we have five more minutes before the session starts.

I grumble. The sooner this starts, the sooner it will be over. I warrant stereotype to the women who do this. If someone is desperate enough to find themselves in this situation, they must either be unattractive or have a lot of issues. Guiltily, I dismiss the thought.

Enoch and I mock the system in which this is conducted. The questions that are asked on the form are extremely invasive and although we both won't admit it, we try our best to answer honestly. I skip questions number nine and eleven and a few more.

17. Eye color: Blue
18. Hair color: Blond
19. Annual salary:

I skip question number 19 and look over at Enoch to see if he answered it, and of course he has, boastfully so.

"Really?" I contest.

"Why should I be ashamed of what I make? I'm not a jerk because I am not poor."

A gong dings indicating for us to take our seats, and we are given random numbers. The lady dressed in blue takes our papers. We make our way to the long rectangular table. I sit next to Enoch wondering whether he feels as ridiculous as I do. The room is full of smartly dressed males, and they look hungry to make a connection. The rules are thoroughly explained to us by Greer and her assistant before we are ushered into a bigger room full of women and food.

Enoch brushes the shoulders of his blazer before acknowledging the woman across from him, whose number matches his. All the men peel off to their respective partners and all of us join our counterparts; according to the numbers we've been assigned.

Greer comes in and reiterates the golden rule to us all. When I look around me, all the men at the table with me look hungrily at the women, and again, I can't help but feel pathetic.

"This is the lowest we've ever stooped," I whisper to Enoch.

"You are so judgmental. This is how people who don't have time to go out and look for the man or woman of their dream do it. There is nothing low or degrading about speed dating. It's faster than online dating and more dignified than pheromone parties."

I almost start choking with laughter when I look at his serious face as he adjusts his collar.

"You're an artist and a businessman and I'm...well, look at me."

He smirks boastfully.

"You have a beautiful house and a promising future. You need to find yourself a beautiful, intelligent woman to share those things with."

"I have a beautiful, intelligent female in my life that I share those things with."

"Dude, Skylar does not count. I did say woman."

"My daughter is the peak of my happiness."

"What about your other needs?"

"What other needs?"

"Don't make me say it."

"Why are you worried about my *needs*?" I make air quotes with my fingers at the last word, "besides, we own the hottest nightclub in two different states; it's not that hard to take care of those needs."

The gong sounds again, and we turn to face our dates and ignore each other for the rest of the session. Time passes moderately slow as we talk to different women and change seats every time the gong thuds.

When, finally, the excruciating interviewing is over I look around once more as the men make their way to one side of the room and the women to the other. My mind is reeling from all the women I've talked to in such a short time. So many things said, I don't remember who said what, and I confuse the name with the face. I am exhausted from all the women trying to sell themselves to me. The only face, the only name I remember is Luna's. She has an exotic name, and she came out and cut through the bullshit.

"I'm Luna, I noticed you when I first walked in. I don't want to play games; I don't want anyone else here. Find me when this is over," she had said.

Greer scurried over to us and quickly took the piece of paper that Luna handed me. "Ma'am if you break the rules, you will be expelled from the program and won't receive any refunds."

Luna rolled her eyes at Greer who remained planted beside us until Luna walked to the other side of the room.

"You too, Sir," she said with smile on her face and she looked me up and down before she popped her hip and sashayed away.

I scoff but find myself intrigued by Luna's bold move. I love a woman who knows what she wants and who isn't afraid to go after it. I periodically steal looks at her as I make my way further away from her, all the while paying little attention to my perspectives who introduce themselves with minor soliloquys.

"I do believe I have me two matches that I shall be calling," Enoch announces as we make our way to the door.

"How did you do that? You are not allowed to exchange numbers."

As someone who has it all, the looks, the sense of humor, the money, Enoch's confidence knows no bounds. His all-American dark hair and green eyes are a magnet, not just to women but to anyone who is part of his audience. Not just his looks, but his personality as well calls attention to the room. I, on the other hand, am more of an acquired taste; my charm is in my silence, my quiet demeanor. Unlike Enoch, I am the type that grows on you.

"Oh, but tattoo, I have my ways." He stifles a Mr. Miyagi accent.

I don't even bother to entertain the matter. Why I thought he would take this seriously is beyond me.

"Dude, one girl came right out and asked me how much money I make," Enoch chimes.

"And you were only so proud to answer?'

"Of course."

"Yet you probably wouldn't even give her your last name."

"Precisely!" he says as he fishes his cell phone out of his blazer pocket. "I took her number instead, as only a gentleman would do."

Greer returns and announces how everyone would be notified, via email, of their matches. She reiterates, for the tenth time, the most important rule of all and that is not to exchange personal information *for our own safety*. She announces to everyone to have a good time as they catered hors d'oeuvres for the evening, her ruby-red lips touching the microphone.

Just like in middle school all the men flock to one side of the room while the females occupy the other. I look around to find Luna but see Greer following her to the next room where the office is located. Yes, this does feel like middle school; Luna has been called into the principal's office.

I find Enoch who is now sampling some *Ahi Tuna Tartare served on cucumber chevron*, and I read this out loud on the side of the platter as he spits it into his hand and he makes a sour face.

"Dude, this is lame. Let's get out of here. All the respectable women left, only the desperate ones remain."

I look around and the crowd has thinned. We decide to leave.

As we get closer to the car, I see Greer is leaning against it seductively, and she bats her eyelashes as we walk up to her.

"You forgot to fill out question numbers 9, 11, and 19." She says, pulling out a pen from her cleavage. Enoch's jaw drops, and I catch mine before it does.

"But I recall you telling me that I didn't have to."

"Not question 19, I didn't."

She takes my hand in hers and lingers for a second before she closes it around the pen and easily drops it in front of me.

"And what happens if I don't want to fill it out?"

"No biggie. Just making sure I'm doing my job. Thoroughly." She smiles seductively, emphasizing the last word.

"You can be thorough on me anytime." Enoch leans against the car behind her, xeroxing her *behind*.

As if she doesn't notice that he's there, she continues prowling at me: she the lion, and I the lamb. I read question number 19 that she has highlighted.

19. Annual Salary:

"I prefer to leave it blank," I declare.

"Humility is no longer a virtue you know," she declares as she closes the gap between us. She takes the piece of paper from me and tucks it between her elbow and her ribs. She takes my hand and scribbles down her number and then kisses it.

"In case we don't find you any matches," she purrs close enough so Enoch can't hear her and then walks away, leaving us both stunned.

In the car, on the way to *Blue Baby*, a club that both Enoch and I own, Enoch merges onto the middle lane without looking, and I decide to bite my tongue but hold on to the custom leather seat as he gushes about Greer and how I not only need to call her, but *I need to keep a girl like that on reserve because she is the kind of toy that you can always bring out to play.*

We get to Blue Baby, and I am ready to part ways with Enoch. He won't stop yapping about Greer and her hot friend Piper. Out of the blue, he changes the subject when we pull into Blue Baby's parking lot.

"Do you think Llarel has a date? Maybe she and I can go to Cornelia's wedding together."

"You two hate each other, and none of you is that desperate. Besides what about the numbers you scored tonight?"

"What about them? Llarel is way hotter."

"Stop talking about my sister, or I'll kick your ass."

"You act like she is too good for me or something."

"She *is* too good for you."

"Don't forget, I let you date my sister in high school even though you were a scrawny loser."

"I dated your sister, but not because you let me. Dude, why are you trying to get under my skin? You and I both know that you and Llarel hate each other."

"You're right. You're just such an easy target." He jabs me in the ribs with his elbow.

We walk into Blue Baby and head straight to our box upstairs. It's 11:30, and the club is already packed, even the private booths downstairs are full. I scan the crowd, and it seems to be the usual anonymous faces. I turn back to Enoch and find him standing next to me, staring down at his prized trophies for the night: the two numbers he acquired in one hand and his cell phone on the other.

"But why bring sand to the beach right?"

He puts the piece of paper and his cellphone back into his pocket and walks over to me, and we turn our eyes back to the wall-to-wall, ceiling-to-floor one-way mirror. I stand with my hands folded across my chest, and we both scope the crowd in silence, both relishing at our success. Less than three years ago, we were both ready to give up, feeling like we were in over our heads. Enoch had convinced me to go in on a club after our restaurant, Baby Blue, started doing well within the first two years. We almost failed.

All of a sudden, I see her. July, on the dance floor moving like a gazelle; her long legs evident inside her tight jeans. She is simple and yet a complication of lines that curve and spin my head dizzy while I'm trying to decide on where to look at her. She is music itself as she lilts under and over the invisible beat that carries her and uses her as a conduit of sound. She moves her hips from side to side, her body making love to the music. Her neck is elongated and stroked by her curls. I want to paint a picture with her hair. Her slender brown arms are long and move in waves above her head. The arch of her dips into a small round butt that draws a perfect curve, a line that simply could not be a mistake. She is wearing a lose pastel top that highlights her skin tone and hangs light on her torso so I have no choice but to stare at her hips. She moves them from side to side, snaking her body into a series of S's.

She oozes sex and paints a picture of what she would do with her naked body if I were naked with her. She is confident, adamant, and wholly autonomous. I strip her down in my mind and stop when I feel myself getting stirred. I lower my eyes to the floor and think, *This is July. Skylar's July.* But she dances like a woman and makes me feel like a man, a man with carnal instincts which are now awakened. I clear my throat and turn away from her, but her image haunts me and is heavily embedded in the back of my eyelids until I have no choice but to look back at her again.

"You know her?" Enoch asks following my gaze.

"No. Yes. Kind of. She's my nanny."

His jaw drops.

"Holy cow. That's your nanny?"

The lights go off, and darkness momentarily steals her from my sight before the neon lights come on: a tradition of Blue Baby's. Now everything is in bright flashing neon colors, and I can't help but prey on July and marvel at her vivaciousness. She closes her eyes and just lets the music carry her. She changes colors from neon green, to blue, to pink, to orange and purple, but her stance remains the same as she snakes and jives to the rhythm of music. I don't know for how long I just stare at her playing with music as they are both visible and tangible, and I don't even notice her circle of friends around her until I finally have to blink to moisten my now dry corneas.

The midnight hour marker is announced by the pitch blackness and the silence of the music. All there is now is a pulsing beat and a bunch of bright blue figures, wearing night vision goggles giving out glow sticks.

When the lights went off and July disappeared from my vision, since then, since that night, I've never looked at her quite the same.

I close the door behind me, ridding myself of any distraction. *July is your nanny, what are you thinking?* I've had her taking care of Skylar for months now; I hate that I am all of a sudden looking at her from a different lens. I fire my computer on and start back to work. I start with the emails and save the most dreaded one for last.

Mr. Benson,

It is empirical that we have a final decision about your traveling arrangements by tomorrow afternoon. I have yet to book your

flight and Madame Lefévre is anxious to find out the details of
your arrival. Your accommodations have yet to be confirmed as well.
Looking forward to your prompt response,
Prudence Rose.

She's attached a copy of my schedule for this month, and I take some time looking over it before sending an email back to her in response to her request. While I'm at it, I send Jane an email detailing my upcoming schedule and thank her in advance for taking care of Skylar during my absence.

Jane is the mother of my daughter, Skylar. She and I met and dated in college and were engaged for a year before we split up. She is now married to a childhood friend of mine, Brady, and they've been happy together ever since. Brady is an architect and has been a great stepdad to Skylar, and we have somewhat of a friendly relationship.

I decide to travel and be back before the first day of Skylar's summer camp and decide that Madame Lefèvre will be happy with me attending to her request so promptly.

I met Madame Jacquilin Lefèvre over three years ago at the opening night of my art gallery, and we've been fans of each other ever since. She is an older lady in her early to mid-sixties and although she talks an awful lot about her husband, I have yet to meet him. Going to Paris to sketch her has been a routine of mine for the past two years. *Vanity does not expire,* she always says.

I look at different portraits of her that I've done in the past. I examine every one of them in microscopic detail, every eyelash, every wrinkle. She always has the same ring on her right thumb, all kinds of jewelry, but always the same ring. I notice the portrait of her touching her face isn't accurate: the stone on her ring is off in scale and knowing my client, I know she's noticed it as well.

I look at the sketches I've done of her and testify that I prefer them over her paintings, although I must admit that I always think my paintings come out better larger than they do smaller. Her face is under the shadow of her hat, and she looks different over the years. It's as though time improves my vision of her, as if the longer I stare at her paintings, the more evident she is.

She is ugly, but there is a beautiful confidence about her. She always wears her hair in a neat tight bun and has a wattle and excess skin under her eyes and behind her ears. The texture of her skin has a rubbery look to it, and her voice is thick and horse, as though she has lived on coffee and cigarettes for most of her life. She is a little on the heavy side with sagging breasts, but her laugh is a stamp of approval that even grown men seek from her, and I've tried to make all of that evident in my portraits of her. I make detail notes in my ledger where I should focus close attention to on my meeting with her again.

I look at my first portrait of her. She is looking directly at me as if scolding me, and no matter whichever way I move, her eyes follow me. She is classic, pure proof of sophistication and *Frenchism*, whatever that is, she is. She holds her head high and her shoulders back, and even when she is sitting, her posture is precise.

She always smells like a mixture of coconuts and ylang ylangs, and she wears her blouses really low so her cleavage stares back at you. Her overstated jewelry and the clothing she wears, there is no other sight but her that that look can work on.

I look at my clock and realize that I've been at it for almost three hours. I get up and stretch starting with my neck, shaking my shoulders and then playfully shaking my hips and legs then wiggling my toes as if moving the stress through my body and finally kicking it off.

I hear July screaming, and Skylar giggling her little heart out. This puts a smile on my face, and I grab my phone and open the door, walking out passed the living room, through the kitchen and stop to watch them through the French doors. Skylar is splashing away at July, and July playfully screams and tries to get away from her. Skylar is circling the pool and shooting July with a water gun, making sure she stays wet even though half of her is submerged in the pool.

"Okay, you got me. I surrender! I surrender!" July is shouting.

I admire how good she is with Skylar, and I am so grateful that they get along so well. Before I even know it, I start admiring more than her interaction with my daughter.

July gets out of the pool, and her long muscular body glistens. Her brown skin agreeing with the curves it covers. Her long neck hiding behind a ponytail, part of her soft wet curls meeting her square shoulders and her tiny breasts; I can tell that her nipples are hard as they protrude through the yellow triangles that cover them. Her washboard stomach is so flat, and hard, and beautifully contoured by the muscles beneath it. Just as my eyes make their way lower my phone vibrates in my hand. I startle, feeling like a Peeping Tom.

"Benson."

"Dorian, it's Prudence Rose."

"Hey Prudence Rose. I gather you got my email."

"Yes, I just did. Please make sure you check all the info that I forwarded to you, and let me know as soon as possible. Since you want to travel so soon, we don't have much time. I assume you'll be traveling alone?'

"Yes. Of course."

"Alright then. As soon as I hear from you, I will move forward with the finalizations and confirm all the times and dates."

"Thank you."

I hang up and walk outside to the screaming girls. I find myself avoiding looking at July's naked shoulders, lingering at her mouth, assessing how her lips fold when she says certain words. In attempts of exerting control, I immediately dismiss July for the day, and she confirms tomorrow's schedule before she dries off and puts on a pair of shorts and layers two tank tops.

"So then, I guess I'll just go over to Jane's, and you'll drop Sky off there at noon."

"Yes. She'll be spending the whole weekend there, so I'll just see you on Monday evening when I get home."

We arrange for her to have Skylar all day Monday while I run some errands and finish some work in the office. Skylar and I have dinner with Llarel and have an early evening.

I weigh the brush in my hand, and it feels inaptly heavy. I pick up another one with a lighter head, but it's too wide. I search in my drawers but cannot find the right paint brush. Frustrated, I walk over to my drawing board and sharpen a brand-new pencil; I dip the tip in a glass of water and dull it by coloring a scrap piece of paper with its sides. I draw a circle and am satisfied with the size of the lines it creates.

I decide to sketch the curves of her legs; to refrain from exaggeration and embellish only the texture. I soften my grip on the pencil and extend my arm, making long lines. I darken the insides of my pencil woman's thighs and leave the long lines of her calves light and thin.

The trombone and the bass starts as Louis Armstrong's "St. James Infirmary" penetrates through the tiny speakers surrounding the room; his raspy voice singing, *She laid out on a cold white table. So so cold, so white, so fair.*

I train myself to concentrate and look only at the small segments of the drawing and not the picture as a whole. I make a dip and then hollow out the contours with convex strokes, evening it out with my pinkie to create a 3D effect. Making the outside of her calves more concave, I thicken the shadows around her silhouette and tease the insides with a hint of gray. Time passes as I try to perfect my lady who has no torso, no head but is only legs, legs that are covered with a cloth at the top of her thighs and entwined at the ankles.

The bass continues, and even though I've listened to this song a million times before, I always think, *What a prick*, as he turns these beautiful lyrics, this deep song around and says, *She'll never find a sweet man like me*…although I can't help but also think, *What a genius.*

Almost two hours later, I remove myself from my seat and step back to inspect my work. I walk a few more steps back, so I can zoom out and see the sketch with reality's background: Jazz. She looks like jazz. I couldn't be more pleased with myself. I walk back to the sketch and pick it up heading to the bathroom; I throw it in the tub and set it on fire. My pencil woman set afire.

I stare at the small flame as the throaty tune of Louis Armstrong pollutes my ears, the same way that the smell of smoke does to my nostrils. For a second, I feel guilty and worry about my housekeeper, Selena. She always complains about how the bathtub in this room is constantly black and is getting harder to clean.

I hear July's car pull up in the driveway and curse under my breath. I forgot to call her and cancel. Now that Skylar's not here, there really was no need for her to come. I decide that I won't waste her time and will write her a check for the hours she was supposed to be here. I walk over to the door and usher her in before she even knocks. I look at the clock, and it's 5:30.

"Hi Dorian."

"Hey July, come on in."

She looks around as she hangs her purse and coat in the mud room, expecting Skylar to come running to her like she normally does. I walk over to the kitchen where I keep unopened mail and keys and retrieve my check book, dodging the messy kitchen island full of ingredients that Skylar left all over the kitchen.

"Jane picked Skylar up and decided to keep her for the night."

"Oh okay," she says a little disappointed.

"It was a spur of a moment thing, and I totally forgot to call you." I don't look up as I sign her check. "I don't want it to be a total waste of your time, so I'm writing you a check for those hours."

She looks at my outstretched hand with a check in it, hesitant. She starts to accept it, but then drops her hand back down her side, ironing her shorts over her hips.

"No worries. You don't have to pay me for hours I didn't work."

"No, I insist."

She looks around, ignoring my hand that's still stretched out in front of her.

"Well, if I take this, then the least I can do is help you clean up this mess."

She scans the dirty countertops. I smile, inching the check closer for her to take it. She slowly retrieves it, folding it in half and putting it in her back pocket without checking the amount. We put stuff away and wipe down the countertops, and she moves around my kitchen with ease as she puts away items at their exact location.

"I had already set everything out for dinner because Skylar had insisted she wanted my spaghetti and meatballs. Have you eaten?"

"I love your spaghetti and meatballs."

"Perfect. I hate eating my own cooking alone. I'm sure the meatballs are done thawing by now." I prepare the ingredients.

"Yum." She rubs her belly.

This makes me smile and then for a second, just for a brief moment an image of her dancing with her eyes closed and her hands in the air emerges in my mind's eye, blinding me from the now. I blink it away speedily and busy myself by checking on the spaghetti sauce, which is now bubbling and ready for the meatballs. I add the meatballs to the now bubbling sauce and the pasta to the boiling water and dust my hands together before turning to look at July, guiltily and deliberately taking a long time to face her again.

She washes the lettuce and prepares the salad while humming a tune, and I am somewhat astonished by how at home she seems. She walks to the refrigerator and pulls out the cucumber, holding it up for my approval, and I nod yes, and then she does the same with the green olives, the red peppers, feta cheese, and I shake my head no to the tomatoes. I pick up a string of wheat spaghetti with a fork and pick it with my fingers and then throw it against the backsplash and it barely sticks then immediately falls off.

She cocks her head to the side, placing her hand on her hip.

"Didn't your mother ever tell you not to play with your food?"

"Playing? This is not playing."

"Okay, that's gotta come with an explanation."

She looks at me fascinated with a huge smile on her face and I notice that along with her big smile she has two deep dimples sinking into each side of her cheeks.

"What! You've never heard of this method before?" I distract myself.

She shakes her head no, still waiting for an explanation.

"That's how you test if your pasta is done." I look at her in surprise. I always thought this was common knowledge.

"And if it is?"

"If it is, then it sticks and does not fall off." I assess her. "You don't believe me?"

Her shoulders move up and down, and she tends back to cutting her cucumbers. She has the thinnest and longest fingers, and I worry that she'll cut herself because of the uncanny way she holds the knife. I take another piece and throw it again, and it doesn't stick. She sucks her teeth in mock confusion.

"You could just taste it, you know."

"Where's the fun in that?"

"I suppose nowhere, but at least we'd still have some spaghetti left in the pot to eat." She crosses her eyes as though one of us is crazy, and it's not her.

I smile wider, marveling at her playfulness. All along, I've never had a real conversation with July. I've always talked to her about Skylar's schedule: where Skylar needs to be, what time Skylar needs to be dropped off, I've never really considered July as anything but Skylar's nanny, and now I am realizing that there is more to her. She is interesting and funny. She is actually fun to talk to, and I realize now why Skylar is so taken with her. It's unnerving.

We talk about Skylar's progress in school and her newfound love: ballet. We also talk about July and her school and how she likes North Carolina.

"I love the South; people have cool accents, and 'Southern hospitality' really does exist."

She has this endearing laugh and an underlying confidence about her. Something about her appears genuine and vulnerable; she is kind of tom-boy-ish but feminine at the same time. She is fascinated by human behavior and people in the South, which makes her fascinating. I had no idea that she was from Colorado, which according to her is *a Christmas state*. We crowd everything on the counter, making our plates and sitting at the bar to eat.

I learn that she is on her third-year double majoring in math and chemistry, and I make a face.

"So, you like science?"

"Yes," her eyes grow wild with excitement as she explains her passion for the periodic table and the different substances it makes up and how she is the only person she knows who loves the *smell of sulfur.* "I can sense your distaste for the sciences, but this is how I see it: You're either into the arts or sciences, and you obviously use the right side of your brain."

"And of course, you use your left." I add in agreement.

"Totally," she concurs between bites. "Smart and witty, and we dominate in sports."

"And us, people who use our right brain?"

"Too emotional, too slow, too prudent, and too soft."

"Nothing good about us, huh?"

"You are also very sensual and virile," she cautions.

"And you are totally making this up."

"Totally," she jokes. "Hold still." She abruptly silences me.

She picks at my eyelash and then sits upright with her eyes closed. After a moment, she sighs and opens her eyes and then blows on her finger.

"Did you just make a wish with my eyelash?"

"Yes," she admits shyly.

"How do you make a wish with my eyelash and not even ask for my permission?" I scold playfully.

"I don't know. I saw it first," she defends herself, completely embarrassed.

"You saw it first?" I laugh very hard and extremely loud. "But it's my lash!"

She shrugs, evidently ready to be swallowed by the ground.

"I don't know about people in Colorado, but us southern folk don't steal other people's wishes."

"I can give you one reason why I think my actions are fair."

"How is it fair to steal someone's eyelash?" I stretch her shame.

"My wish was for the both of us." She is so shy, I think she is blushing.

"Huh?" I'm speechless for a change. She cannot be all that selfless.

"I…" She looks away out of the corner of her eye. "I wished us both well."

I don't care that I don't believe her. I lean in my seat close to her, to listen closer to what she is saying, to smell her, I don't know; I just linger beside her, torturing myself with this new yearning that takes me by surprise.

"I think I might kiss you," I hear myself say, with all honesty.

"I think I might let you," she permits with a shaky whisper.

We both fall silent, and the mood in the room changes. The lights seem dimer, the air expectant. I breathe out, and she breathes in, and when she breathes out, I breathe in, as if in exchange of something unspoken. I steadily lift myself off my stool beside her, locking eyes with her as I do so. Everything silences. No noise, no sound, not even my heart beat. She stares at me, into me with those dark mahogany eyes, and I want to look at her; no, I want to stare at her until the thirst in the back of my throat subsides. I want to smell her; I want to taste her. I have to kiss her. Now.

Slowly, I move my hand over to her knee, and her eyes follow eager to see what I might do next. Gently, I push her leg to one side, but she doesn't open her legs like I anticipated; her right knee follows her left, keeping her legs closed. Gently and slowly, I spread her legs apart and walk into them in the same motion as a person opening a gate and then entering, but the look she gives me, the burning stare on her face is more haunting than any ghost, any memory that exists in my actuality.

I stand closer to her, deliberately invading her personal space, so close that I can make out the rhythm of her breathing. She keeps her stance; I see her face change as she arms herself with bravery, and I catch that shift which pleases me when she looks directly in my face. Those eyes, those haunting eyes have so much fire; I now melt under them and close mine as I do so. I cup my hand under her chin and only gently, just gently motion her to stand up. She obediently erects herself, locking those immense gorgeous eyes with mine. I gradually motion for her to close the gap between us, and when she does, I notice that she is almost a foot shorter than I am. I calculate in my head, if I'm about six foot two then she is a little over five foot three. Her heart betrays her brave face and beats loudly against her chest.

I lean in and whisper into her ear, "Do you not want me to?" hoping that it's no longer an option to stop.

She simply gives a shy smile, her eyes telling me that she definitely wants me to. I take a moment to study her, keeping my face so close to hers I can feel her breath. She chews on her bottom lip, and her dimples dent her cheeks deeper, her mouth so soft and delicate, like the skin of a plum, inviting me to suck on it. I draw in a long breath and finally let it out inside her mouth. Yes, as suspected, her mouth is dangerously soft and deliciously sweet.

Both her tongue and my heart in my mouth, I find I don't need to breathe. I kiss her and linger in her mouth for a moment, waiting for her body's permission. She responds to me and I take this as a sign to carry on. I kiss her again, and she parts her lips, ready for me to taste her, and I slowly seal her kiss with mine. I let myself be kissed by her, and all my senses halt, I just let the moment take over. I close my eyes and kiss her till we're both drunk. I pull her close, playing with her full lips until she lets out a small moan from the back of throat and inches closer to me. The feel of her tongue, the taste of her lips, I stop myself before I lose myself in her. I take a deep breath while still in her mouth and withdraw with some of hers as I abruptly and rudely eject my tongue from her mouth and her puckered lips take a moment to acquaint to my retraction. Soon after I open mine, I am slapped with reality. She opens her eyes the same moment she conceals her disappointment.

"You should go home," I state as guilt unwillingly lets itself known in my chest.

I notice a shift on her face from deer caught in headlights to a hurt look of someone who has just been rejected, and then to a strong woman who now hides her weakness.

"Yes. Perhaps I should." She swallows hard and disappears into the mud-room, leaving me alone in the kitchen with my guilt. I hear her exit the house and drive off before I sit down with my hands on my head and chant:

"Shit! Shit! Shit!"

CHAPTER TWO

I make it to the address just in time. As soon as I knock on the door, the rain thickens. A new girl I haven't met before wearing all white opens the door and smiles, offering to take my umbrella and trench coat before she's even said hello.

Another girl much younger comes in from behind and offers to show me to the great room where I will be meeting Madame Lefèvre. She purposely walks fast, in front of me as if given orders that I should follow, and I do; I just follow behind her, taking in my surroundings.

In the hallway, right after the foyer entrance, I notice a new piece: a dilapidated Herm. I walk past it and rub it with my right hand, as only tradition would follow.

"Isn't this house so lovely?"

"Yes ma'am. It's beautiful."

"You can call me Marjorie."

Marjorie is very petit with long wooly hair that jackets her back, and she walks with her head down, but her posture is very well put together, and she has an elegant grace about her.

Her voice is very mousy and quiet, and her English is heavily accented with a French intonation, but I can guess what she is saying because she gestures as she speaks, pointing at different pictures around the house as we climb the stairs.

Little does she know that I am already educated about the history and the story behind most of the pictures that hang on the walls with the exception of the newer ones. She is not aware that I am no stranger to this house, and the old girl Anna would always keep the conversation light by telling me about them as she walked me up these very steps. I find myself wondering what happened to her but dare not ask.

The house has a huge hallway which reminds me of the historic libraries in England; and it smells like a library, too, which is a smell I have come to grow fond of. The floor is marble and poetry echoes from wall to wall, and the colors envelop you with their warmth, and there are white drapes everywhere that tower from the tall ceilings. It's like a museum but better.

"You meet Monsieur Filipe? This one is his favourite." She points to sculpture of a crying Botticelli angel, who holds his hands under his face as if catching his tears.

"It is beautiful," I say in my own daze as I marvel at all the too-beautiful and extremely expensive art pieces from all over the world.

"Personally, this one is my favorite." She points to a seemingly out of place piece at the end of the hallway of a hippopotamus wearing a tutu waltzing with a meerkat.

She lowers her head as if realizing that she is not supposed to share something personal with the guests.

We walk into a great room solely designed for art and statues and music. We walk in, and there is a soft lull of white and ivory everywhere. The huge room with tall ceilings is covered in marble pillars and drapes of sheer silk. I remember reading somewhere that this building used to be a publishing warehouse in the nineteenth century.

"The Madame will be right with you. Please help yourself." She points to a table with colorful fruit and water and crackers and all kinds of cheeses. I think she almost bows before she walks backwards to the door and closes it.

Alone in this massive room, I walk over to the window and watch the rain. It is raining heavily, and Paris hides from me as I try to look past the rain and into the deserted streets. I only see the traffic light change from green to orange to picture perfect blurry dancing lights.

Somebody, a man clears his throat, but when I turn around it is Madame Lefèvre. I turn around and relax my face into a smile, and she walks over to me and kisses both my cheeks without saying anything else. I clear my throat.

"How were your travels, young Dorian? Good to see you again."

"Madame."

"Please darling, call me Jacquilin."

I nod but worry that I may not annunciate her name as fluently and as elegantly as she does.

"This is where he finds himself." She turns to look at me for the first time since we left the first entrance way. "My Filipe."

She looks directly at me and makes no secret of it. I, in turn, divert my eyes and look around, hoping this awkward moment is fleeting, but the moment lingers, and she makes no point to look away or say something.

"Your house remains as beautiful as always." I clear my throat again.

"Do you enjoy having sex, Dorian?"

I look up not sure if I've heard her correctly, and for some reason, I feel like a pervert for having thought she said what I think she said, but then she confirms it when she asks again.

"Well? Do you?" She's never been one for small talk.

After a long pause, I reply, "Yes I do." I answer with a stunned expression and a strained voice, training my eyes not to look so guilty, and for what exactly?

"Are you promiscuous?"

"No. Not at all."

"Have you ever experimented with men?"

I poise myself but remain indifferent.

"No. Never had the urge to."

"Do you think about it?"

I smile and try to swallow my own embarrassment and some annoyance at her boldness, "Can't say that I have. No."

"What about another race or age group or body type?"

"All women are beautiful in their own way. I don't think I've ever discriminated."

"So, then you've been with women outside your age group, no?"

I shake my head no.

"And you've never been with a woman outside your own race?"

I automatically clench my jaw refusing to break eye contact with her but say nothing.

"So, you have then, no?'

"Have what?"

"Discriminated against certain types of women."

"I guess I've never really thought of it." I didn't even know I had a preference.

"I mean you are a beautiful man with a magnificent body and gorgeous eyes and a head full of that hair. You have all the choices in the world, with women and with men. Why choose to limit yourself?"

She looks at me as if agitated, waiting for an answer or an explanation, but I am on empty. She sighs in exasperation and gets up from her seat as if she's gotten bored. She rubs her lower back as she strolls past me.

"Close-minded people miss out on life, no?"

"Yes. Yes, they do."

And by admitting that, I am aware that I am admitting to her that I have been close-minded.

"So, what are you going to do about that then, Dorian?"

I shrug, feeling like an altar boy in boarding school. She steps in front of me and turns her back on me.

"Would you like to be liberated, young Dorian?

I swallow hard, trying to detect my invisible prison.

"Unzip me please."

I oblige and watch my hands as they unzip the back of her dress and the opening of her zipper exposing inch by inch a long scar, on the center of her back from the base of her neck, all the way down to her lower back. She wiggles out of it and steps forward, leaving room for my eyes to wander. She is completely naked. Her leathery skin sags on each side of her torso and her buttocks have given in to gravity. The scar on her back is not completely healed and still has a purple tint to it.

"Do you know what my Filipe gave me from my sixty-fifth birthday?"

She still has her back turned toward me as she adjusts her massive jewelry that drapes around her neck and over her chest and breasts.

"A scar."

I don't know what comes over me, but suddenly I am walking over to her and running my fingers down the length of her scar; she shudders as I do so. She turns to face me. Without giving myself some time to think, before I can register what the rest of me is doing, I caress her face and kiss her hard. On her lips is a hint of mint and menthol.

When we both pull up for air, she looks into me through her deep sunken eyes, not shocked at all.

"I just knew you would have soft hands."

She takes them in hers and studies them.

"You have an artist's hands. But of course."

She turns and faces me, and she is not at all ashamed of her body or any imperfections she may have; about her size, her age, her scar. She places her hands on my face and caresses it and then brushes my hair with her fingers.

"You are so beautiful. So young."

She kisses me before I can say anything else, and her lips are not so leathery; they are soft and have a residue of her peppermint tea that coats her tongue. She untucks my shirt and unbuckles my jeans. She puts her hand on my stomach and presses lightly with her fingers.

"You are like the sculpture of David; those muscles, that skin...so young." I look at her hands anticipating her claw-like nails to dig into me. "Look at me. Look at me with those pretty blue eyes, I want to feel young again."

I do as I'm told but find I cannot keep my eyes open when she vacuums my mouth into hers.

She lifts her arms and removes several pins from her head, and her hair falls, cascading down her back and just barely kissing her backside; and like the chosen one, I feel like I have been let in on a secret, a secret that she reveals only to a chosen few. By the oversized chair on the corner of the room, she sits me down, and she undresses me. And like a king whose servant kneels before him, I watch her as she disrobes me item by item and then she lays me down on the crisp white futon by the window where the rain makes vertical shadows on our bodies.

She has hair so gold, so long, so thick and so sensual, it's young and mighty erotic. For the first time, I see why hair can be a secret weapon that women can use against you, such an amatory attribute to have. For the first time since I've known her, I see her in her true form: beautiful; because of her hair, because of her confidence, because of her nakedness and her ability to be a woman with a man and doing what it is that women do to make a man feel like a man.

She stands over me and watches me without saying anything, and I watch her as well, watching me, admiring me, lusting over my youth. She flattens me on my back and lowers herself on top of me letting her hair fall over her and onto me. Her thick blonde hair smells like ylang ylangs, and she sweeps it over my body as if it's some tribal ritual known to seduce men. She starts from my head, and she sweeps her hair all the way down my body and then up again, making me tingle in a way that I never have before.

She wraps it around my neck and lifts her head making me rise with her and she sits me on a chair and straddles me. She nibbles on my neck and then my ears and then turns and stares directly at me. She doesn't make love to me, or sex me, she puts her hands behind her on to my knees and rides me and fucks me, groaning like a diesel engine as she bobs and weaves on top of me. She is so animalistic, so wild and so ripe with age and experience, and isn't ashamed of being instinctual within her lust and her carnal cravings.

Her confidence is so elegant, so intoxicating. Even though she is not the most beautiful woman I've ever been with, she is by far the most captivating, the most potent in her ways, and very sexy and seductive, and right away, I change my perspective about the way I view her.

After we've both climaxed, she gathers her hair on top of her head and adds a few bobby pins to hold it in an untidy bun while she is still straddling me, and I am still inside of her. She follows my eyes to her chest.

"You like my décolletage, no?"

I simply kiss her enormous breasts, and she stops me after a while and grabs a cigarette from the side table next to us. She sticks a long cigarette into her mouth and looks at me. I take the lighter from the table and light it for her and watch her as she pinches her eyes while drawing in a breath and continues to look at me through the smoke.

"You have the body of a boy: no hair, no fat, no gut. You are so youthful, so raw of life."

She speaks to me between puffs, blowing her smoke into my face as if christening me and performing some sort of baptism. Her face distorts from behind the smoke, and she looks beautiful, goddess-like, and I can see how beautiful she was when she was young. She takes a long puff while staring right at me and kisses me, exhaling slowly into me.

"So young. So beautiful." Her French accent, sounding more poetic with each syllable. Through puffs of smoke, I see her beauty only too clearly.

She repeats the same action, taking a break to ash out her cigarette on the ashtray next to us, "So young." She lets out a toxic breath into my mouth, "So beautiful." She kisses me again.

In a matter of minutes, Madame Lefèvre has transformed right in front of me; from a woman with leathery skin, tight uniform hair and bags under her eyes to a nymph, a beautiful sex deity with long, long hair and a confidence that is well deserved and very desirable.

"You should paint a picture of yourself and stay frozen in time. Like Oscar Wilde's Dorian Gray. The name is quite fitting too, no?"

She stands up, exiting me out of her body as she takes another cigarette.

"I don't suppose we'll get anything done today. How about we reschedule for tomorrow. Let's say 1300 hours, yes?"

She remains naked as she approaches the window puffing her cigarette. She watches the rain and ignores me, and so I dress myself and exit quietly and let myself out into the rain and walk to my hotel.

In my hotel room, in the shower, the thought of her makes itself known, keeping me in the shower longer than anticipated. I quite enjoy myself with her as a tool to my pleasure. I think of myself to be ridiculous to find her unconventionally attractive, but for some reason, this is no surprise. I decide that I can't wait to see her tomorrow.

The flight back is excruciatingly long. I have the whole section to myself, so I spread out and unfold without being disturbed or disturbing anyone. I replay everything that took place in the last couple of days: kissing the nanny, sleeping with my client, I need to practice some self-control.

Who would have thought that I would find Jacquilin Lefèvre sexually appealing? I have always thought she was the perfect muse for a piece of art, but never in a million years would I have thought that lust and sex would be part of the equation, and now I understand why one of the richest and most powerful men in Paris would want her and why she is able to keep him. This merely brings me to my lack of morals; the fact that she is married.

I can still smell a hint of ylang ylang if I think about it hard enough. Ashamed; I make myself feel guilty.

I was worried about how things would transpire between us after our fuck session, but everything seems unhindered. Jacquilin Lefèvre let her hair down, as if that is cue for seriousness to cease and time to let things of the flesh be known and taken care of. Once her hair goes back up, so does business as usual.

After some unorthodox foreplay, with no shame and no guilt, we did what only comes naturally. We fucked until we were soaked and out of breath.

"Do you ever feel guilty?"

"No." She didn't ask me about what, but I knew that she knew to what I was referring. "A great portion of our melancholy comes from denying ourselves of what comes naturally to us: sleep, food, sex. If all things are done in moderation, a balance is acquired."

"But where does that balance exist? Shouldn't Filipe be that balance?"

Her answer, to my astonishment, was Biblical and should be a philosophy.

The rest of the flight home is rather smooth. I lean my head against the cold window and close my eyes. Enough about Madame Lefèvre; too much of her can never be a good thing.

Being home with my daughter grounds me. I have a sense of who I am and what my purpose is in life. I don't wander around aimlessly and forget right from wrong. I have thought about last week and Jacquilin Lefèvre but have decided that it was my moment of weakness, and it will not happen again. Surely if I never mention it again, she won't either. That way, we would be able to maintain our professional relationship. I look outside to the beautiful Spring day and convince myself that it's good to feel guilty, that way I still feel like I have some morals.

I stand up and walk to Skylar's room and find that she is still sleeping, so I lean over her and rub her back, waking her up for school.

"I don't feel so good, Daddy."

I sit on her bed on her side and examine her. I put my hand on her forehead and feel her for a fever, and she feels normal. She does feel a little damp, like she's been sweating all night.

"What's wrong, Binkie? Where does it hurt?"

"My belly feels like the spin cycle of the dryer, and my head hurts."

"Okay, baby. Daddy's going to let you sleep a little bit longer, okay?"

She turns and lies on her belly, and I place my hand under her shirt and rub her back, which feels a little too hot and somewhat damp as well. She rolls her eyes and closes them.

I decide I will let her sleep for a little bit and take her to school late today. I walk over to the other side of her bed and kiss her forehead before I exit her room. I am certain she doesn't have a fever but decide to call Jane anyway, as a precaution.

I walk out of her room and leave the door ajar as I walk to the study where I can make a phone call quietly without waking her up. I look at the clock: 6:45. I decide against calling Jane so early. I set the alarm clock on my phone for another hour and go back to bed.

The alarm goes off. For a minute I am disoriented and startled, but I turn off my phone and find Skylar next to me fast asleep. She really must not be feeling well because she is a morning person and always gets up early, and also, she doesn't like missing school.

I tiptoe out of bed and walk out of the room after checking her forehead again, and she is still fast asleep, but her body temperature feels normal, and she doesn't seem to be in any pain.

I walk to my study and dial Jane's number before checking to see what time it is. It's almost 8:30, and so I make the assumption that she is up and ready to go to work.

"Dorian, this better be good," a groggy voice answers after a few rings.

"Ah, hey Jane, did I wake you?"

"Yes."

"Aren't you going to work today?"

"What do you want, Dorian?" I am reminded how Jane is not a happy camper in the mornings. *I sure don't miss that*, I think sarcastically.

"I was thinking about letting Sky skip school. She doesn't feel very well."

"Oh crap. She has it, too?"

"Has what?"

"Brady's nephews were here yesterday after school, and Cody and Myra conveniently forgot to mention that they had a stomach flu less than 24 hours prior. Now I have it, and apparently so does Skylar."

"Shit!"

"I know," she continues to complain.

"Do you think I should take her to the doctor?" I whisper into the receiver.

"Nah, it'll pass before the end of the day. Just make sure that she eats healthy and keep her hydrated. Let her get as much sleep as possible." I make a mental note as Jane enunciates everything. We hang up, and I call Prudence Rose and let her know I'll be working from home today. I decide to go over some paperwork while Sky sleeps. Selena comes in, and I inform her of the current situation of the house.

Close to noon, I've done the majority of my paperwork, made some phone calls and showered, and a groggy Skylar walks into my office with messy hair and pink ballerina pajamas.

"Daddy, I don't feel so good." She comes and sits on my lap. I make room for her as I steady her over one knee, and she lays her head on my shoulder.

"I know, honey. Do want to eat something and take a bath? I think you'll feel a lot better after."

"Okay." She doesn't protest but continues laying on me as if she has no energy to even move her limps. I lift my baby up and take her to the kitchen where Selena has laid out some bagels and cut some fresh fruit.

Skylar decides on a cinnamon bagel but eats it plain. She takes a few bites of cantaloupe and eats a few strawberries.

"Are you feeling any better?"

She shakes her head. I eat next to her in silence and watch her every move, contemplating whether I should ignore Jane's instructions and take her to the doctor.

I take her again into my arms and lead her to my bathroom, where I run a bath for her, and she does not even ask for bubbles this time. She does not even want the jets on, and I worry that she might be really sick. I sit on the toilet next to her while she soaks in the tub; she dips her face in and out of the tub. I notice her personality finally emerging towards the end of her bath, and I start to relax.

"What would you like to do today?" I ask her.

"You are not going to call July?"

"No. Today's just me and you."

"Oh," she says, and for a second, I think she is disappointed.

"Is that okay with you?"

"I guess. I love it when it's just me and you, sometimes, Daddy."

"I do too."

I help her out and dry off, and she goes to her room and picks out her own clothes and does her own hair, and when she emerges again in the living room, she is her own self again; only a little sluggish. She walks over and sits on the couch, and Skylar's black poodle, Neo jumps up and sits next to her.

"Do you want to watch a movie together?"

"Only if I pick."

She picks her obvious favorite, which we've watched at least three times, and we share the couch, but she decides she doesn't want any popcorn. When the movie is over, it's close to three in the late afternoon, and we both decide to take Neo for a long walk. This pleases me when she agrees because it means she is feeling well enough to burn some energy. Jane calls to find out how she is doing and asks if I can keep her till tomorrow so that Brady doesn't get sick and I gladly oblige. She informs me that she called school, and I am grateful because I didn't even think about it at all.

During some chicken noodle soup and crackers, I note that Skylar's sense of humor is nothing like mine at all, and as she talks, walks, and gestures, I try to find myself in her, but I can't be so sure, but I notice only a few things that I can claim as traits that she may have acquired from me or my side of the family.

"Daddy?"

When we get to the dog park at the top of the hill, she doesn't seem to be out of breath.

"Yes Binkie?" I call her by her nickname when she is being really sweet.

"Do you have a girlfriend?"

This catches me by surprise, but I am not at all astonished because I am used to my daughter's forwardness and her lack of timing.

"Why? Do you have one for me?"

"I was just thinking…you know, it's okay for you to get married again like Mommy. She's never lonely."

I laugh a little wondering how someone so small can have such big ideas.

"She and Brady laugh all the time, and sometimes Mom laughs so much she starts crying."

I smile at my little sunshine, who wants to pour it down on everyone who has any kind of gloominess in their lives.

"And you don't think I'm happy?"

"You don't laugh all the time the way Mommy does. Even salt makes her laugh."

"Salt?" I look at her quizzically.

"The other day she bought the wrong kind of salt for her ingredients, and when she and Brady started cooking, they realized it, and they both sat on the floor and laughed so hard tears were coming out of her eyes."

"Really?" for a brief second, I have an image of a young Jane who laughed so hard, she peed in her pants. She was always so easy to laugh; it didn't take a lot to make her pee in her pants. I'm glad to know that that part of her still exists.

"So, they decided to fill my boots with the salt and put them outside in the rain and we are going to wait and see how long it takes for the salt to desperate."

"Desperate?" I ask a little amused and marveling at how cute and innocent this little being in front of me can be and how much space she takes up in my heart.

"Yes."

"You mean dissipate?"

"No, Daddy, desperate, because salt can do that, you know. It means to disappear."

I find a dictionary app on my phone and pull both words up. I motion for her to follow me and she does after rolling her eyes. I find the word *desperate* and hold it with my finger while I pull up the word *dissipate*, and we both look them up together.

"Oh, I am so glad that you are the first person I tried my new word out on, or Marybeth would have made so much fun of me," she says in relief, and amazingly, I see a little of Jane in her worry face. I laugh but secretly watch her talk and make gestures, so glad that I had something to do with the existence of this amazing little girl in front of me.

"You never do silly stuff the way Brady and Mommy always do."

"Only happy people do silly stuff then?"

"Yes. All kinds of silly stuff."

"Like what?" I ask her out of curiosity as to what goes on in that household but relieved to hear that it's a happy environment for her.

"Like Goofday."

"Goofday?"

"Goofday is when we take turns picking out each other's clothes, and you can't complain or say no when someone picks out something that you don't like. Last week, I had to dress like a boy, and I didn't like it at all, but when I tried to get Brady to wear Mommy's clothes, he changed the rules and said it had to be from your own closet."

"Cheater!" I gasp.

"That's what I said!" she says, and she is so animated. She is sitting on a gigantic rock in front of me. She wiggles her nose as if it itches, and I can't help but laugh. I am relieved that she feels better.

"Dance with me."

"But there is no music."

"Happy people can make up their own silly music, can't they?"

"Yes. They can do anything they want." She laughs.

I start humming a tune and take her hands, and she holds my hands and follows my lead. I think that she might have grown a little taller since last week. I move from side to side, motioning in the same direction, and after a few seconds, she stops.

"Daddy, you are a terrible singer."

"Okay, then I have an idea."

We walk back home, occasionally racing on one foot. I take her hand and lead her to the art room, where I walk over to the record player and pick up an MP put it into place and gently place the needle and start the song.

Louis Armstrong's raspy voice sings *What a Wonderful World*, and I pick my daughter up and dance with her, holding onto her for dear life. I like the smell of her hair; she smells of innocence and purity, and for the first time, I dread the day she will bring home her first boyfriend, the first time she drives, and the first time her heart is broken, the day she leaves for college, and her wedding day, oh gosh; her wedding day.

We spend the whole day together swimming, jumping on the trampoline, chasing Neo, and it turns out to be one of my favorite days so far.

Around dinner time, Jane calls and checks in. We decide that I should keep her, and I agree with no reservations, wanting to spend a whole full day with my daughter without any babysitter or Jane.

By the time I put her to bed, we are both so exhausted having had a day full of activities and her going back to school tomorrow. Neo crawls into bed with her, and they both embrace the night. I walk to my bedroom, and after taking a shower and turning off all the lights, I fire up the computer.

Chapter Three

How far I've come. I think to myself as I sit at my desk while Prudence Rose gives me the news about the new project I've been offered by a non-profit foundation in Denver, Colorado.

Only four years ago, I was graduating from grad school with a degree I had no intention of ever using. I was a young dad, and for as long as I've fought it, I was almost pressured into joining the family business and giving up on the core essence of my being. I had no confidence in my talent and didn't know what I wanted to do with my life. I had come out of a relationship and finally accepted what I couldn't change about that horrible accident. The nightmares were still there, haunting me every night. I was a kid who was raising a kid and combating his dark past and an uncertain future.

"You will have three months to work on it if you agree to do it." Prudence Rose brings me back to reality.

It would be a great opportunity, an honor even.

"But painting a portrait is a lot of work, and I don't think they understand how much time this is going to take. Three months does not give me a lot of time."

"It's negotiable as far as I'm concerned. Once you decide on whether you are going to do this, then I can call them and see if they can give you an extension."

I think about it for a second. I don't have any clients in Colorado. This would give me a chance to start new relationships and build a clientele in another state.

"When are they expecting an answer?"

"In three days."

I look at my map on the wall and all the green pins of all the places where I've done and sold work.

"Alright. Let me sleep on it."

Prudence Rose turns on her heels to the door, and her jet-black hair held up by a yellow pencil that's twisted into it. When the door shuts behind her, I stare back on the map on the wall and notice that there are not many pins on the West-coast, and I wonder if this would open doors for me.

My phone rings, and it's Jane. I've gone a whole month without having to summon July for her services, and to keep my guilt at bay, I would have preferred to prolong it indefinitely, which is why I am now very annoyed at Jane when she calls me and tells me what her plans are for the day.

"July is going to be bringing Skylar back, and she is going to stay at your place with her for a few hours before you get there because I have a meeting with Brady and his bosses. I just thought it would be easier to give them something to do together."

"So, you organized to have them stay at my place without consulting with me first?"

"I know, I'm sorry, but I didn't think you would mind."

"I don't. I just really would like you to consult with me first before you make any decisions that concern me."

"Dorian, I didn't even think you'd be home."

"Which is all the more reason to consult with me first?" I realize I'm whining.

"I guess I would expect the same courtesy from you," she says. I breathe a sigh of relief when I realize that this is not going to escalate into an argument. "So?"

"I guess that will work." Since I don't have a choice in the matter.

"And you are fine with keeping Skylar for the rest of the weekend then?"

I agree to that, too. Jane would have a fit if she knew the real reason why I am upset.

I finish things up with Prudence Rose who assures me that I don't have to travel anywhere for the next month unless I accept the offer. She reminds me of the upcoming art show at our gallery before she leaves at the end of the day. I deliberately take my time leaving, prolonging inevitably facing July.

I make it home, hurriedly opening the door and shutting it behind me and leaving the angry wind beating outside the door.

"Whew!" I sigh in relief, glad to have made it home when I did.

I set my portfolio samples on the counter and pull off my blazer, setting my keys and wallet on the counter. I walk over to the living room to find July's back turned to me, and she is monitoring the weather and there are red warning signs all over the TV screen.

"Hey July."

She reluctantly turns to face me, her body rigid and uncomfortable.

"Hello Dorian. You are here." She looks around uneasily. "Skylar is already asleep, and since you are here, I better get going before I get caught in this thunderstorm heading our way."

She is nervous, and I know it's because of the other night and the kiss that transpired between us. Before I can say anything, the TV screen flashes, and there is a voice that announces that our county is under a severe thunderstorm warning, effective until one 1:00 AM. I turn my wrist to look at my watch, and it's a quarter after 10:00.

"Stay," I offer, waiting for her to protest but hoping she doesn't.

"Is that okay with you?" she asks sweetly, unsure of herself.

"You might not make it home in time." I offer, surprised at my own gratitude for this natural disaster. She looks unsure of herself as if contemplating on what she should say or do next, and then she nods lightly.

The image of her on the dance floor appears, and I blink it away inconspicuously. I shake my head to clear it of that image completely, but then a new thought invades me: the other night; the taste of her kiss.

I notice her face contorting to several different expressions as if she is having an internal dialogue with herself. She is not sure what to do with her hands, so she pulls on her sleeves with her skinny fingers.

"Did you already have dinner?'

"Yes. Skylar and I had chicken alfredo," She answers formally.

"Okay, I've been craving something sweet all day. Would you like some?" I cringe at the connotation of that sentence but remain indifferent.

"Sure." She only shrugs implicitly.

She sits down at the far end of the table and crosses her legs under it. I, in turn, take everything that's sweet out of the refrigerator. I lay everything out in front of her and sit down diagonally to her.

"Dig in." I point at the ingredients for a stomachache laid out on the table.

"Oh, I was planning on it." She has a light beat to her voice and an excited look in her eyes; all the awkwardness gone. She picks up the ice cream and the chocolate syrup and then looks at me with her hands full. The mood between us morphs to relax mode as though a switch was turned.

"No spoons and bowls?"

"No, none. Now that we are both sitting down, I think it's best if we just use our hands."

She eyes me skeptically and then shifts in her chair.

"Use our hands? Okay." She smiles mischievously.

She opens a box of popsicles, takes two out and holds them up.

"Which one do you want?"

I reach out for the green, which I assume to be lime, and she picks the red one. Then she looks at the different flavors of ice-cream and again asks me which one I want.

I pick up the rocky-road, and she smiles and hugs the mint chocolate chip closer to her. She squeezes a good amount of syrup into the container and digs in with her popsicle, plopping a big amount into her mouth before looking up at me with a smile.

"Yum."

She is very animated and has a light air about her like that of a child. It's no wonder why Skylar is taken by her.

I make a face but don't protest. I scoop a small amount as I study her actions. She is all lines and circles. Her posture is formal and polite, her movements are wide and carefree, her smile—big, and those dimples. Her eyes are a velvet dark brown, so large and happy. When she laughs, she hangs her head back and bobs her curls behind her ponytail. Her neck is long and narrow, and her shoulders are square. She keeps her popsicle clean when she is speaking, and I find myself having a hard time listening. We engage is small banter, and

I find her pleasurably likeable.

"My father is Jamaican and my mother Egyptian. Between the two of them, I have an interesting upbringing."

Right away, I have an image of her mother singing and swaying her hips on stage. Sade.

"How exotic." I say to her. "Do you have any brothers and sisters?"

"No, although I've always wanted an older brother." She smiles at a distance, but her smile quickly fades, and she turns to face me, "Do you have any siblings?"

"Yes. I have a twin sister."

Her eyes twinkle, and she erects herself as though, I have finally gotten her undivided attention.

"Really? I bet she's beautiful."

"She is." I deliberately leave out the part that she's blind, justifying the thought that that's not what defines her.

"What about you? Are you close to your family?"

"No," she says it a little too quickly and leaves no room for any more discussion on the matter. I only have a moment to think that, *That's weird…* before she draws me in with something else that's interesting about her.

I learn that she is training for the nationals in track, and she is a sprinter, does hurdles, and may also qualify for high jump. I note in my head how this explains a lot about her athletic physique.

She asks me about my parents, and like her, I dodge the subject.

I keep looking inside her mouth trying to catch sight of her tongue. After a while I notice, she's been silent. I look up at her and notice that she is waiting for my response.

"Huh?"

"What do you like?"

It would be great if I had been paying attention to what she's been saying or what it is that she said she likes, so I can respond accordingly.

"I like pasta."

She laughs and drains the stickiness on her popsicle.

"Pasta rhymes with Rasta and buster, but not with please or kiss or me." She looks to the floor as she closes her sentence.

Whoa! My eyes automatically widen but I correct myself immediately.

What exactly did I miss while she was talking? I foolishly stare at her lips and remember how soft they are, how warm, how sweet. Finally, I become self-cognizant, but the moment has fled, and she is standing up, clearing the table, sure that I have rejected her.

I stand up and start helping her put everything away and loading the dishes from earlier, and when I bend over at the dishwasher, she turns quickly from me to the refrigerator, and I catch a whiff of her nectarine hair. I remain hunched over and foolishly staring at her. She stops what she is doing and just stares back at me until I straighten myself up.

"There are fresh sheets on your bed, and of course, you already know where everything is." I could swear my voice sounds like a prepubescent boy.

"Right." She looks down to the floor and squeezes her lip between her right thumb and index finger. I want to take her hand in mine and remove it from hurting her mouth.

All of a sudden, she walks over to me, stands on her toes, holds my face in her hands and kisses me, deep and hard, and then walks away before I can catch my breath.

"Goodnight." She looks to the floor and disappears on the right to the hallway without looking back. I gain my composure and run my tongue over my mouth.

I attempt to tidy up by throwing everything in the sink including the syrup and sprinkles before throwing the two tubs of ice-cream in the freezer. I pace back and forth by the sink and then finally walk over to my bedroom somewhat in a daze. I take my shoes, socks, and shirt off and lay on my back on top of the covers. *She kissed me.* Was that her way of telling me that she wants me? Of course, it was.

I sit up on my bed and shake my head no. But why wouldn't she? I know I want her. A shadow catches my eye from the crevice under the door, and I know she is standing behind it. I wait for her to knock but instead the shadow lingers for a moment and then disappears. I maintain my composure and stare at the door. Nothing.

I can't ignore the signs now. Can I? This was definitely a sign. I didn't just imagine that. I stand up from my bed and weigh the consequences: Skylar's in the room right next to hers, I am her employer, wouldn't that be taking advantage of her? I sit back down on the bed, clenching and unclenching my jaw.

I am apprehensive now; I can't sit still, and my body is invaded by an invisible force that insists that I stand up and walk right over to her room. I resort to going to get a glass of water, hoping to run into her in the kitchen, but instead, I head left of the hallway. I tiptoe, making sure that I don't creak the floor. The hallway stretches, seeming longer than usual, but when I reach her door, I hesitate before touching it. I knock once then slowly let myself in. The side lamp next to her is still on.

I walk over to her bed, and she is facing away, with her wild curls spread all over the pillow behind her. She turns to face me, not really surprised to find me hovering at her side. Slowly, I push the covers down to her ribcage and take her hand, ushering her out of bed. She is in her white cotton underwear and her white tank top that was underneath the grey one. I place my finger on my mouth.

"Shhh," I inculcate.

I take her hand and lead her to the door, to the right in the hallway, down the steps and into the basement. I halt in the middle of the doorway and release her hand. I look at her: her face, her eyes, her mouth, her neck, her shoulders, and the outline of her breasts through the thin fabric that covers them.

"Kiss me again," I whisper to her.

Say yes. Say yes. I subconsciously beg her while I wait for her to answer. She, in turn, only nods her head as she purses those full lips of hers that I prefer over anything sweet. I do what I've been wanting to do since that evening when I first kissed her. I take a hand full of her hair and inhale it before sealing her kiss with mine. She smells divine, like the ocean and the mountains and everything in between.

I envelop her in my arms as I pull her closer, first kissing her softly and then firmly. Making my mouth hollow and making room for her to fill it. I hold her face instructing her not to move, not to move, not to go but keep the suction tight. She responds by kneading my tongue with hers, and she inebriates me, making me forget who I am. July simply dissolves into my arms, and I catch fire as she ignites me, lights me up, and scorches my throat with her scent and her mint chocolaty kisses.

I sachet her with myself, my arms snaked around her petit body. I lift her up and sit her on my lap as I sit down on the edge of the leather couch that sits by the sliding door leading to the pool. *Gently.* I remind myself, and so I slightly release her, safely lifting her left leg over and around me. I open my eyes for a second only to find her physically there with me but absent in every other way; somewhere else that only she sees with her eyes closed and her hands now knotted behind my neck. I place my hands to her lower back and staple her to my pelvis in one languid movement and she obliges as she breathes frantically in my mouth. A fire consumes me, and I feel myself increase.

"I want you. Do you want me?" I mumble, somewhere between asserting and pleading.

When she doesn't answer but simply bores those beautiful chocolate eyes at me, I am at her mercy. I take her face in my hands and in desperation I quill her mouth with tender kisses between breaths,

"I want to kiss you where you are sweet. Touch you where you are warm."

She lets out a sound from her lungs. It sounds like a hum or a sigh or a combination of both.

"Do you want me?" I ask, not wanting to wait for an answer.

"Yes. I just don't know how," she whispers.

"The only way you know how," I coach, not wanting her to fear, for her sake and for mine, her carnal cravings.

I kiss her jaw line heading to her ear as I slowly suck her earlobe before completely encircling her earlobe with my mouth. She hums and sighs again, making that sound more urgent. I notice that I am no longer in charge of my body, that I am in custody of it. I will myself to slow down, and I know I should stop but at this point, I don't want to, and I don't even know why I should.

I push the strap of her tank top off her shoulder leaving it naked. I kiss it then blow on it, kiss it, and then blow again. I continue doing this, and she continues to let me until I feel her crumble in my embrace.

"Wait," she says in a voice so small I'm not convinced I heard it.

I stop. I lift her up and set her down waiting for her to state her case while still panting and holding my hand.

"This is wrong," she states softly as she pats her full lips willing the heat I left on them to subside.

I simply squeeze my eyes shut and stand up to put my arms on her shoulders.

"I know. I'm sorry," I utter, sounding defeated.

"You're my boss. I nanny for you," she mutters back in a soft voice, and I now cringe at the realization that I've made her feel uncomfortable. All the heat leaves my body and a cold chill threatens.

"July; you're Skylar's nanny," I resonate, instilling it to myself more than anything. "I wasn't trying to take advantage of you. I just assumed…" I now discredit my assumptions with my agitation.

I hug her as if she is Skylar or somebody very fragile.

She backs out of my arms and dodges my embrace.

"I don't want you to see me that way. I don't want you to see me as a child."

She looks away from me and searches the floor for bravery because when she looks back at me, it appears as though she has found it.

"All this time I've fantasized about this moment, and now that it's here, I am ruining it. I don't want you to stop."

"But July, you deserve better. You deserve someone who can stroke you like it's your first time, someone who can love you, someone that you love." I imagine I sound like her father at this moment. I internally scold myself for introducing us both to the dilemma we now face. I step back from her to assess the situation clenching and unclenching my jaw in exasperation.

"I've wanted this for a long time now. Please," she pleads with me, which frightens me. "I'm not asking you to love me. Right now, right here, I am asking you to let me be the reason your veins are engorged, for your heavy breathing, and for the ignition of your desires." She sounds like a woman on a mission and I am a man who cannot refuse her.

"July, I—"

"Please." She whispers.

She drops her long arms to my naked chest, spreading her fingers apart against my sternum.

"I want you," she uses my own words.

"I want you, but I know I shouldn't," I preach.

She closes the space between us pressing herself firmly against me and whispers again, "Please."

My body, right there and then, makes up its mind to give in without my consent.

She kisses my neck…

"Please."

My fingers…

"Please."

She sits me back down on the coach and kisses my face.

"Please."

The seductive way she says such a simple word. The way she whispers it and plants it on my skin with her lips sends me to a place where logic does not exit. I kiss her mouth, her nose and her eyes, and I prop myself up on my elbows and watch her slowly shed out of the item that covers her hard nipples as I anchor myself securely on the center of the couch. She has brand new skin, so soft, so new, and so brown, as if you just peeled her out of her wrapper from the box. Never been touched by the sun or damaged by weather. She walks over to the door, pushes it shut, turning the knob and turns off the lights so only the bathroom light invades the room through the cracked door from the right. Her slender frame is so delicate, and I can only make out her silhouette in the dim lights.

"I want to see you." I want to turn on the lights and admire this magnificent bronze creature in front of me.

"No. I want you to feel me," she responds softly.

Her skin is warm and soft, her lips full and tender against mine. She smells like men's cologne; of wine and roses. I remind myself to go slow and gentle as she straddles me. My eyes have somewhat adjusted to the darkness, so I can faintly make out her face, and it looks calm but also bewildered. She looks at me, into me, through me, and I know that she is consumed with the same desire that courses through me. She takes both my hands and gently places them on her breasts; her tiny, firm breasts.

Again, I wish I could see her in vividness, the size of her areola, the pattern of the little hairs on her neck, the line on her navel. I tenderly kiss each of her breasts and take my time tending to them and then leave small traces of wet kisses past her navel, making my way to her fragrant pudenda. I kiss her over her panties and am dizzied by the smell of her sex. She softly coos and purrs, and the sound is hypnotic.

She pulls me back up by my hair, her kiss deepening when I touch her breasts, her breath quickens, and there is movement, but no space between us. She steals a wet kiss from my lips, kissing me all the way down to the middle of my chest and then back again. I gently pull her to me, for I can't get enough of her kisses. She unbuttons the last three buttons of my jeans while she's in my mouth and slowly slides back down. She slips my pants to my knees and blows through the fabric of my briefs, creating a warm cloud that lights a fiery flame in my crotch, and when she stops, a cooling sensation makes me want her whole mouth there and everywhere else on me.

I am at attention and firm. I am at a point of combustion. She slips her hand into my briefs, and with one move she releases me and the sudden exposure has me wanting her immediately and absolutely. Infinitesimally, I withdraw my wallet, pulling the flaps apart and dig out a condom before throwing it behind the couch. I lean all the way back and pull her on top of me. Still with her panties on she wheels on top of me with no resistance. I pull her to my mouth and hold her torso as close to me as our bodies will allow. She purrs and stirs as I slowly slip my fingers under her panties from the back and into her and find her wet and ready for me.

I rip the wrapper with my teeth and left hand, while my other hand is occupied inside her and as my patience wanes, I dress myself with the latex while owning her with my mouth. Pulling her panties to the side, I slowly enter her, making sure she is letting me in as she is taking me in. She molds into me oh so sweetly and soughs as I dig myself deeper into her; her warm pudenda receiving me and welcoming me to stay. Her insides mold around me as if begging me to stay, not to go, to build a nest inside her and never leave. She squeezes her thighs with me in them, and I hold on to them and will her to squeeze tighter. I am sealed in the V of her thighs, and I might want to make that my permanent home. I pull, and she pushes; I push, and she pulls, and my pelvis cannot suffer any more pleasure.

I kiss her shoulders and her arms and try to keep her as close to me as I can have her. She tosses her hair to the side, and I get a whiff of it: a delicious citrusy July. Her curls fall on my face, curtaining us both as she hovers above me, and I hold on to her hips and watch her silhouette jive on top of me. I run my fingers on her smooth back, which is now textured with tiny beads of sweat. She moves on top of me as if she knows my body, and it responds to her all the same.

The hectic sound of our breathing, her kisses, her pleading is an aphrodisiac. Our breathing gets louder and louder until I hear her hold her breath as if she is running out of air. She is silent for a second and then lets out a long sexy sigh as I feel her constrict, and like a remora, she clenches on to me one last time before releasing her inner muscles. My body shatters and collects it-self while hers bends backwards 180 degrees. She leans back to me and kisses me oh so softly, both her hands cupping my face as her hair curtains us in a little world where our lips and tongues are dancing to the sound of our panting. At this moment, with her as company, guilt is of no consequence.

CHAPTER FOUR

The morning light penetrates through my eyelids, and I wake up to the sound of the lawn mower and birds chirping. I find myself spread on the couch with a kink in my neck and a surfacing regret. In a moment, my mind is aware of my indiscretions and I cringe at the sight of the condom wrapper on the floor as scenes of last night play themselves to me in vivid motion picture.

I had sex with the nanny. By the looks of it, she regrets it, too. Why else would she have left before I woke up? I rise and rub my eyes as I slowly make my way upstairs, tiptoeing, so I don't wake Skylar up. I go past the kitchen and realize a big mess on the counter. I figure Skylar is up, and as I make my way to her bedroom, I hear playful voices outside that stop me in my tracks. I head to the direction of the voices and peek out the window to find July and Skylar racing to the trampoline. *Shit, she's still here.*

I head over to my room and realize it's almost 10:00. I'm surprised I slept in, but I feel relaxed and rejuvenated, so I decide to take a quick shower and face what awaits me.

⸻

I walk over to the two girls, and they are lying on the trampoline and talking softly; they don't even realize I am there until I clear my throat, feeling like I've intruded their world.

The grass is still wet, and there are fragments of wounded trees as a sign of bad weather. The trees are skinny, and all their leaves are spread all over the yard. The thunderstorm never did hit, but some damage was done by the rain, obviously.

"Good morning girls." I wait for their response, not exactly sure of how I should approach July.

"Good morning," they say in a chorus, both with smiles on their faces.

"Daddy, I have to show you something."

"What is it?" Skylar climbs out of the trampoline through the small opening of the net that surrounds it. "You have to promise to say yes, please Daddy; July already said she would take me."

"What is it?" I ask again, this time looking at July, who simply shrugs her shoulders.

"Wait right here. I'll be right back."

She runs to the house, leaving July and I alone feeling awkward in the open air. July climbs out and stands next to me. She puts her hand on my arm.

"Hey. Are we cool?"

"Of course, we are," I say, very much aware of the foreign object hanging on my arm.

"Good, because nothing has changed. I know that."

I am relieved to hear that, but I fight to make my relief visible, so I smile a strenuous smile and pat her hand on my arm with my other hand. Skylar runs back holding a colorful newspaper article.

I quickly release July's hand, and she steps back, gaping the distance between us before Skylar stops in front of us.

"Before I show you this Daddy, you have to remember you promised." She hands me the piece of paper with the Wilmington Zoo logo and a picture of a baby elephant.

"I didn't promise anything." She is jumping up and down as I read the flyer.

"Please Daddy. I'll match my socks, so Selena won't have to do it," she begs and pleads until I have no choice but to give in. How can I resist?

We arrive at a crowded zoo parking lot. At the gate, there are kids everywhere and women with strollers and small kids. There are a few dads here and there. I have half a mind to convince Skylar and July just to see the baby elephant and then go back home.

"I want to see the giraffes and the monkeys, too. What do you want to see, July?"

There goes my plan, I think to myself as July and Skylar deliberate.

"I want to see polar bears and penguins." July is almost as excited as Skylar. "What do you want to see, Dorian?"

The inside of my car and the highway back home.

"Snakes and lions." I try to think of something manly instead.

Once inside, the day is actually tolerable. July and Skylar walk ahead holding hands, and my presence is barely acknowledged, which leaves me to my thoughts. July is handling things maturely and not making a big deal out of things. We go through the petting zoo as our last stop and then head to the exit, having had lunch at the zoo cafeteria.

Not even 15 minutes into the car, Skylar falls asleep, leaving July and I in the front seat at our own device. July turns and looks at her before making a maternal sound. She looks at me and smiles.

"She's a jewel, isn't she?"

"The apple of my eye," I respond.

She sighs in exhaustion and turns to look out her window. We drive in silence, and it's not an awkward silence: it's not comfortable, but it's not expectant either. I notice for the first-time what July is wearing.

<hr>

After unloading the car and putting Skylar to bed, I walk downstairs and find July gathering herself and taking her bag and keys from the mudroom. I head straight to the counter and write her a check for today and yesterday. I fold it and give it to her, and she takes it and puts it in her pocket without checking the amount.

"So, I will see you next week then?"

"Yes. I already have my schedule from Jane."

"Okay."

I can tell that she is ready to leave before things get awkward, but it seems we both don't want to say goodbye or talk about last night. I am unsure as to whether I should hug her, shake her hand, or wave goodbye, and thank goodness my phone rings and I answer, and she just waves as I occupy myself with my phone.

"Enoch."

"Benson! What time are we going tomorrow?"

"Going where? I told you that I was going to see Llarel's solo tomorrow night."

"I know. What time are we going?"

"What do you mean we?"

"We are going to watch Llarel twinkle her toes tomorrow, aren't we?"

"I am."

"Me too then."

I know this is some sort of ploy for something else, or he must have some ulterior motives.

"Why on Earth would you want to go see Ballet?"

"I'm being supportive. Why not?"

"You know both Burr and Selena will be there right?"

I ask him knowing very well that Enoch has hooked up with both my housekeeper and Burr, who's Llarel's matron since they were kids. I can't exactly call what he had with them relationships because Enoch does not have relationships: he merely has flings and hook-ups.

"It's time I make amends and let the past be the past."

"You are serious. You really are planning on coming tomorrow night, aren't you?"

"Yes. How long are we going to keep talking in circles?"

"Right after you answer me this. Why? Why now?"

"Like I said: I'm going to support your sister and make amends with Burr and Selena."

"But you hate Llarel. Why would you want to support her?"

"I don't hate her. I merely dislike her. That's all."

Enoch and Llarel have hated each other for as long as Enoch and I have been friends. They just clash. Neither of them would be able to tell you why. They are always bickering and making fun of each other. Truth of the matter is that they are just too similar. They are the opposite genders of each other.

I reluctantly give Enoch the details and decide on not saying anything to Llarel with the hopes that Enoch is just bluffing and that he will in fact flake tomorrow night.

The flutes flutter and the symphonic chords make themselves familiar as Vincenso Bellini's Casta Diva fills the air. Llarel starts out curled up and small in the middle of the circle of light, and she makes herself bigger as an opera in a woman's voice paralyzes the audience.

She is graceful, a note in the ballad. She is a single raindrop purposed to rain over the whole Earth. She dances, multiplying herself so she touches all of the stage and the hearts of the people watching her. The faux winter background absorbs her as if it were her natural habitat.

She extends her arms and closes her eyes as her body transforms into music itself. My heart strings are pulled, my guard completely down. I turn to find Selena with a teardrop that now makes its way down her finger. Llarel is lethal and absolutely captivating.

I am transported back to childhood as I watch the music take over her. I dig my toes into the toes of my shoes and anchor myself as I watch my blind twin sister see into herself and grow bigger than life. She reaches with her hands while her whole body shakes and her toes remain firmly pointed, waiting their chance to dig into the ground. I forget she's blind, and I know she does too as she dances like a feather that is blown by Aphrodite herself. She resembles a leaf that endlessly falls but never reaches ground.

The light nests in her hair as she collects food for it. I look around me, and all the women are on the verge of tears, and Enoch looks paralyzed. Llarel, like a Persian mermaid, an African diamond, she dazzles and astonishes, and it's hard to believe that she is not some mythical creature that has yet to exist in some unfathomable universe.

The angelic voice screams into the sight of Llarel, and she, in turn, turns into the melody itself: the music dances, and she is the beat. The wind stirs around her as she closes her eyes and paints rivers and deserts with her long, lithe limps while the gold chignon stays steady and tight on her head.

She closes her eyes and is transported into an invisible world that only she knows about. I envy her; serenity is around her and inside of her. She stretches her body and then her fingers to an invisible object that she just can't seem to touch, and the screams of the violin in the background scream as the pain in her expression makes you, the viewer, imagine your own pain.

Her pink slippers bare into the ground but can't seem to penetrate it as she dances lightly like a feather or a butterfly's wing, whispering to the air as she twirls around and her tutu dances in the middle of her length. I watch from the corner of my eye and find Skylar in wonder and in tears. In her eyes, I see Llarel climbing up and sitting on a pedestal.

As the lady with the big lungs screams her final note and the song comes to a soft lull, Llarel folds herself until she is half her size. The song's tempo changes to a soft lull, and the harp strums sharply and the volume lowers until the song comes to an end, and Llarel is laying on the ground, covering her head and making herself as small as possible.

There is a composed or a shocked silence before everyone rises and claps. I rise as well and partake in the well-deserved standing ovation. Even though the story behind the song is about two lovers, I give Llarel credit for the way she portrayed the melancholy of a broken lover.

Waiting in the limo, Skylar wants herself next to her aunt, the star of the night and her role model.

Burr ushers Llarel in and climbs in after her, and everyone starts clapping for her, and Skylar hands her a bouquet of purple tulips that she picked out herself.

"Let's hear it for twinkle toes," Enoch shouts over the applause.

"Ugh. What is he doing here? I thought I smelled something foul." Llarel's smile fades.

Those two have never liked other, hence my surprise when Enoch volunteered to come not only to some *ballerina thing*, but one that actually involved having dinner with Llarel after.

Skylar places herself on Llarel's hip and asks her question after question about her music, her costume, her stance and dance technique, making it impossible for Llarel to participate in any of the adult conversations.

Burr and Selena both quietly avoid Enoch and talk among each other as they both have a common enemy. Enoch, being the male slut that he is, managed to hook up with both of them, and now all three women in the limo hate him.

"You know you want me," Enoch instigates.

"Dorian, I thought this was supposed to be my night. Why did you bring this pompous idiot with you?" Llarel gestures to the direction where Enoch's voice came.

"He insisted, although I'm not exactly certain why," I defend.

"I didn't want to miss an opportunity to be surrounded by my fans."

All three women roll their eyes, and Selena sticks her tongue out at him.

"Don't flatter yourself," Burr mutters quietly but loud enough for all of us to hear.

"No one likes you here." Llarel points to his direction.

"And that is why I have seen half of the people in this car naked."

Burr covers Skylar's ear, which only alerts her. All three women ignore us the rest of the ride to the restaurant, and I scold Enoch for putting me in the doghouse with him.

We arrive at Ruth Chris and are immediately assigned to our table; Enoch deliberately places himself between Burr and Llarel, and Llarel's other side is occupied by Skylar who is her number one fan for the evening.

"So, twinkle toes, are we going to share a dessert?" Enoch's sarcasm has no limit.

"There's that foul smell again. Brush your teeth why don't you," Llarel fires at Enoch.

"Are you sure it's not your own sweat you're smelling? I mean, you did just dance up a storm."

"You are such an idiot, Enoch. Why are you here?"

The whole dinner is bickering back and forth between the girls and Enoch, and everyone ignores me for bringing him and ruining the dinner. This makes the evening long and dreadful, and by the time I am done dropping Skylar off at her mom's, Llarel's driver takes me and Enoch home. I am exhausted and in no mood to hang out.

"So, your sister really hates me."

"You think?"

"I'm not really that fond of her either."

"And?"

"And nothing. I was just trying to be supportive that's all."

"Since when?"

"Since I had nothing better to do with my Friday evening. You know that speed dating thing was a crock. All the girl's they matched me with were either hot but crazy or normal but ugly."

"You are such a douche," I assert, with no hint of humor.

"This douche has been making sure that both *Blue Baby* and *Baby Blue* are running smoothly this week. You haven't checked in at all this week."

"Yeah. It's been a crazy few days. Want to swing by right now?"

"I better get going. I have an early morning tomorrow."

"You? First one to call it a night on a Friday evening?" I am shocked.

"Yes. We are going out to the country with Cordelia's in-laws. I was told that it was compulsory for me to be there, or I would be in the doghouse with her again. At this rate, I'm about to be uninvited to the wedding."

"Have you not met his family yet?"

"My parents have, but Cordelia had this great idea that all the immediate family get together for the weekend. It's such a drag. Now we all have to put our lives on hold and start this spoiling-Cordelia-marathon until her wedding is over."

"Yeah, your sister can be a princess sometimes," I offer my two cents.

After Enoch leaves, I walk over to the art room and sit facing the south wall where an unfinished portrait of Jacquilin Lefèvre stares back at me. I spend the whole weekend working on her vacant eyes and the big ring on her thumb. I study my old work of her and try to concentrate on her mouth and eyes this time, making her ring the focal point. When I feel myself getting agitated with the same face, I walk away fighting the edge to throw the whole thing in the tub and burn it.

I spend the rest of the weekend going back and forth between *Blue Baby* and *Baby Blue*, and on Sunday, I drive 64 miles outside of Wilmington in search of a new art gallery that is rumored to have an original statue of Auguste Rodin. I am surprised at my confusion when I find out that the rumor is not true. I am disappointed not to have the honor of being in its presence.

It's been a crazy week at work. I am flooded with phone calls and trying to make sure that all the art gets in on time and that the gallery is big enough to accommodate the guest list and all the major pieces.

I give Prudence Rose my final decision about doing the portrait in Colorado, and she leaves right away to make the phone call to confirm dates and sets up a meeting for me to meet with the coordinator in person. She returns after a few minutes.

"Julian is the person seeing this project through, and he is the one you will need to meet with."

"Great. When would he like to meet?"

"This week."

"Not great."

"He is going out of town on Friday, and he would like to meet with you before he leaves if you want to give yourself enough time for this project."

"I have a child. And I do have other clients you know."

"I know, and I'm sorry. He was expecting you to get back to him last week, remember. They can book you a flight for Wednesday and have you back Friday evening."

After having worked out the details with Jane and making sure that Skylar is taken care of, I walk out to Prudence Rose's desk and let her know that she can confirm the travel arrangements, even though she did say that I would not be traveling this month.

The meeting with Julian goes well, and he gives me pictures and the background story of the honoree. Denver weather is a little bit different and a little bit off-sorts for my taste, but I have dinner with a sculptor, David, from France who's seen my work from Madame Lefèvre, and we both talk about how brilliant she is and her love for the arts and the aesthetics. I wonder, for a moment, if she has bedded him, too, but quickly derail such childish foolery. We exchange numbers and promise to call each other whenever we are in each other's town.

Arriving home, I have a new appreciation for the weather here. I call Enoch back and take a nap. I find out from Jane when she will be dropping Skylar off.

"We are coming from Cody and Myra's, and July left her car at my house. Do you mind dropping her off to pick it up later?"

"Yes. Sure."

"We will be there in a few then."

I sit down and examine how I feel about seeing July. We never did talk about what transpired between us, and I am honestly afraid of what her stance is on the matter. I haven't had time to make sense of it or think about how to approach things when I see her. Is she going to want to know what happens from here on? Or like me, maybe she wants to forget the whole thing and pretend it never happened; I hope it's the latter.

Automatically I walk over to the basement, and it looks normal; nothing out of the ordinary, and no evidence of our unspeakable affair. I imagine Jane would kill me if we lost a great nanny for Sky because of me. How do I feel about July? I don't. It was only a spontaneous indiscretion, and it will not happen again. I just need to find a way to get us both on the same page. She acted normal at the zoo; surely that means we've moved past it as adults. Could it be that easy?

Chapter Five

"July, Skylar hasn't had a snack yet, and she needs to practice her pirouettes before she can play. Where's Dorian? Dorian!"

Jane throws her commands at July without really acknowledging her. She walks back and forth unloading Skylar's backpack and ballet bag off her shoulder.

"Oh, her ballet class is cancelled tomorrow, and I'm taking her to a birthday party at the boat club, so I'll pick her up here at three."

July simply mentally notes everything that Jane instructs to her.

"I have to go, tell Dorian to call me later." She waves, still without looking at July. "Bye sweetie, Mommy will call you later." She directs her voice towards Skylar, who is in the restroom.

July simply waves to her, having had no chance to say a word since they walked in the door. Jane slams the door behind her as she picks up the phone and starts barking orders at someone else.

Skylar comes out of the bathroom and calls for Neo, who comes running for his treat. She sits next to July on the kitchen counter with her little black poodle in her arms.

"July, you know I'm going to miss you this weekend."

"Hey kiddo, I'll miss you too."

They sit with their legs folded on the quartz counter, and they talk as though they have a lot of catching up to do. July pulls Skylar closer to her taking off her shoes and massaging each of her feet while she asks her about school and her weekend. I walk into the room unnoticed and watch from the side, marveling at how good July is with Skylar.

"I'm upset that they cancelled ballet tomorrow because now we have less time to practice for the recital," Skylar vents to July, who simply listens and nods on cue.

"If you want, you can practice, and I'll watch." July offers.

"Okay. I can show you the new way I do my pirouette," she squeaks excitedly.

"I'd like that," July concurs.

"Hello girls."

Both girls turn to look at me, moving their feet off the counter as if they are accomplices against my rules.

I walk over to Skylar and give her a hug, grateful that she is still not too old for public affection. She tucks her blonde hair behind her newly pierced ears and looks at me in anticipation. I purposely take longer to look at July by looking around the kitchen.

"We are going to your favorite restaurant tonight, and you can eat as much dessert as you want."

"No Daddy, really?"

"Really!" I affirm.

"Can July come, too?" She looks at me with bright begging eyes.

"Of course, she can. That is, if she wants to?" I look at July for confirmation.

"I would love to." She looks at Skylar as she answers.

"Aunt Llarel is coming, too. We are meeting her there."

July's eyes widen, and I gather that she feels like she is intruding. I give her a nod and a smile, assuring her that it is not a big deal.

"Yay! July you'll finally meet my cool Aunt Llarel. She is blind, but don't be scared, she can smell anything and tell you what it is just by smelling it or touching it. It's so cool."

She looks at me again with a surprised but reprimanding look, I assume, for me not telling her about Llarel's blindness.

"Daddy says it's a special gift that only pure hearted people have." Skylar continues excitedly, unaware of the silent conversation transpiring between July and I. July looks at me once more for an explanation, but I motion with my eyes that there is none.

Once there, we claim our reservation, and our waiter sits us at the balcony overlooking the water. Llarel has not yet arrived, and I find that a little disconcerting since she never is late for anything. As our waiter brings our water, I excuse myself from the table.

"I'm just going to call your aunt quickly and see what's keeping her."

I walk outside with the phone glued to my ear, and she picks up after three rings.

"Dorian? Is everything okay?" Llarel sounds concerned.

"That's what I was calling to find out. I thought you were meeting us here at 6:30?"

"Didn't you get my voicemail? That explains why you never responded. I left you a message explaining that I wouldn't be able to join you tonight after all."

"No, I haven't listened to my messages. Is everything okay?"

"Yeah, no I'm fine. Something else came up that's all."

"Oh okay. Do you want us to bring you something afterwards?"

"No. No thank you, I'm meeting…err…an old friend out to dinner. I have to go Dorian. Give Sky kisses for me."

She hangs up. I look at my phone for answers with a flabbergasted look on my face. What is she up to? And what old friend? Why is she being so mysterious? I wonder.

I forget about it as soon as I sit down.

At Connor's, Skylar's eyes are dancing with excitement. Before our food even arrives, Marybeth Hudson, a little girl who's friends with Skylar comes over to the table and asks if Skylar can sit with her and her family at their table.

Skylar knits her fingers together, chanting, "Please Daddy! Please!" with her puppy dog face, and I can't help but say yes. They scream and squeal and dash to the table on the far back of the restaurant, and I wave at the parents, and they wave back.

I excuse myself to July and walk over to the table. I introduce myself to the father, since I've met the mother on several playdates and ballet practices. I talk briefly to Skylar's friend's parents before walking back to July. By the time our conversation is over, the two girls have convinced both me and the parents that Skylar should spend the night at the Hudsons'. We confirm that they will take her to ballet, and Jane will just meet them there.

I feel conned as I walk back to now July and I's table. I apologize for leaving her alone as I scoot myself into the chair next to her, I accidently lean in too close to July, and my nostrils are bathed in her scent.

"What is that smell on you? You smell like that all the time. It's divine."

She smiles her crooked smile and her dimples sink in mischievously.

"Cologne."

"Men's cologne?" I raise an eyebrow, surprised.

"Yes. Bora Bora."

"Why?"

"Why not?"

"Why not perfume; like normal women wear?"

"Because I am not a normal woman."

This intrigues me. I wonder why she doesn't consider herself normal, why she sets herself apart from the norm.

"Is there a story behind it?"

She shifts uncomfortably in her chair before meeting my eyes.

"Okay. I wear men's cologne, this one in particular, because it reminds me of my father."

I cock my head to the right, coaxing her to go on, feeling her reluctance to offer the rest of the explanation.

"This was his scent, and when he died, I got into a huge fight with my mother because she started washing his clothes and hanging them back in his closet as if waiting for him to come back. I, on the other hand, knew he wasn't coming back, but I felt him with me when I could smell him."

"Were you close to your dad?"

I am surprised at my need for this knowledge. When you ask such questions to a person, you are looking for your way into their lives and giving them permission to do the same to yours, and I know I am in no position to be doing that. But I want to know.

"Yes. I'm starving. Let's eat."

She changes the subject, and I decide not to push because if I do, I pretty soon would be answering the same questions, and that is something I would rather do, second to sucking on a burning piece of coal.

"Yes. Let's." I announce as I dig into my plate.

I wonder for a second about the similarities between July and I. It seems she, like me, is more eager to share herself physically than she is emotionally. My intention is to keep her out but enjoy her more tangible attributes, and the idea that she might be doing the same disappoints me. Is that how she would feel, too, were to discover my intensions for her? I wonder.

"You want to know how I pictured your mom?" I try to lighten the mood.

"My mom? You've thought about my mom?"

"When you told me your mom was Egyptian, I thought about her on stage."

"You thought about my mom on stage? Doing what?"

I can't decipher her look. She looks rather amused but could easily be offended. I try to finish chewing and swallow fast so I can explain to her before her assumptions get the best of her.

"No. No," I say, swallowing before I'm done chewing.

"I mean, I pictured her on stage in front of a crowd, swaying her hips from side to side with her hands in the air and her eyes closed."

She tilts her head to the side, waiting for me to say something that makes sense.

"Sade. Do you know who she is? She's from Egypt."

A smile forms in her mouth, and I am relieved that she has understood and is amused at my incoherency.

"You imagine my mom as Sade?"

I nod, fighting the edge to cough as I feel my throat close around my steak.

Halfway through our meal, the Hudsons wave goodbye, and Skylar doesn't dare come to say goodnight, in case I change my mind. As soon as they leave the restaurant, the dynamic changes between July and I, as if the restaurant suddenly dimmed the lights.

In a restaurant full of people, she sits across from me, staring at me while she chews on her Dijon chicken. I notice that the light hits her profile in such a way that there are hills and valleys in the middle of her face. Her neck is long and her curls dance around her head, making playful shadows on her cheeks. The air between us is charged, and there is no need for conversation. I stare back at her watching her mouth spread into a smile and her throat swallow. She stabs a fork into my steak and immediately retrieves it. Her face horrified, and I watch her with amusement.

"Two seconds less and this cow would still be breathing," she asserts in disgust.

"Come. Sit next to me." I pat the padded red cushion that extends from beneath me.

She scoops a forkful of garlic mashed potatoes and deposits it into her mouth, and then she scoots all the way to the left until she is next to me.

"You look amazing tonight." I stare her down as I compliment her.

She looks at herself as if trying to see what I see. She looks up seemingly dubious. I let out a long breath as I surf the crown and notice the crowded room full of people with lives to attend to and bellies to satisfy. We both let the silence travel around us until I finally break it.

"Spread your legs," I say nonchalantly as if telling her to pass the salt. She looks around, making sure no one heard me. She stabs a spear of broccoli as she follows my instructions.

"Now, hike up your skirt all the way to your waist." This time, I keep the same volume but my eyes surf my surroundings as I turn my body to face her.

She shakes her head no, and my smile lops to one side as I catch her nervous expression. I run my hand on her cheek, and she catches it and kisses the inside of my palm. I run my thumb on the outside of her lips, dip it in my wine, and then put it in her mouth, she keeps her teeth apart and lets it linger there.

"You have a beautiful mouth," I state.

I remove my thumb from her mouth and let my hand drop to her knee. I trail it on her inner thigh and stop at the center of her. She starts breathing fast and shallow when I squeeze the inside of her thigh.

"Your skirt!" I reiterate my earlier request.

She pulls on the tablecloth until she is covered from the waist down and then pulls her skirt up to her waist so it's in full view from where I sit. Her breathing is chopped and audible, and she paces the room with her eyes while she keeps her hand on me, squeezing for me to stop. I take a sip of my wine with my free hand as if I am not doing anything out of the ordinary, and she watches me and mirrors my composure.

"Does this excite you?" I whisper close to her ear.

She looks around again and then at me. She moistens her lips with her tongue and then grabs her water and takes a big sip.

I press into her with my thumb and her body tenses, and she lets out a small grunt.

"Do you want me to stop?"

"No," she whispers.

"Do you want my fingers inside of you?"

Her breathing accelerates, and her big brown eyes dig into mine in disbelief.

Slowly and tenderly I massage her with four fingers through her satin panties, and she folds and squeezes her legs shut trapping me with her thighs. I take another sip using my right hand and turn to look at her. She stabs another spear of broccoli and attempts to put it in her mouth, but the act of normalcy fails her as she now places the staked broccoli back on her plate and strains to control her breathing.

I make fast and circular movements with my fingers, and I feel her panties moisten as she jams my hand in the middle of her thighs. She is agog, orgasmic. Her lips start to quiver, and she rolls her eyes back, and so I slide my fingers under the cotton and slip two inside her. And in a matter of seconds my fingers are sopping, and she shudders. She takes her napkin and hides behind it as if she's coughing.

I remove my left hand from under the table and lick my fingers one by one while keeping my eyes steady on her. She looks away shyly and then looks back at me amused.

"Mmmmm," I tease her.

She takes another gulp of her water and doesn't stop until she drains the whole contents of the glass. Our waiter comes and asks if everything tastes alright as he considers our half full plates.

"Check please." I ask politely.

I settle the check and walk out with July in my arm. Under the black sky, under this moonless night, July trustingly follows me. Instead of walking towards the parking lot where the car is, I pull her towards the alley and on the side. There are two buildings an arm's length from each other: *GlassGlow*, a glass shop, and *Petunia's Petunias*, a flower shop. There is only a narrow separation of space between them and July and I tuck ourselves inside of it, kissing and giggling like two drunk fools in love—or in our case, lust. I start kissing her and pull her skirt up to the top of her thighs and she stops me.

"What do you think I am... Easy?"

"Yes please." I nod excitedly.

She laughs but pushes her skirt back down. July simply looks at me and playfully kisses me all over my face, everywhere on my face but my lips, and I move with her trying to catch her mouth, but she dodges and bobs her head, teasingly avoiding me.

She smiles her wide, all teeth smile, showing off her dimples as she unzips my pants and slides down pulling them down with her. She kisses my hip bone, my hip, and the ridges on the side of my stomach, and then moves on to the other side, licking a long line along the top of my thigh. She bites hard on the side right above my left thigh. My erection grows with every touch and every sound she makes. I cannot see what she is doing with her mouth or her hands; I just see her head bobbing, and I anticipate her quest as my mind awaits the obvious. But she does not take me into her mouth, and I ache as she plants a small kiss on my muscle. She rises and looks at me with a devious look on her face.

"Dessert? Where should we go for dessert?"

"No!" I grunt in frustration.

She starts walking away without looking back, and my eyes widen in panic. I look around the deserted alley and conclude that she cannot just leave me here in this state. She wouldn't.

"You are not that cruel," I call after her.

"No, I am not, but I do have other plans for you."

"And what might those be?"

She saunters back to me, and I am relieved, for her wellbeing as well as my physical state, although part of me knew she would not leave me with my pants down to my ankles.

"I want you to please yourself, and I want to watch."

What! I am taken aback. I have always known that most men have this fantasy to watch a woman masturbate, but I always thought that women find it disgusting. It really isn't that sexy when a man does it.

"I'll do it if you do it."

"Ok. You are to, under no circumstance, touch me."

"Ditto," I reply, playing a little hard to get, although I suspect that she knows she could have me if she wanted me. Anytime.

This seems like bizarre behavior. Especially for me: to have a beautiful woman right in front of me, to watch her pleasing herself and be unable to touch her is not something I would consider to be fun, but why not? My pants are down to my ankles and my erection awaits. She makes it easy for me by dropping her purse and jacket between us, leaning against *GlassGlow* opposite me, and she looks intently at me as I press my back on the side wall of *Petunia's*

Petunias, facing her. She puts her hand in her blouse while staring at me and biting her lip, watching me watch her.

I stare intently at her as I hold myself in my hand and slowly stroke up and down, imagining it is her hands on me, and she is relishing playing with me as she is enjoying playing with herself right now. She unzips the back of her skirt and strokes herself from behind, spreading her legs and pushing her back against the wall and moaning.

I ache as I wonder where her fingers are and what they are doing to her, and my own hand changes tempo on my throbbing tendon. We both stare at each other as we rub ourselves, and our breathing is in sync as if I am touching her and she me.

I make an O with my fingers and thumb, and begin thrusting prudently, pretending it is her that I am thrusting into, although not as warm and as sweet and soft, but...ah...the look she gives me, those eyes. Like candle wax, I melt and burn under her stare. To watch her, to witness such a private show humbles me. She throws her head back and moans my name, which sets me off at the thought of her pleasing herself using me as her instrument.

Her body frantically shudders as she comes into a frenzy, panting and effervescent right in front of my eyes and I have yet to touch her. Her eyes don't leave mine but mine soak her whole body in, and I, for the first time, am given insight as to what she looks like or how her body reacts when she lets go and acts as though she is alone. This sets a feverous stinging deep within me, and I just come undone; I split in two and detonate like cherry confetti. We both hum and buzz right in front of each other's eyes.

She puts her hand on the side of the wall of *GlassGlow* and leans down panting while waiting for her frantic breathing to subside. And I lean against *Petunia's Petunias*, putting on my trousers and watch her while I try to control my own breathing. I turn myself now at opposite walls, and I push myself forward and step over to her. I kiss her hard, and she kisses me back and then she puts her aromatic fingers in my mouth and the sweet taste of her, of her sex and cum. She takes my right hand as well and inserts it into her mouth, sucking oh so gently.

"I'm ready for you to take me home now," she says to me with a voice of an insatiable sex goddess.

"And do what to you?" I ask with a dark smile.

"Turn me inside out," she says as she zips the back of her skirt back up.

I nod my head as she gathers her belongings and follow her out of the alley and to the car. I don't take her hand but simply place mine on the arch of her lower back and steer her towards the parking lot. We enter the car and drive home in silence as it starts to drizzle.

———

Silence becomes us as we approach the street to the house and pull up in the driveway, electricity ricocheting between us. It must be the storm as I catch glimpse of her face each time it's lit up by lightning. Her fingers touch mine, and she quickly retrieves her hand holding it closer to her, and I am afraid that the heat radiating from within me had burnt her; somehow that doesn't seem impossible. I insert the key and twist the lock, both of us walking in cautiously as though intruding into a stranger's house. The rain is at a steady pace as we close the garage door behind us.

I grab a bottle of white wine and two glasses, leading her to the living room. I set the glasses down by the TV and walk to the center of the room. She walks behind me leisurely, looking around as if she has never set foot in the house before. I turn the lights on, dimming them, and then pick up the remote controller and start the fire.

I turn to look at her and walk over to her and sit her down on the couch. Still no sound from either of us, but her last words echoing in my head; *turn me inside out*. I kneel before her and take off her left shoe and massage her foot and then kiss her heel. I repeat the same motion with the next foot. She looks at me and moves slowly and deliberately, watching and waiting for me to coach her to move, to breathe, to do as I will. I lean closer and rest my cheek on her knee and enjoy her hand on my head while she moves it slowly against the sequence of my hair.

I listen to the false fire from the fireplace crackling and move my cheek up and down her soft smooth legs. Having spoken not a single word since we got into the car, I much rather delight in the presence and the silence of July. I look up at her as I kiss her knees, and she looks down at me, and for a split second that makes me uneasy. I lift myself off the floor, pulling her along with me. She scoots off the couch and levels with me as I take her hand, and we dance to the crackling of the fire and the silence that envelops us. She looks at me, the brown in her eyes turning gold as the fire reflects on them from behind me. I unbutton her shirt revealing a black bra with intricate red lacing. I unzip her skirt and let it pool to her feet, uncovering a matching pair of panties that pleasantly hug her hips.

I take a step back to admire her, and she twirls around, allowing me full view. I kiss her shoulder and leave her standing solo while I walk over to my prized possession: my classic record player; an original. I remove Louis Armstrong from the disc, scanning my collection and deciding on one, I place the record and soupçon the needle to it.

Sade's voice fills the room as the spread of gold and candle glow colors the walls around us.

"Sade!" she grimaces, and we both laugh at our inside joke.

I walk over to her, untucking my shirt and throwing it by the fireplace.

"Does this music turn you on?" she asks as she studies me, steading when I reach her.

I unbuckle my belt and bend over to take my shoes and pants off. I kneel before her and kiss her naked thighs as she rubs her hands on my now sensitive scalp. I close my eyes and concentrate on feeling her hand as she rubs my head. A snaking thought sneaks into the surface again, and I open my eyes to push it away before I can even comprehend it. This is strictly lust and obviously carnal.

"Music doesn't seduce me. You do."

I unhook her bra, slowly and seductively running my hands down her arms as I free her from its restraints. I put both my hands in the back of her panties, cupping her butt before I pull them down.

"How?" she smiles mischievously as she steps out of them.

She is completely naked and totally vulnerable, as am I. I pull her to me and lower myself, so I'm level with her.

"Your scent. The way you move." I breathe her, I just inhale her and keep her under my skin.

"What about the way I move?" she whispers seductively.

We sway back and forth, skin to skin, pelvis to pelvis, my hand on her lower back and her hands gently kneading mine. The volume of our voices, the rawness in hers allows the music to pierce deeper within.

"The way you extend your lines. You're like a flawed painting that corrects itself."

"So, I am flawed?"

"No. You're perfect."

"What about me is perfect?" She looks up at me from under her lashes, teasing me with her voice.

I lean in and kiss her throat after tucking her curl behind her ear.

"The way you breathe."

"And what about the way I breathe?" she purrs against me.

"It's rhythmic. Evident. You let people know you're alive."

"And you don't."

I pull her closer and run my hand up and down her back and pull her hair out of her ponytail.

"No." I breathe against her neck.

"Why not?"

"Because I'm defective."

I let her hair torrent around her face and the fragrance of it sends me into a small trance. Sade's The Sweetest Gift serenades, and I lean down and kiss her. Hard. I hold her as close as I can have her and devour her. The strumming of the guitar strings wrap around us and make us a note that sings along, we are diluted with the song.

"Would you like for me to turn you inside out now?"

"Yes. Yes please."

Surrounded by a beautiful melody, I lay her down on the carpet in front of the fire and make her wish my command. I simply turn her inside out.

CHAPTER SIX

July has spent the night, and we've spent all morning avoiding the inevitable. We play around and ignore the fact that at some point, there is another world outside of these walls, and that life comes with definitions and explanations. I ignore my logical self and just cling to the now and enjoy her presence for as long as I can, knowing very well it won't last.

She walks out through the French doors, wrapped in an oversize towel. I try not to stare by busying myself with the garden umbrella. I remove my shirt and right away the sun bores into my shoulders. I wear my baseball cap and sunglasses as I reach for the sunscreen. I only put some on my nose and ears and decide to humor myself.

"Would you, could you please?" I extend my hand to hand her the tube of SPF.

She drops the towel and saunters over to me, wearing my favorite yellow bikini. The bright color on her dark skin looks amazing: her hips, her thighs, I ache for my paintbrush.

She takes the tube of SPF and sets it down on the table. She picks up her giant glass of lemonade, wrapping her skinny long fingers around it as if she is someone coming in from a cold rain who takes a sip of cocoa to warm her bones. She closes her eyes and not like a girl with manners, or a lady with an audience; she takes the glass and pours the lemonade down her throat without taking a break until it's half empty.

How adorable, I think to myself. I love that she is not afraid to be herself. She sets the glass down and rubs her wet hands to her naked thighs to dry them, unaware of what she is doing to me, and I push the thought aside as I continue to marvel at her subtle but bizarre behavior. She squeezes a white paste into her palm and motions for me to turn around, and when she touches me, I close my eyes and concentrate on her cold hands running in zig-zag motion on my back. My skin absorbs the feel of her hands on me before it absorbs the sunscreen, and I wish, I just wish…

I brusquely open my eyes and stop the wish from materializing in my head. I take her hand and lead her to the pool.

I love the feel of her skin when she is soaking wet. Water just does something to it. She feels amazing. I love how she smells, too; her natural scent is brought out by the water, and her essence sips through, no longer a secret.

"Why are you so hot?" I ask.

She goes under the water and emerges after a second.

"Because I'm not cold," she teases.

I immerse myself under water and come up with my mouth full of it. I squirt it out of my mouth in a long arch getting her chin and then swim away from her.

Across from her on the other side of the pool, I watch her for a second and playfully try to splash her, but the splash does not reach her. I take off my swim trunks and throw them at her, and she catches them in her hand, smells them, and throws them out to the side of the shallow end. She takes off her bikini bottoms and throws them to me; I catch them and then ball them up into a small cluster and put them in my mouth. I dive under and swim back to her keeping my eyes open under the water.

When I reach her, I am almost out of breath, but I stay under a little longer and admire her naked thighs and her hairless pudenda. As I come up for air, she swims away from me to the steps. I hold my breath and go under again and swim to her, and when I reach her, she has her legs crossed. I spit out her bottoms and impishly ask,

"Are you gonna let me in?"

"Password," she inquires.

"Abracadabra."

She shakes her head no.

"Open Sesame?" I second.

She shakes her head no again, this time holding her finger up and mouthing "one word."

I think for a second wondering what it could be; her name? Too obvious.

"Demerara," I eat the word.

"I like that word. What does it mean?"

"You."

She looks at me and patiently waits for an explanation.

"It's something that resembles the look and the taste of your skin."

She smiles and uncrosses her legs and walks over toward me. As she saunters over, I stretch out my arms in wait to receive her. We curl fingers and receive each other, her drawing to me and me pulling her closer.

She takes my hand and kisses my fingers one by one and then without skipping a beat she takes my thumb and licks it and then my index finger and then my ring finger and then my pinkie. She returns to my middle finger and then puts all of it in her mouth and starts sucking, moving up and down simulating something else that I would like for her to suck on.

I take cue to be my turn to tantalize her. I kiss her ear and then suck on her lobe and then trail kisses from her jaw line until I reach her lips and then I slightly nibble on them before I repeat the same process starting with her other ear. I dip my whole head under the water and come up to her chest where I lick her from her navel to the middle of her breasts and then under them. I push the yellow triangles to the side, revealing her teardrop breasts, and I tease her by not touching her nipples but run my tongue around her areolae. I keep doing this until I see her chest rise and fall in small heaves, and so I pull on her nipple with my teeth, slightly stretching it until she moans.

I cup her butt and gently squeeze it, and as I move my hand to the crevice between her butt and thigh, she pushes into me and knocks me out of balance. In turn, I whirl her around and place her against the wall. I lift her leg and suck in a long breath; I let it out leisurely as I slowly ease into her. I squeeze as I push in and relax when I pull half of me out. She hisses.

I pick up my shorts laying outside the pool by her head and press her against the wall using them to cushion her back. She rakes her fingers in my wet hair while she showers me with her urgent kisses. I fold her into me and pray her like a psalm. When her breath starts breaking into small stitches, I pull out of her and walk over to the steps. I sit on the second step and motion that she sits on my erection, and she faces away and obliges, prudently swallowing me. Her up and down motions creating glugging noises with the water and my thighs, and that's music to my ears.

The open air, the sun penetrates my back and shoulders, and the heat spreads through me and settles on my thighs. I remain steady, holding July's weight as she bobs on me. I kiss her back and fist her hair.

The skin on my back rubbing raw against the third step of the pool, but all I can think is that it hurts but oh so good. It hurts so good as July and the water and the sun and the openness liberate me. The feeling that the neighbors are secretly watching through the trees and envying us as we sex out of control only fuels my carnal cravings.

July is thrusting steadily on top of me as I fill her with myself, and she squeezes me in and breathes out of control. I watch the muscles on her back come alive as she leans forward and rides me. Her dark skin glistens under the stare of the sun, and I watch her move, every muscle under her skin following her while I am inside of her.

It hurts so good, and I feel the skin on my back shred into threads against the wall of the pool, and the water soothing it as we make small waves between the two us. The friction and the water are medicinal opening a portal to my mortality. July plus the water plus the sun equals my very own recipe of ecstasy, and I am drugged and high and soaring. I feel her stiffen, and I know that she is about to detonate. While she breathes in and out in small stitches, I put my hand on her belly and feel her vibrate. Like carbon that is shaken in the confinements of a small aluminum can, we both are let out, and every feeling, every thought comes gushing out and becomes free. We both sough and moan the noises of freedom, and there is no better sound in this world at this moment.

Her back shifts and shapes into a C, and then she shudders before I close my eyes, losing my sight and self momentarily. And then, the water, the sun, and July on my side, and no longer I inside of her. Tomorrow is another day but for now…Right now, I just want to float in the water with my eyes closed and July next to me.

After, she showers in the guest room and I in mine. We resume in the kitchen. I know this is wrong, but again I allow myself to be stupid and solely worry about the now. There's no reason why we can't milk this since we've already blurred the boundaries. Just this one time, just today; we can't undo what we've already done so far, so I make up my mind to compartmentalize it into one moment and redefine things tomorrow.

"Tell me the most abnormal thing about you," I ask her, pushing my worries aside.

She kisses her shoulder and looks up at me shyly. After a moment, she inhales as she shakes her head no.

"Come on."

She drinks from her bottle and looks at the fire.

"Okay."

She shifts from her seat, bringing her legs closer to her and tugs on the hem of the bottom of her jeans before unfolding it and revealing a word written with permanent marker, but she puts her hand on the word, so I cannot read what it says.

"I used to feel abnormal. I'm not really sure I've overcome that." She looks away and laughs at herself but continues with her explanation. "One night, I heard my best friend describe me to her boyfriend, and for the first time I saw myself through her eyes."

She stops and lets the anticipation build as she brushes the inked word on the bottom inside of her jeans.

"She didn't know I was there and that I could hear. That is why I was so sure that she meant what she said. Up till this day, I never told her about that night."

I take a sip of my wine and brace myself as I wait to find out from her what she discovered that night that shapes her normalcy.

"I had never heard anyone say such nice things about me. At that time, I hadn't even considered her my friend, but after the night, I knew she was my best friend. Anyway, she called me brilliant. Brilliant. Even I hadn't considered myself that. So, when I got home I looked up the word and carved in on the bottom of my vanity. It became my new favorite word."

She smiles again as if another thought suddenly occurs in her head, "I wrote it on the hem of my skirt and then on the right helm of the right leg of my jeans. Ever since then, I would write my favorite words on the inside of the right side of the bottom of my pants, but the ink would always bleed through, and people would always ask, so I resorted to just doing it to my jeans."

"So, what does that one say?" I point to the hem of her jeans where her fingers play as she keeps folding and unfolding her hem.

"Desiderata."

I raise my eyebrow, waiting for her to explain further.

"That's all. That's what it says." I feel her reluctance to give a detailed explanation, and that makes it all the more important for me to know.

"Desiderata?" I urge for her to continue.

"Yes. My father's favorite poem by Max Erhmann."

This is the second time I notice her difficulty mentioning her father and to speak of him and anything that has to do with him.

"What does it mean?"

"To me; everything."

I watch her fiddle with the hem of her jeans without any indication that she will continue. I introspectively struggle with whether I should keep probing but decide against it.

"Two things from the poem that my father made sure I lived by," she surprises me because I had already given up on her adding anything else to the subject.

"'If you compare yourself with others, you may become vain or bitter; for always there will be greater and lesser persons than yourself.' He would quote this verbatim and made me memorize it, and I didn't fully understand what it meant until later."

She laughs as if she is recollecting a distant memory.

"Oh, but I did. I learned the hard way. 'You are a child of the universe, no less than the trees and the stars; you have a right to be here. And whether or not it is clear to you, no doubt the universe is unfolding as it should.' This was my father's mantra raising me."

She looks at me as if expecting a reaction. She tilts her head to the side and repeats, "'The universe is unfolding as it should.' Even to this day, I strongly believe that."

"So, you don't believe in mistakes?"

"Small faults, yes, tiny miscalculations, but not revelations or life altering errors."

"So, you don't believe in chance."

She shakes her head from side to side.

"And neither did your father?"

She repeats the same motion, this time looking at her fingers as she knits them.

"Was your father a religious man?"

"My father was a lot of things." She smiles at me as she exhales, "When did this topic get so heavy?" she jokes, but I know she is ready to close the subject. She unfolds the hem of her jeans and stands up, dusting the seat of her pants, as if she'd been sitting on a dusty surface.

"I should go."

I look at the clock on the wall, and it's already 8:30.

"Stay."

"I have training early tomorrow morning."

I can tell that our conversation took a turn to where she didn't want to go, and it appears to have upset her. I conclude that it has something to do with her father, and that makes me think she is not done grieving him.

"Are you okay?"

"Never better." She doesn't turn as she says so but disappears into the kitchen, and a few seconds later, I hear the back door slam. I run after her and find her fidgeting with her keys with glass in her eyes.

"Did I upset you?"

"No," she simply answers defensively.

"What's wrong then?"

"Who says anything is wrong?" She sniffles a little bit.

"You're crying." I say, as if revealing to her something she doesn't already know.

"No, I'm not. I'm just reminiscent, that's all." She smiles a sad smile and then tucks herself into me. "A hug. That's all I need. Is that okay?"

With her heart on my chest, I just let out a breath and let her breathe for a moment. She retracts as I'm getting used to her against me.

"Come on. No more heavy stuff." I nod as I acquaint myself with the cold air she left on my chest.

Before I can stop myself, before I even know what I'm doing, I ask, "You want to stay?"

"Only if you do me a favor."

"Is it going to cost me?"

"Maybe. But I'm sure you can afford it."

I nod. July simply takes my hand walks me slowly to my bedroom. I follow her lead and count the curls at the back of her head as I forbid any thought of guilt or anticipation. Having talked to Jane earlier and knowing that Skylar was picked up and is safely with her mom, and Enoch is at *Blue Baby* tonight, I let myself believe that there is nothing else to worry about today.

July walks over to the opposite side of the bed and then looks at me.

"Ever turned the most ordinary thing into something phenomenal?"

"That depends."

"On what?"

"On what you mean by ordinary."

"How about I show you what I mean."

"Okay." I salivate as if I can taste the sweetness of whatever it is she is promising.

She smiles at me, shyly at first but then she gets an intense look on her face before she mouths the words as she says them.

"Take. Off. Your. Clothes."

This is one command, I can never resist from a woman. We both freely and unhurriedly take our clothes off while we watch each other as we perform the most simple and everyday act, but this moment is so pregnant with anticipation and erotic promises that the air is charged with tiny fibers of electricity.

"Turn off the lights," she instructs.

I walk over to the door, and I can feel her eyes boring into my back. I turn off the lights. I tune in to my breathing, expecting to hear hers, but all I hear is shifting and my pupils dilate as they try to absorb as much light as they can in the darkness.

"Come to bed," I hear her say from a distance.

I prudently walk over to my elevated California king, and when my knee touches the bed I stop and feel around with my hands, well aware that July is on the other side of it.

"Get under the covers."

Her voice is soft but commanding, in control and not at all pleading. She is demanding but gentle in her commands. I feel myself get excited at the thought of letting her take control of the situation; of me. I do as I am told, and the feel of the sheets on my skin is amazingly cool and soft on my torso and thighs and feet. I just want to tuck the fabric between my toes.

She scoots close to me until I am behind her, and we are in a spooning position. She tucks herself into me and her skin is smooth and soft and her hair smells like citrus and rain and fog and mountains and…

"Wrap your arms around me."

I shift and move around and she lifts herself up, so I can put my arm underneath her and the skin on skin, the darkness, and the silence diluted with our breathing has me anticipating and guessing what sound is going to occur next. She takes my hand in hers and places them on her chest.

"Cup my breasts."

Instantaneously, I start kissing her neck and burying my nose in her hair. I squeeze her breasts, but she places her hands over my hand and applies pressure onto my wrists.

"Gently."

I stop and let her barely audible voice guide me.

"Now, I want you to loosen your grip and just follow me where I lead you."

I kiss her back and run my tongue along the length of her spine. I repeat, only this time running my nose along her spine and not my tongue, taking in my saliva diluted with her coffee skin. She takes my right hand and lowers it. She places it on the apex of her thighs and folds my fingers in excluding my middle finger.

She sucks in a deep breath and holds it as she leads my finger into the center of her, making this the most profound and intimate moment that two people can share. My finger along with hers inside of her as if we are both entering a journey together inside of her, somewhere where only one person can go at a time.

She flips my finger around and bends it inside of her as if making the *come here* gesture by bending and straightening the finger along the inside wall of her. She lets out two quick breaths before finally letting out a long sigh.

I only hope to see her face as she pleases herself with my hand, my finger. She pulls our fingers out and grabs hold of the rest of my fingers. Gently and conscientiously she moves my hand to a point where I can't stretch anymore, she gently sucks on my middle finger and holds it with her teeth while she makes small circles with her hips, grinding and rubbing the frontal part of my pelvis with her bare skin.

I hold myself steady and push forward, so I can feel as much of her as I can take. The darkness gives the illusion that she and I are creating a secret together, something only she and I will share against the rest of the world. I like the thought of the two of us against the world.

My tendon inflames and responds with a burning that lets me know that the only way to ease the aching is to bury itself inside of July. She releases my hand, and I take it from her and gently caress the roundness of her gluts, her soft skin responding to my touch.

She finally turns around, and there is nothing in the room but darkness and heavy breathing and moaning and skin rubbing on skin, mouth meeting mouth, tongue kissing tongue, breasts, thighs, me and her ignoring the night and the world that it envelops.

While kissing July, I climb on top of her, propping myself on my elbows so as not to weigh heavy on her. I sweep my bottom lip from her throat to her mouth and gently suck on her bottom lip and then draw it out with me when I retreat. I lower myself to her, so I can feel her bare breasts on my naked chest. I kiss her mouth and listen to her breath catch as she tries to control her thirst for me. She places her hands on my naked butt and pushes me into her while she spreads her legs, but I want to kiss her and touch her and feel outside of her before entering her, and I do just that.

I urgently unwrap and dress myself with the latex before I finally find my way home. I make sure that the invitation fully stands and I, I do what everything south of my body tells me to do; I find her, and I enter her, and July's south mouth clamps around me as if I am something that belongs to it, a treasure never to be seen outside of it. Slowly, I ease myself into her and feel her take me in. I hear her let out a soft sigh, and her breath caresses my jaw as I lower my head and kiss her softly, slowly, and delicately squeeze her chin between my teeth.

"Have me, Dorian. Only this way."

I don't try to understand what she is asking me; I simply let myself follow her commands as she moves me with her breath, her thighs, and her kisses. Like a Remora, she clamps around me, and I move in and out of her, kissing her teardrop-shaped breasts.

"Make me come alive, Dorian."

She licks my name as she says it, and I taste the sweetness of it from her tongue. I kiss her with all of my mouth as if any other way wouldn't suffice, and she returns my kisses only the way that she can, tenderly but firmly, wholly but sweetly, maddingly and abundantly. With my eyes closed, I am finding light. In this dark room, on this soft bed, we turn something so ordinary into phenomenology.

I thrust into her, and she inhales, and when I pull out she exhales, we re-peat the same motion over and over until we are both out of breath and ex-plode at the slightest trigger as every nerve in my body screams under a plethora of sensations. This, unlike before, feels like we're making love.

I wake up in the middle of the night in a small panic. *What am I doing?* This is the second night in a row that July's spent the night.

I look over at her, and she is sleeping peacefully. I am an asshole; I'm lead-ing her on. This is not a woman who is taking things lightly. Does she possibly see this as a start of something that is going somewhere? I hope not. I try to calm myself down until I fall asleep.

CHAPTER SEVEN

She ties her scarf around me, and right away my nostrils are bathed in a sweet but musky fragrant.

"Is that too tight?"

"No."

"Okay, good." She spins me around for a second before she releases me and runs away from me, her giggles sounding from a close distance.

For a second I think of Llarel; she and I used to play this game as kids, and she took less time to find me while she would remain in the same spot and would not say a thing for the longest time, and at one point, when I finally caught her, she had fallen asleep on the corner of her bed.

July, with her most alluring voice seduces me. If only she knew she didn't have to, but for my own indulgence, I let her.

"Come to me, darling, I'm over here," she coos.

I stretch out my arms in front me, careful not to bump into anything and follow the direction where her lyrical voice came. I know I am close to the bed since I have walked about five feet diagonally from the door. I prudently move my legs, so I don't hurt my shins.

"You must not want me, or you would have found me by now," she purrs from behind me.

I know I am heading back to the door, and there is not much furniture there, so I hurriedly and blindly charge toward her, still with my arms stretched in front of me. I try breathing through my nose, forbidding myself to use my other senses but my hearing.

"Oh well, I guess I'm going to have to put my clothes back on," her voice teasingly threatens coming from the right toward the bathroom.

At the thought of her nude, I feel like I'm wasting time playing blind when I should be staring at her naked body and doing things to it.

"It's your birthday today. Find me, and you can do anything you want with me."

Like a deer perking up its ears to find the sound of a waterfall, I try to silence my breathing, my now throbbing veins and try to catch her proximity on the left where her voice just came. On cue, I begin salivating, well aware of the veins pulsating under my skin. I don't argue that today is not my birthday, and whether she knows it or not, her voice makes it clear that it makes no difference.

"Tick tock, you're running out of time," she mummers seductively.

This game is excruciating, but my overbearing ego does not let me give up. I have to win. The mixture of frustration and anticipation has my skin textured with goosebumps, and every bit of me is at attention.

"Oh the things I'm going to do to you once I catch you," I promise.

"Too bad you won't," she declares with a smile in her voice. She is not too far behind me, and I play dumb to get her to inch closer.

"When I find you, what do you want me to do to you?" I become very still and wait for her to give up her location.

"Turn me inside out," she declares, still in her previous location.

I calculate her position to be about five feet to my left, and without warning or caution, I spin to the left and enclose her between the dresser and the leather chair. I barely miss her as she dives past me, and I catch her by the arm. She giggles like a school girl, and I chime in as I hold on tight in case she decides to cheat. She pushes her scarf down to my neck without bothering to untie it. I am glad to have my sight back and muse at her white teeth as she tilts her head and laughs with her whole body.

"I thought you said you were naked," I point out, disappointed.

"I lied."

I press myself against her so she can feel my excitement.

"You are such a tease. Now. My winnings."

"Me. All of me."

She repels from me and slowly walks toward the bed, kicking the bulky duvet to the floor. When I follow, she motions for me stop. My dark grey sheets and her in them is my favorite color scheme. I watch her as she makes her way on top of it, crawling like a gazelle and elongating her slender body, revealing new curves in its lines. I watch, making sure I steady myself where I stand. She stands on top of the bed, and her silhouette is flawless in the dim lighting of the room. She turns to face me, arresting me with her big mahogany eyes. She takes off her grey crewneck and throws it on the floor revealing her signature white tank top. She takes it off and throws it at me, her eyes never leaving mine, and I catch it and suck her aroma into my lungs before dropping my arms beside me and letting it fall to the floor.

"Now…" she whispers and trails off without finishing her sentence.

Now what? Now what? All of me wants to know.

She unhooks her bra, freeing her breasts, and I swallow a gulp of my own saliva. She turns around and gives me a view of her back as she slowly slides out of her panties. Turning back to me, she cautions again for me to stay where I am. It takes a lot of restraint to keep myself from leaping to her.

"Now…" she continues where she left, "I want you to describe me," she instructs. "Describe the way you see me," she reiterates.

"You're beautiful," I instill, almost in a whisper.

She shakes her head.

"No, describe me as you would in a letter to a close friend. As you would to a blind man who's never touched a woman. Start from head to toe."

"You are… She is exquisite," I start. "Every curl in her hair is not a mistake. The texture of her skin is made only of butter and honey, of satin…"

She smiles at me her most innocent smile while tilting her head, as if she adores me.

"…Your skin…" She tucks her hair behind her ear and listens attentively. "Her skin is a demerara. Your mouth…her mouth is full and soft and sweet and delicate."

I zoom in my focal lens to examine my favorite body part for me to describe next.

"Your neck…her neck is long and slender. No veins intrude it…" I stop again to examine her face and she is captivated.

Without blinking, she asserts, "Don't stop," engrossed in my verbal letter.

I swallow hard and continue,

"Your shoulders…her shoulders are happy, like they have yet to carry the weight of the world. Her belly…always hungry, tighter than a rubber band that's been stretched to maximum capacity. Her hips, her hips curve exquisitely, even better inside a tight black dress."

"What about my breasts?"

I look at her face and then her breasts.

"Your breasts…her breasts are perfect in no other size. They—"

And before I continue, before I can disarm her with the rest of my drivel poetry, she runs to me, taking me in her arms and seals my thoughts with her desperate and uncontrolled kisses. She wraps herself with my arms and right there, right then I lay her on the floor, and like a musician who fervently loves his cello, I polish my instrument; I take her in my arms making sure that my fingers caress her every curve. I hold her along her sides and strum her strings and push her buttons. She sings her song against my fingers as I dig when I should and brush her to change the tempo. Her toned body doesn't resist me, it merely abides to the command of my hands as I mop and polish, push and pull. Together, she and I make jazz.

I lay spent and soaked in sweat, and I am content. Now would be a good time to take up smoking. I look over and marvel at July's body next to mine. My skin seems pale and hairy next to hers. Her beautiful brown skin is flawless and smooth and soft. I run my middle finger along her spine and she shifts and sighs in her sleep. I lift the duvet that covers the rest of her and assess her perfect round butt; it's so firm and round, I want to cup it with both my hands but decide I should let her sleep. I think about how great it would be if I could smoke a cigarette. I take in a deep breath and let it out slowly as I watch July do the same next to me as she turns over and her ribs rise and fall. I cover her up and brush her curls out of her face.

"Sleep, you beautiful sex goddess," I kiss the words as I say them.

I wake up in the morning, and I am feeling guilt, the worst kind. I run the most recent happenings in my life. I try to convince myself that I have nothing to feel guilty about. Guilt feels like coming from a cool pool and walking into a sauna where you feel the heat travel through your body in a slow speed. I feel my feet heat up, and the heat travels to my knees, my stomach, my chest, and then to my head. My head is full of thoughts that blur my vision for a moment and then steam my ears.

There is a churning in the center of my stomach, a knocking on the base of my spine. This agitates me, and I wake up in a bad mood. I know this feeling all too well. Guilt feels like a burn in your tongue from a hot cup of coffee except it's a burn that starts in the middle of your torso and gathers in your throat before it goes to your head. I don't feel hot, but I feel a burn that makes me feel like steam is about to come out of my ears, as though I'm a pressure cooker.

What is it that I feel guilty about? July. I slept with the nanny, not once but over and over again. I am about to jeopardize the perfect situation for Skylar and I.

July stirs next to me, and I can't believe that she actually stayed, that I let her spend the whole weekend with me. I recall last night in slow motion, fast-forwarding and pausing as I go. I didn't even feel guilty about it the second time around, which explains the suffocating that I now feel.

Suffocation: What am I thinking? This girl who now lies beside me is something unstable, and I am certain that I don't want to stabilize it. I cannot mess with someone's emotions, and it's quite obvious I'm about to hurt her.

Guilt: I feel a pain on my lower back and automatically start rubbing it. I prudently exit out of bed and walk over to the bathroom to examine the rough red patch on my back that's now starting to peel. The pool scenario plays itself fast in slow-motion, and I am aggravated with myself for being so careless; what's gotten into me lately? Jacquiline, July...

Since when did I turn into Enoch?

You have got to get your shit together! I tell the face that stares back at me from the mirror. Guilt; like a physical, tangible object that sits on my chest and presses down on me until I feel that breathing softly is not an option. I breathe loudly and evidently to remove it from my chest, but it only climbs up to my throat, and I cough loudly sending a shooting pain through my temples.

"What are we doing?" I hear myself say as I sit on the bed next to the now awake July.

"What do you mean?"

"I mean you and me. What are we doing?" I hear my voice; I hear the words, but I have no control over what's coming out of my mouth. She looks at me, not at all shocked that I'm freaking out.

"We're starting something that we both can't finish." She smiles mischievously, unaware that she is only confirming my fears. "Not everything has to have an end. Let's not finish it if we both don't want to." She is playful and could care less, as if she is not worried about where this might lead.

"July, I'm serious. This…" I point to the space between us, "…whatever it is…is…what are we doing?"

"Doing a little dance. Making a little love," she sings as she pulls her hair up into a messy ponytail. I frown when I realize that my concerns are in vain.

"Relax, Dorian. We are only doing what's natural: succumbing to what's natural to us. We don't feel guilty about eating or sleeping, sex is as part of human nature as eating is. It's the body's need to release and connect. You like it. I like it, and we're both single, so why not?'

"So, there are no ulterior motives?"

"None."

"From either side?"

"You're okay with this?"

"What's this? Two people agreeing to offer each other some release?"

"That's all it is?"

"Release me, please," she jokingly teases.

"You're so hot when you know what you want."

"I know."

We both laugh, but somehow, I doubt that this gnawing feeling is not deserved and won't eat at me when I'm alone.

As if on cue, the phone rings, and when I look at it it's Jane. My heart speeds to a million miles a minute, and I am afraid we've been found out.

"We just got home, and July's car is still here. Did you not bring her to pick it up?'

"Yes. I mean, no." I comb through my hair fighting the urge to pull it out.

"Did you or did you not, Dorian? Should I worry, where could she be? Do you know if she's okay?"

Jane's frantic voice hammers at me, "I tried calling her, but it goes straight to voicemail."

July's staring at me, biting her bottom lip with an apologetic look on her face.

"Yes. I mean no, don't worry, she asked me to drop her off at her friend's house instead," I blatantly lie.

"Well, do you know when she'll come pick it up?"

"I think she said sometime today."

"Oh okay."

We figure out the week's schedule for Skylar between her and I, and I hang up first chance I get. I turn to face July, and she is already out of the bed and gathering her stuff. We both collect ourselves, aware of the outside world that consists of other people and responsibilities. Our bubble finally bursts.

<hr>

We look at each other as if at camp and we were caught making out with cigarettes in our hands. We reluctantly enter into the realm of reality, and July emerges from the bathroom with wet hair and some of her clothes in her arm, and her phone in another hand.

"I spoke to my roommate, and if you don't mind dropping me off at my place, she can take me to pick up my car."

I simply give her a slight nod. I realize there's so much I don't know about this girl. For starters, I don't even know where she lives. She navigates for me, telling me where to turn and what shortcuts to take. We stop at a carwash hub close to her neighborhood and wait in line behind a car as I am very anal about my car, and the green film of pollen covering it agitates me.

It seems that neither of us is willing to break the silence after that.

"You want to?'

All of a sudden, she turns and looks at me, folding her lip in half smile as she projects the thought that animates her face. My eyes widen, and I am stoked. I watch her for a second without saying anything, making sure that I am not imagining what I think she is asking me.

"Here?"

"Here! Now." I am a little skeptical about reverting to this chapter, but I convince myself that it's all in the name of fun, and no labels are obligated. We decided, as adults, that we can have fun, and no one said anything about a relationship. The only expectation that we have for each other is that we have fun. Where is the harm in that? Right?

I relax and watch her watching me, and she unbuckles her seatbelt. She reaches across my lap and pushes the button that retracts my seat back in slow motion, and I have to unfold my leg at the knee to keep my foot on the brakes. Her curls graze my chest, and I lean in closer, so I can bury my nose in them. She rises from her seat and carefully jumps over to mine. I push the gear from drive to neutral as instructed. She towers over me and then looks down on me and declares,

"No kissing."

She bites her top lip with the lower tray of white teeth as she takes off her bra without so much as lifting her shirt. The car in front of us pulls away, and ours is automatically injected into the ingress full of soapy water. The giant brushes suck us in with me on the driver's seat and July on my lap. I crawl my hands under her shirt and scoop her bare breast in my hand and watch her body rise as I do so. She bites her lip ready and willing for me to ravage her. She slowly grinds on me while planting me in place with her eyes. I put my hands on her lower back and try to draw her in for a kiss, but she resists me, shaking her head. She simply stills me with her mahogany eyes and unzips me without looking. She pulls her panties to the side and slowly injects me inside of her while she continues holding me under her provocative stare.

The confinement of our small quarters has us vibrating and erupting with a humming echo and the air stales. The windows are fogging up, and I am turned on by the fact that I am now breathing in recycled air, the breath from her body now coming into mine and her, the same. The swishing and swashing outside the car makes it easy for us to fall into rhythm.

Now engulfed in her sweet warmness where I now consider my second home, I am pinned to my seat as she takes control by moving up and down, round and round. The big blue pieces of cloth beat on the car, and the drumming speeds up our thrusting as we both feel the urgency for some release.

The rinse cycle continues outside the car while we fuck each other until we both collapse and are quickly brought back to reality as the red light has long turned green and the car behind is honking impatiently. I'm sure they won't have as much fun, and I keep that comforting thought as we pull all the way out before she climbs out of my lap and into her seat. I take the car off neutral and hit the gas, slowly exiting our naughty rendezvous but taking the sex smell in the car with us.

She rolls down her window and looks out. Such a normal act as if nothing out of the ordinary just happened. She's so relaxed and so natural, and for a second, I wonder if I have just imagined the whole marvelous experience, but the satisfied throbbing in my pelvis testifies that I haven't.

We drive about three miles without saying a word, and I finally decide to look at her instead of sneaking looks from the rearview mirror. She refuses to look at me, but when she finally turns to look at me and we lock eyes, she giggles. Her laugh: contagious, and I find myself laughing along with her.

"That was awesome!" she exclaims loudly, shyly covering her eyes.

"I concur." I face her. "But why no kissing?"

"It's the thrill of being deprived of something. Forbidding something to you creates a different kind of yearning. A foreign sensation. Right?"

I don't respond but give her a look that answers her question.

Chapter Eight

Three weeks have gone by, and I've avoided July like a plague. Summer break started a week ago, and Skylar has had a lot of playdates. Since July also has summer break, she's been helping more, but spends most of the time at Jane and Brady's. Between Llarel and Selena, I am able to have Skylar without having any contact with her, and it works out for the most part aside from a few awkward moments when she comes with Jane or changes from Jane's house and drops Skylar off here on weekends when Selena is not here.

I spend the next two weeks distracted with Enoch working on the bar and restaurant, and the gallery showing that's coming up in two weeks. The weekend, I reserve for Skylar. On Sunday, Enoch calls me, and we have to meet with vendors for *Baby Blue*. *Who the hell wants to meet on a Sunday?* So, I make sure to schedule July to be here with Sky for when Jane comes to pick her up.

I come home from the meeting to find July's car in the driveway, and my stomach churns. Both girls are still here. Jane's tardiness is annoying at times. It's harder to avoid July when she has the key to my house and cannot leave until Jane does her part.

"What are you two doing here? I thought you'd both be gone by now."

"Mommy is running late, but she's on her way."

I look over at July, and she simply shrugs. She is wearing a pair of cotton shorts that hug her curves. The khaki cotton halts at the top of her toned thighs, I notice before I abruptly change the direction of my thoughts. She is wearing a green tank top under a yellow one and a baseball cap. The relaxed nature of the way she is dressed reminds me of childhood, summer camp, and I smile to myself about some naughty fantasy that I had at that age that I would like to make a reality right now.

"When did Jane say she would be here?" I ask July, trying to focus my attention.

"In the next 30 minutes or so."

She jumps up and down the trampoline, and Skylar jumps along with her. I decide to go inside and avoid Jane.

"I'm gonna go take a shower if you don't mind staying till Jane gets here."

"Not at all."

"Bye sweetheart. Have fun this weekend with your mom and Brady."

With the water massaging my scalp and back, I decide to entertain myself using the thought of July in those cotton shorts that hug her butt so impeccably snug, thoroughly holding it in place. I imagine her thighs sweaty from the heat, the smell of it as it seeps out of her pores. I imagine the wind blowing it dry, morphing her skin into goosebumps while her tendons firm under her skin. I much rather enjoy the thought and spare no time feeling guilty about my filthy whims.

After my relaxing shower, I come around to the backyard to find July and Skylar still on the trampoline with their legs crossed facing each other and giggling like two best friends sharing a secret.

"She's still not here?"

"She'll be here soon." July says, not bothered by Jane's tardiness.

I climb into the trampoline with them and leave my flip flops next to theirs. I sit down next to Skylar, careful not to trigger any suspicions about July and I. July is teaching Skylar a hand-clap game from her childhood, and I listen as they sing along, both looking like they are about the same age.

By so by Love to Baby
To Baby Boo the Sun
The Sun Boo the Yona
The Yona Boo the Man
The Man Boo the Boo The.

"What does that even mean?" I ask both girls, and Skylar looks at me as if I am a really old person who has no clue.

"Whatever you want it to mean, Daddy. Tell him July." She rolls her eyes as if that was so obvious, and everybody knows that.

Jane calls out as she opens the screen door to join us outside.

"Skylar, don't make me walk all the way there in my heels. We need to go we're late." Both Skylar and July hug, and Skylar gives me a quick hug before she climbs out of the trampoline.

"Coming," she yells back to her mother.

"Don't forget your bag and the rest of your stuff's by the front door," July yells to her as she runs to join her mother.

"Sorry I was so late, July."

July waves a manicured finger nonchalantly.

Jane waves and walks back inside before Skylar even catches up to her, lifting up her sunglasses and putting them at the top of her head. July and I simply watch the mother and daughter duo make their way inside. As soon as the door closes, I turn and look at her. I just stare at her and after a while smile. She smiles back and lays back, facing the sky. I lie beside her, mimicking her sigh. It's harder not to want to be around her when she is next to me. My body goes to autopilot, and I find I don't have control over what happens to me in her presence.

We just stare up at the sky and just breathe. I scoot closer to her and look at her before turning my eyes back to the sky. She lets out another breath.

"Dorian?"

"Hmmm?"

"The other night; when you said you were defective." She is still looking up at the sky and she cautions as she finishes her sentence, "Defective how?"

I don't move or look at her, I simply continue staring at the sky alongside her. I take in a long breath and let it out slowly.

"The way a cow would meow and a bird would bark." I am someone who, without rhyme or reason, is chemically imbalanced and ironically damaged.

She is quiet for a second as if weighing my words and putting them in an order that she can understand. Neither of us have turned to look at the other, but she shifts lightly, and the springy material beneath us shifts under her weight. She turns to look at me while propping her head in her hand and putting all the weight on her elbow.

"When I was young, I had a cat who thought he was a dog."

I choke with laughter when I notice that she is in fact serious, my contagious laugh infects her, and she starts laughing with me. We are quiet once again, and she assumes her prior position next to me, and we both stare at the thinning clouds.

"You're not going to tell me, are you?"

"Nope," I simply say, humor carrying my voice.

She shifts her head, and I can see her from the corner of my eye studying my face, and when I turn to look at her, she turns her eyes back to the sky. I look back again at the sky with her and just listen to her breathe without her knowing that my attention is on her, even without looking at her.

"Do you want to stay the night?" I find myself saying.

"Yes."

An uncomfortable silence charges the air, and we continue to occupy ourselves with whatever images the sky presents to us.

"Stay here."

I jump up and run inside and grab pillows and blankets and hurry back outside to find her in the same position, still staring at the now darkening sky. We order pizza and inform them that the delivery guy should come around all the way to the back of the house. The pizza guy arrives with our pizza and our wings. I walk over to him and pay him and walk back into our springy world enclosed with a net. We sit opposite each other and eat in silence. She gathers the garbage and climbs out of the trampoline, walking over to the big garbage can and throws away everything.

She flaunts her legs as she stretches them in front of me. I admire her skin against her cotton shorts: the length of them, the subtle way that the fabric rubs against them. I admire the green and yellow in contrast to her hair and her eyes and her mouth.

We waste hours just talking and eating pizza. Ironically, we both learn about each other's idiosyncrasies and talk about light subjects while we both, with some effort, avoid mentioning the real and personal matters that make us who we are. I don't mention my baggage, and she avoids bringing up hers.

"I've never camped out before. This is fun," she chimes excitedly.

"Never?"

"Never."

"Not even as a kid?"

"Nope."

"That's the saddest thing I've ever heard."

She looks at me as if making up her mind whether she believes me or not.

"If that's the saddest thing you have ever heard, then I am utterly envious of you." We both laugh. "Seriously though, I would love to be the one to show you what you've been missing." A light bulb goes off in my head, "I am going to take you camping."

"Yes? Yes." She stands up and jumps up and down as though she were Skylar and the springy material between us and the ground causes my body to leap in the air with every impact her feet make on the springs. She flops back down next to me and looks at me, "When?"

"Whenever. Wherever. Whatever." I catch myself from making promises that I cannot keep.

She looks at me with a concerned look on her face.

"Seriously. Would you really do that for me?"

"I would do that for you."

"Well then. I'd like you to do that for me."

"Then I will."

Her eyes flicker, "Maybe with Skylar. Yes. Skylar can come with."

"Maybe."

The now dark sky appraises us as we huddle together and stare back at it. She sighs and tucks herself closer to me.

I get the feeling of a teenager at band camp who sneaks off behind the bushes with his geeky best-friend as they make a pact to take each other's virginity, except this moment is a hundred times better; I am with an attractive girl under no pretense or secret pact. We are both willing and consensually succumbing to this beauty that surrounds us.

"I love that we are enveloped by the darkness with crickets and all the creatures of the night spying on us." She dreams.

I take in what she is saying and simply listen to the music of the night and fold myself in to the comfort of this moment. She continues after a long pause.

"I love that there are no walls or ceiling caging us in, and that it's you and me and nature."

I think about our fucking in the rain and internally smile but continue to say nothing. The space around us suddenly stretches beyond our grasp...no confinement, no hiding, but still, we do what people do in private, in secret. We can hide, but we chose not to. We choose to let the night paint our naked bodies with shadows while the moon openly stares down at us. The smell of the moist grass, the sound of the night and the slight possibility of having an audience intensifies our muffled sounds although another part of us feels free and unconfined.

Like a flute, she whistles when I place my mouth and caress her where I should. She makes the most beautiful music to my ears, and she responds to my touch as if I am the only thing holding her in place, as if without me, gravity would swallow her.

In the open air, on this beautiful night, under the moonlight, I do my best to make July feel like the only woman in the world, and if I haven't, I've failed trying. Her breathing and her moaning give me sign that I may not have failed at all.

We fall sleep under the summer's moonlit sky with the chorus of the crickets and the stars and moon and sky as our audience, leaving the ground beneath us, our only suspension; the springy fabric and nothing else. The trampoline, our vice against gravity and we stay suspended as though the rules of the world, of nature that pertain to everyone else are excused to us.

The more I do this, the less guilty I feel about it. I'm going to hurt her; I know I will. I don't know what she expects from me; I don't want to know because I cannot deliver. I don't ever want to tie myself to any more people. Sky is my only deliverance. I do not want to attach my happiness to another human being.

Jane brings Skylar back on Tuesday, and since Selena has been off sick, I make no excuses, but spend my time between the office and Sky's activities. I find myself avoiding July, once again.

Jane has been telling me that she wants to sit down and talk to me about something. I figure she wants to talk to me about summer plans for Skylar and about camps and their summer vacation with Brady. I'm blindsided when we finally sit down, and I learn of her plans for the summer.

The conversation starts off casually, and I should have realized that it was just Jane trying to butter me up. Granted, the relationship that Jane and I have is relaxed and uncomplicated, but there is a lot of things that we don't see eye-to-eye on. Brady has been our greatest arbitrator when it comes to finding a middle ground, especially on things concerning Skylar. Otherwise, we know little to nothing about each other's private lives.

"Brady and I would like to take Skylar to Europe."

"Okay. That would be a great opportunity for her to learn—"

"For the whole summer."

She looks at me as if waiting for a reaction, but I have none to offer her. I simply gather myself as my stun courses through me.

"I don't know, Jane. The whole summer?"

"Yes. Leaving three weeks from today. We will be living in Barcelona."

"Why so soon? And why are you only telling me this now."

"Because Brady just got the offer last week.",

"What offer?"

"I can't talk about this now—"

"What offer?" I repeat. Afraid that there is a lot more that she is not telling me.

"Dorian, just think about letting Skylar go. We'll talk about everything else later."

"WHAT OFFER?" I press, for the third time.

"Your only concern is making sure that you get accustomed to the idea of being without Skylar for such a long period of time."

"And if I say no?"

"Don't be irrational. I know you would never deprive your child of such an opportunity."

"If it's for two months, I will."

"Please take it into consideration that it is not about you, but about Skylar."

"I know. Two months is too long though. Maybe I can think about going there halfway through the summer and bringing her back with me."

"Maybe. Just think about it, although I would like for her to stay the entire time, so she can travel."

"I'm trying to meet you halfway here."

"I have to go, Dorian; Brady is waiting in the car." She turns and grabs Skylar's stuff and calls for her before turning to me finally.

"We are going with her."

Skylar comes running down the stairs and I hold my tongue.

"Daddy, will you tell Selena that I can't find my black ballet slippers, and I know I left them in my bathroom yesterday."

"Okay, sweetheart."

"And also, please play with Neo, Daddy. He gets lonely when I'm not here."

"Sure."

She hugs me and gives me a peck on the lips, walks over to join her mother who has already opened the door and is stepping out into the darkening day.

I walk over to the living room and can't shake the feeling that I am forgetting something that was tremendously bothering me not a while ago. I sit down on the oversize couch and retrieve my vibrating phone from my pocket. I have a text message from Enoch.

The offer still stands.

Offer. The word triggers my memory about the gnawing feeling that I can't shake. What did Jane mean when she said that Brady got his offer last week? What offer and what does that have anything to do with them going to Barcelona, and with Skylar staying with them the whole entire time? I make a mental note to find out, although I am certain that there is no way I am going to let them keep my daughter for a whole summer without me. I text Enoch back.

Good. Time to do some serious negotiation.

Drinks at Blue Baby?

Now?

10 minutes

Make it 30.

CHAPTER NINE

Work on Monday is as usual. I go back and forth between *Baby Blue* and the gallery and pick up Skylar at the end of the day. I give July the week off and spend as much time with my daughter as possible. I spoil her a little more than I normally would, and of course, as bright as she is, she notices.

"How come you are being so lenient towards things this week, Daddy?"

"Lenient?" I marvel at her big word.

"Yes. My new word for this week. It means accepting or kind or less strict."

I laugh as I watch her. She is sitting on the barstool at the kitchen doing her homework, Neo on the floor next to her. Selena is already gone for the day, and it's just me and her, and Neo.

"Less strict? I am not too strict...am I?" I ask her, doubting myself momentarily.

"No, but last night you let me stay up past my bedtime, and I had ballet camp early in the morning, and now you are cooking my favorite meal, and I never even asked you."

"Oh okay. Would you rather I made chicken and vegetables every night this week?"

"No, I like your spaghetti and meatballs."

"I know, that's why I am making it for you."

She is quiet for a moment.

"I love you Daddy."

I look up at her, and she is on floor, patting Neo.

"I love you too, Binkie." I walk over to her and give her hugs.

We've had a few more conversations with Jane, and we decided that she goes to Spain with them and see how it goes. She can come back any time she wants, or I can come get her if she decides that she wants to come back to the States. I knew it was a losing battle when Jane reminded me about all the opportunities there. I've spent all week with her since she will be leaving in a couple of weeks, and I will be busy with the showing next week, at the gallery.

On Friday, I was such a drag, and Enoch could not understand why it was such a big deal for me to let Skylar go to Spain. Having no kids of his own, I do not think he understands how hard it would be to have Sky so far away from me and for so long.

"But she will be with her mother. No one can keep her any safer than she can," he had said.

"I know. I don't think it's her safety I'm worried about."

"What is it then?"

"I don't know. I just cannot shake the feeling that she would be better off here with me. I mean, she's too young to be away from me for that long."

"Dude! She will be with her mother and only a phone call away. You could also go over there and visit, correct?" Enoch looks at me like I am being such a girl.

"Yeah, I guess you're right. But…"

"But you get to spoil her before she leaves and after she comes back. She will get to experience a new culture, learn a new language, see the world. Don't deprive her of that for your selfish reasons," Enoch asserted with confidence. As much as he is a smartass, he can be a good friend when he wants to be.

I get it now. I do not want to, but I will agree to it. I'm still uneasy about the fact that Jane and I never finished the conversation about Brady and the offer he got.

The week goes by smoothly with no issues as we get ready for the art show, next week.

"Ready?" Prudence Rose asks as the ushers open the doors.

"It looks amazing. Prudence Rose, you are amazing!" I exclaim. She has been the person behind every success the gallery has had. She makes all the important decisions, and she is great at her job. She is a private lady though; outside of work, I know nothing about her.

"All the works displayed are from local artists, and the proceeds go to the children's program at the local art center," I hear Prudence Rose reiterate to a local newscast after I have been interviewed.

Jane, Brady, and Skylar show up and support, which they always do when it comes to my bigger events. I appreciate them showing up since they are busy packing up to leave in a few days. Brady and I have a drink together, and he thanks me for agreeing to let Skylar go with them.

"You know I respect you as a man and more so as a father, so I appreciate you trusting me." He shakes my hand.

"Thank you for being dependable and always being there for both of them." I have always been appreciative of Brady's presence in our lives. He has made Jane so happy and has been a great stepdad to Skylar. As I start to ask him about his offer, Prudence Rose pulls me to the side to meet a few artists.

The evening goes on in a blur, and everything goes smoothly and Prudence Rose makes an exceptional closing speech. I stay and help clean up a little bit before leaving to meet Enoch at *Blue Baby*. On my way in, I see two of the girls that July was with the first time I saw her at the club. I wonder if she, too, is here and find myself looking for her every chance I get.

"You won't believe this chef I'm hooking up with! She is friends with Miss Ruby red lips," Enoch chuckles.

"Who is Miss Ruby Red lips?" I roll my eyes.

"The lady with the red hair and lips. Remember her?"

I stare at him blankly.

"The hostess at speed dating."

I vaguely remember her, but I am too busy searching the crowd.

"Are you expecting someone?" Enoch quizzes me

"No, why?"

"You just seem distracted, that's all. Anyway, this chef…"

I tune him out and just weigh different options I have about going to Europe and visiting Skylar while inconspicuously hoping to run into July.

For the last week, I've insisted on spending all my time with Skylar before she leaves for Europe. I've tried to memorize everything about her before she leaves. She grows up so fast, I'm sure she'll look different by the time she comes back. We invite Llarel to go to dinner with us the last night before she leaves, and we have so much fun. I pick Llarel up, and we give Burr the night off.

Skylar absolutely adores her aunt, and they are both in love with each other. We go eat and go back to Llarels and play some games. Llarel and I are both talked into swimming, and Burr comes in to join us. After a lot of splashing and playing around, I can tell that Skylar is starting to wind down. Jane did make me promise to not overtire her and get her to bed at a decent hour, so she is not overly exhausted.

"So, Aunt Llarel, do you and Burr promise to come and visit me?"

"Of course. We'll talk to your mom about the details." Llarel looks like she really is committing to going.

"Remember, Burr, a promise is a promise. You guys can't back out now." Skylar shakes her little finger in the air.

Once home and in bed, I have a terrible dream about Skylar drowning. I can't find her in the water; I just see her hair floating, and when I get to it, she disappears. I wake up with my heart racing. I sit up and rub my head as I clench and unclench my jaw. A big part of me still feels like it's a mistake letting her go. I walk over to her room and find her sleeping with Neo tucked in with her as if he realizes that he won't be seeing her for a while.

Days pass by slowly, and I keep looking at the calendar in the office, thinking, if it's only been three days, and I already miss her. It's only been a week, and I miss her so much, how am I going to get through the whole summer? Without thinking, I just dial July's number. She picks up after two rings.

"Wanna come over?"

"Well, hello to you, too. Do you know what time it is?"

I look at my alarm clock and it's a little after midnight.

"Please."

I don't know why I'm so desperate. I'll even consider going over to her if I have to. She turns me down, but somehow, we end up making plans for her to come over for lunch tomorrow. I spend the whole night in the art room painting and sleep most of the morning until July calls me around noon.

"If I were a hue, what color do you think I would be?" July asks.

"Yellow," I blurt out without hesitation.

"Is that your favorite color?"

"No."

She frowns and pouts a little, "Why yellow then?"

"Because it's bright and happy and unavoidable…just like you."

"Can I ask you a trivial question?" She looks at me uncomfortably.

"Shoot," I allow.

"Have you ever painted a picture of me?"

"No," I lie.

"Do you want to?"

"Are you asking?" I keep an indifferent composure.

"Please paint a picture of me, Dorian."

I make a gesture as though I need some time to think about it. I remain stoic until I see a tiny fragment of anxiety cross her face.

"What part of you would you like for me to paint?" I finally speak.

"My back…no…" She stops and looks at herself and then spread her fingers wide in front of her, "…what's your favorite part of my body?"

I hesitate for a second with a smile on my face, "I love your ass." I start out slowly and tease her by stretching my words and deepening my voice. She makes a face. "I love your breasts…and your stomach, and your ankles, too, but I would have to say… if I must, your neck."

"Paint my neck, then, Dorian," she pleads softly, "Please."

I walk over to her. I hold her face in my hands and tilt her head. I put my hand on her jaw and slowly float it down her neck letting my fingers fall one by one as my thumb moves further away from her face.

I feel vibrations under her skin as she struggles to swallow. With my index finger, I measure the texture of her neck, the fabric of her throat. I turn her head, so I'm looking at the other side of her face, and her curls fall in my hand. I brush them off and concentrate on a fragment of a vein that threatens to swell. I touch it lightly with my index finger and bring my face closer to her, inhaling her warm neck. I lick the vein and then suck on it until it protrudes from her skin. She quietly soughs.

I inhale and take her in, keeping her within the walls of my nostrils, and I continue my journey, exploring her neck, her long slender neck; the ball at the back of her, just above her spine shifts and dances when she moves her head. I watch my fingers as they graze her skin; ivory on ebony, vanilla on mocha, Dorian on July. I want to whisper things to her, let myself loose and free to her, but I can't; I won't allow myself.

Her skin is perfect, a solid brown with no wrinkles or scars. It has a soft texture, a velvety feel. The ridges of my fingerprints are evident as I graze her with a gossamer of a touch. How do I paint such perfection? How do I imitate such a rare and rich color, and how do I bring the texture to life?

I want someone to look at my portrait of her and imagine what it would feel like to touch her there, how sweet her neck would be on their tongue. Just by looking at her neck alone, I want a man to feel like a man and women to be jealous. I want someone, just by looking at her neck, to feel their mouth water and their fingers ache. The texture of her, the shape, the size of her neck, I want, I want it dripping down with conjectural gold; complete with abstract truism.

I want someone who studies this portrait of mine to see what I see and beyond. I want the bystander to look at the picture and be haunted by the clandestine woman, to wonder about the head where those big curls dangle from. I want to create a yearning, a fire that I feel as I assess her. I breathe loudly as lust inhabits my body maximally and irrevocably; taking over everything that enables logic to assemble within me, and so I sit down beside her and ache to study the rest of her.

My appetite is distilled with her wanting me, and I salivate as I wonder what she is wearing under her oversized sweater, under those jeans, beneath that heart.

"Take off your clothes," I command in a raw whisper.

She stands up and rips off her sweater.

"Slowly," I plead.

In a white room full of light, this beautiful brown goddess takes off her clothes in slow motion, and I watch her, trying hard not to blink, so I don't miss a thing. She takes off each item excruciatingly slow, so I have no choice but to be patient. She is July at my favorite, wearing her boy-shorts and her sports bra. And then…and then July at her most beautiful: nude and natural, and my very own private show.

"Now you," she says.

But I shake my head with my index finger on my mouth.

"I want to paint you," I look her up and down, "just as you are." I point at her.

She shakes her head no but with a smile on her face.

"Please." I rise from my seat and walk over to her. "Please." I use her winning word.

She closes her eyes as though she is contemplating a refusal to my request. "Kiss me."

Her professing her longing for my mouth, for my fingers and parts of me that only want to be engulfed by her 24/7. Something tells me that if I don't kiss her right now, I will regret it for the rest of my life.

"Please," I repeat, kissing her hair. "Please." Her face. "Please." Her mouth, and she responds to my kiss by sealing it with hers.

Her long lashes, her wide smile, and her beautiful white teeth weaken my thought process. She folds her lip between her index finger and her thumb, and I am afraid she will break the skin and start bleeding. She knows how to seduce me, she doesn't even have to try. I am at her mercy, I am disarmed and in wait for her to free me from her mouth, from her limps, from her oozing femininity and bewitching sexuality.

"Only my neck, Dorian."

"Please let me paint you whole."

I pull myself away from her and watch her watch me as I strip out of my own clothes. Her breathing is loud and provocative, which intensifies every desire in me to have her. Now.

I lightly tug her petit naked body close to mine, my fingers dancing on her soft back as her hands grasp my hair, begging me to stay, begging me to be her need, her breath, her everything. I sit on the chair next to the easel, and she sits with her legs on each side of me, breathing me and needing me, but leaving me outside of her. I pull her as close as I can have her, and she looks into me with her warm chocolate eyes while gently and oh so slowly embedding me inside of her warm, delicious pudenda. Between kisses and against her mouth, I beg her once again, "Please, let me paint your whole body."

"Yes," she whispers in my ear before she envelops it with her wet mouth.

"Yes." Between thrusts, she sings again, "Yes."

Just for a few minutes, we let ourselves be all that we need, from each other and from the world.

She is hills and valleys, light and shadows, and a complex of geometrical shapes. I want to sketch her so she appeals to all five senses; the look in her eyes, the taste of her tongue, the weight of her hair, the smell of her skin, and the sound of her breathing, all in paper: my paper July.

She folds her lip between her fingers, and I notice she's uncomfortable. I deliberately train my eyes to attend to her face and not her body: her eyes, her nose, her mouth, and then her dimples, those two beautiful dents on each side of her cheeks but not the rest of her; not yet.

I start with the loose curls that cascade from her head. They hang loose mid-air without a face that they belong to. I don't even have to look at her, I'm quite familiar with the way they hang from her head and how they sit on her shoulders.

She grabs a hand full of her strayed hair and pushes it away from her face, and I notice her hot veins beating against her temples, and I clench and unclench my jaw, willing myself to concentrate on the task at hand, but noticing very tactfully that it's not only her body that captivates me but threads of her that make her the whole fabric. Her presence takes over the whole room, and there is no sound only pencil meeting paper, breath leaving body.

I walk over to her, obeying my body, for it now tells me it won't stop buzzing until I've touched her. I kneel beside her and pull her ponytail holder out of her hair and watch her face disappear behind it. I pull on the hair on the front half of her head and tie it untidily above her head, so that half her hair is up and some of it is down. But I can still see her neck, so I satisfyingly walk back to my station and turn to look at my muse as I continue to sketch her.

I want to capture all her sides and corners and make her come alive on this white paper of mine; the rise of her hip and the dip of her navel, the arch of her back and every wrinkle in her nipple.

Her dulcet mouth meets her lovely shoulder as if to kiss it, her praying eyes fenced in behind her long eyelashes that can fan her horizon and create a windstorm. The ever so evanescent delicateness that is her I make evident by collapsing the lines of her ribs and the slopes of her clavicles. My heart stills at her ineffable, goddess-like loveliness.

My senses cry, but I hold on tight to my pencil; never have I looked at her so directly. So closely, I am honored for the permission. I decide to be obvious but eliminate clichés as I darken the point where her neck meets her shoulders, making that the cynosure of the masterpiece that is her body, climaxed by sharp strokes that make it more evident and solid where her shoulders fall.

She gives me the look of an Ingénue with complete trust in me, and that look alone, along with that body is the dream, or rather a nightmare of an artist who finds a pencil in the dessert and mud instead of paper; such a bitter sweetness indeed. You see such beauty, but there is not a thing you can do about it.

I let my eyes fall from hers and let them travel down the length of her body, taking in every stop. I revel at this blithe moment when I can stare all I want, and she does not turn away or hide even though I know she wants to. She looks down shyly, and I am again at awe by her oblivion to her own beauty. I continue my eyes' journey and halt at the dip of her navel to the north of her south: Eroticism at its best. Her lithe arms move to each side of her as she contorts herself so some of her is hidden.

"Don't hide such beauty. The sun loves you." I draw in a long breath and finish, "Let it."

She obeys by lowering her shoulders in an effort to relax. She looks up, elongating her neck, resting at an angle at which the light hits her skin perfectly. Turning her left breast into a penumbra and making light nest on her shoulders, shadowing her stomach. And just as I see her, I outline a ghost of the bones on her chest, just a fragment of her skeleton and her tight skin that she so elegantly wears.

I look at my paper July, and she looks like a shy goddess hiding from the sun. Her gossamer curls nesting behind her ears as if to whisper confirmation of her being a deity. She is beautiful, untouchable; surely, she has broken hearts, I'm certain of it. If I were of normal candidacy, I too would fall in love with her. Unfortunately, I am not. I involuntarily clench and unclench my jaw, my angry fingers suddenly breaking my pencil in half. I do not pity myself.

Frustration, anger, something, whatever it is builds up in my chest and manifests itself into something greater than the moment I find my mind wondering into. I push my easel to the side and walk over to the window.

July startles but says nothing. She simply looks at me as though I am now the subject under speculation.

I grab some Egbert brushes and a pallet; I walk over to the cabinet and open a brand-new box of acrylic paints as an idea formats in my head. I move quickly and breathe long and deep as I focus all of my intense energy on clearing everything standing in my way until there is nothing left but the bare white wall that awaits my hands to dress it.

If I can't love her, if I can't have her, I'll settle for the next best thing. I clear my workstation and look at July, who has suddenly rises from her post and is now covering herself with the paint-soiled sheet that was lying on the corner of the room.

"What are you doing? Where are you going?" I inquire in a tiny panic, afraid she's changed her mind.

"What are you doing?" she reflects back.

"I am going to take you from this moment and perpetually keep you in it."

She looks at me as if I've lost my mind, and I might as well have because inspiration moves me and I have no time, no need for reason. I respond to her confused expression by stating what I think is so obvious.

"I am going to take you as you are and put you all over this east wall." I all but snarl with passion.

I look at the white wall of the room where the sun rests for most of the day, and I decide this is a perfect and most ideal place, and July? What better subject for a more brilliant and provocative mural?

"But wouldn't you rather…" she drifts off and looks at her feet "…I don't know put something more beautiful and more permanent up there." She concludes her sentence barely in a whisper, and I beg to differ.

There is nothing more beautiful than a naked July who looks at me as I look at her while her breasts are at attention, her skin covered in goosebumps in anticipation for my eyes to reveal my thoughts. I am amazed at her statement but find I don't need to consider it, even though she might be right. Beautiful yes; it's the permanent part that poses an issue.

"Let's worry about tomorrow when it gets here." I smile but know very well that I have not assured her.

She remains standing, covering herself with the paint covered sheet. She doesn't move, but her hands firmly grip the sheet as if she has no intention of uncovering.

"Please don't hide." I gain the softness in my voice.

I walk over to her, and I take the soiled sheet from her and lay it at her feet. I take her hands in mine, kneeling down and tenderly take her down with me. Her body is nimble as I instruct her to sit on the sheet that I have laid out for her. I spread her over it, extending her legs on the side, so her body is long and organic. I see all of her, and she is a sight to see as my breath catches in my throat. I swallow it and walk over to the bare wall. I run my fingers on it, measuring its texture. I close my eyes for a second and envision what I plan to make come alive. I take my palette and mix colors until I have a deep blue.

"Stay still," I command at my muse.

She squeezes her eyes shut to acknowledge my request as if moving her lips would be disobeying me. I paint her exactly as I see her starting from her head before culminating with the delicate protrusion that is her ankle and then ending at her toes. Minutes pass, hours maybe; I don't know, but July patiently poses and I, the artist, try my best to make my painted July as real and as alive as the one who now breathes in front of me. I realize there is no burning this piece. I tell my heart to cough if it's bleeding.

Chapter Ten

The summer is coming to an end, and in anticipation of Skylar's return, I plan to keep my promise to July to take her camping, and then close that chapter for good. I'm grateful that July was a massive distraction, but I have decided that I do not want to jeopardize anything for Skylar by fooling around with July. It's so easy to make that decision when I am alone, but when July is in front of me, I lose all inhibitions. I rationalize that this is our final rendezvous and then we both have to say goodbye. I'm sure she'll understand. I just can't have too much fun this weekend.

I have this gnawing feeling that the venue has some haunting memories that I am not yet ready to confront. I decide that it's better to be with someone that I can't let my guard down with that way my ghosts will be faced with a very indifferent me and then I can move on without having to dig too deep.

The closer we get to our destination, the tighter my chest feels. It is clear to me that there are some unresolved feelings that are associated with this place. My father's cabin; I have somehow blocked from memory that it does not hold happy sentiments for me and my family. And then there was the last time I was here with Skylar, another tragedy I would like to keep from surfacing in memory.

We get to the decrepit building standing in the middle of a green field. There are grape vines wrapped around the whole back wall. and it looks like something from Green Gables. There is so much color, it looks like we have walked into an animated world. The air is cleaner, crisp and the clouds hang low, I think I could touch them if I climbed the giant peach tree that is in full bloom towards the back of the house.

"I just love the last days of summer. Don't you?" July takes in as much fresh air into her lungs as she can.

Suddenly, I wish I was alone. To appreciate such beauty, it must be done in silence and in solitude. The windmill in the far horizon slowly spins, and I feel like I am in the eighteenth century. This place feels and looks exactly like it did growing up and holds some of purest memories: when my parents were still together and Llarel still had her sight.

Nothing about this place has changed. My father still has someone maintain it as though time has not taken place. My mother's favorite chair has a fresh coat of paint and sits in the same place on the porch. This nauseates me.

"I can't believe that your parents own this beautiful land…" I hear July talking, but I move further and further away from her as I try to drown out anything new. I remain in place when earlier, happier memories still existed. The last person I was here with was Sky, and this is the place where she almost drowned and had to be helicoptered out to the hospital, and she almost died. I shudder at the memory as I realize that I had since then avoided this place because it harbored that horrible memory, among others.

I breathe as deep and as heavy as I can, holding the clean air and hoping to store it and take it with me wherever I go because somehow I find it harder to breathe the nearer I draw to the lake. I keep walking towards the lake until I hear July calling after me. I turn around agitated, somehow regretting bringing her here.

"I'll be right there." I call back to her as I turn my back on the calling lake.

Once inside, we find that the air conditioning is not working, and no one can come fix it till Monday. We put away the groceries, and I take our luggage upstarts to the bedroom. I sit on the foot of the bed and inspect what used to be my parents' room. I decide that perhaps it was not a good idea to come here; July is not the person I want to be here with when my demons come knocking. All the pictures are of us as a family smiling at the camera, one of my parents smiling, Llarel and I, our old dog Woolly. I turn all of them face down except for the one of Llarel and I. At least that one is not a lie. I all but sprint downstairs and take her by the hand.

"Come on let's go outside. The sun is about to set."

I grab some blankets and pillows, determined to convince her to sleep outside. Away from this suffocating house.

"Oh okay. Did you see a ghost upstairs?"

I ignore her and just grab sandwiches that we've just unpacked from the fridge. I lead her to the far west of the house where there's less trees, and I lay an old plush comforter down and motion for her to sit. I sit next to her and just stare at the now golding sky. She stares at me for a long time for an explanation, but I give her none. I simply pretend my view of her from my peripheral is obstructed by the beauty that I try so hard to marvel over. Eventually, she turns her eyes to what has captured my attention. We remain vacant until the sun's painted the sky purple. She breaks the silence.

"Dorian?"

"Yes?" I slowly but reluctantly respond. Wishing very hard that I was here alone and amazed at my feelings.

"Are you okay?"

"Of course. Why do you ask?"

"For starters, you haven't looked at me since we got here. You seem kind of preoccupied."

I am. But I say nothing. Instead I just turn to look at her.

"I am not comparing myself to this beauty. I'm not arrogant but it seems like...like instead of sharing it with me, you would much rather be here with someone else or alone, maybe."

I remain facing her, hoping the guilt I suddenly feel does not register to my face.

"I'm sorry. I just got carried away with my childhood memories, that's all."

She starts to say something but then closes her mouth. She sits up with her legs crossed and passes me a sandwich and a drink and then starts unwrapping hers.

"It actually feels good out here; better than it does inside," I say lightly.

"We could just spend the night outside; that would qualify as camping, right?"

"Right," I agree, relieved.

"For someone who promised to take me camping, this place is way too posh to consider it a real camping experience."

"Are you complaining?"

She simply makes a face.

"You don't just take an inexperienced camper and throw her out in the wilderness."

"Are we talking about you or me here?" She banters back, and we both laugh.

"I'll have you know, I was a boy scout when I was a kid."

"I find that hard to believe."

"I have my badges to prove it. I can tie the meanest knot."

"So, you were a nerdy little kid huh?"

"Yes. But I was the coolest nerd."

"Do share. Were you also a mama's boy?"

That stops me from laughing, and I suddenly cannot feel my smile, and I notice in her face that she has noticed the sudden change, too.

I look up at the sky, and the stars are as clear as ever.

"I love how you could always see the stars here. You don't ever see a sky as vivid as this in the city," I divert.

"It is a sight to see."

We talk like this till we both fall asleep. Never once asking her deep-rooted questions for fear that they would be reciprocated.

In the morning, I make sure I wake up early enough to explore the house and any feelings summoned by its memories. I find a note pad in the office and some pencils and pass a sleeping July on my way to the lake to sketch.

My pencil eventually dulls, and I become self-aware again. I hear someone behind me, and I turn around to find July standing there in her spandex tights and her Under Armour sweatshirt zipped halfway and stops midway at her chest so her signature tank tops peak out from the opening. Her hair is pulled back into a tight ponytail and she is wearing tiny diamond studs with no hint of make up on her face.

Such a lovely sight. She is natural, organic, nothing about her is embellished or highlighted. I wonder how someone can ever tire looking at her. She saunters over to me, and I find my curiosity moving towards her shadow. Even her silhouette has a tale to tell. The fabric hugs her thighs as if pulling them apart and as she walks towards me, I keep waiting for them to meet, but they keep their distance from each other, leaving me with the thought that the space between them is where I am meant to be.

"Do you want to go for a run with me?" she asks innocently.

"Are you sure you can take the heat?" I humor her.

"Can you bring the heat?" She takes another band from her wrist and ties her curls securely, eyeing me as she does so.

I follow her eyes and assess my body. I am wearing loose black sweatpants and light sweatshirt that covers a white body shirt that hugs my muscles, highlighting the definition of my chest and abs.

"You look like you've done this before."

I make a face that says maybe or maybe not.

We both take our sweaters off and place them on the bench, catching a glimpse of her eyeing me and that makes me smirk a little as I compress my ego.

"What do you prefer? Distance? Or speed?"

I look at her as if that's obvious, "Speed."

So we warm up together, fighting to ignore the electricity and sexual tension that is ever so present between us, as present and as physical as both she and I. We sit across from each other with the soles of our shoes touching, forming the shape of a diamond between us as we stretch back and forth, and I am suddenly aware of the muscles on my back as they begin to stretch and make themselves known.

"You ready for me to kick your hiney?"

"Are you ready to eat my dust before you see my hiney disappear out of sight?"

I can tell that she is taking this seriously. I deliberate whether to be a gentleman and let the lady win but then decide that she would want me to be fair; after all, this is her turf.

"You're the one who's about to see dust, once I am done running circles around you."

She stretches her arms above her head and then from one side and then the next, making a moaning sound as she closes her eyes and cracks her neck. I am momentarily distracted, but I pull myself together and ignore her attempt to distract me.

"Do you want to do a trail round as a warmup?"

I know for a fact that she is trying to tire me because I am not used to practice runs like she is, and of course, I don't have as much stamina as she does, but I decide that I am going to pull all stops and not take the easy way, deciding that if I beat her, I am going to do it fair and square.

"You are planning on making this as hard as possible, aren't you? I like!"

She starts jogging, and I follow behind her but soon catch up, and we both relax on the first round and engage in small talk.

"So how often do you do this?"

She looks at me as though she is not surprised but glad that I can and am doing this with her.

"At least once a day."

She starts jogging faster, and I follow behind her taking my time to catch up, so I can watch her ponytail sway back and forth. Her legs hold her impeccably as she runs rhythmically, and her butt squeezes and releases with every step she takes. I join her, and she is breathing peacefully as she offers me a sweet but small smile.

We forget about racing, and we jog silently side by side both transported by our own thoughts and the beauty that surrounds us. By the time we make it back to the house, we have both enjoyed a perfectly normal silence, and I have compartmentalized all my thoughts about my past that I had to reluctantly face. We spend as much time outdoors as possible.

After eating lunch at the picnic table outside by the windmill, we go inside to clean up the dishes. The house seems less suffocating, the energy is different, and I have started some new memories.

As I am putting things up and clearing the mess on the kitchen counter, July emerges from behind the fridge door as she shuts it. She takes a piece of ice and sucks on it before running it along her jaw line and then rubbing it on her neck, her shoulders and then her neck. I see her like that, and my primal instincts take over. Sex is not really complicated, and I know that as I look at her crazy body. She is ready to be desecrated, to be penetrated, to be complicated, and I know I have to be the one. My ardor is awakened.

I want to have barbaric animal sex with her. I want to fuck her in every single position our bodies will allow. I swallow hard as I try to control my breathing and silence my pulsing temples. The heat, the humidity traps me in some sort of spell where I can't get out of my head and everything inside it is in sync with what's going on between my legs.

I want to bury myself in her hair and let her consume me. I want to be inside of her and in her mouth. I want her chained on me, locked inside of me. I don't want to speak, I just want her sweating on me, rubbing against me. I want to do dirty things to her and hear her saying she's enjoying every last bit of them.

I walk over to her and run my tongue from her chin, to the side of her face, all the way to her hair line, tasting the salt of her skin. I do it again, this time from the base of her neck all the way to her throat. I do it again and again and again, and when she is wet with my saliva, I take a big whiff of her and enjoy how she smells of me. She shapes her mouth to speak, but I put my index finger on her mouth.

"Shhh." I don't want to speak right now; I just want to do.

I take a big bite of her mouth, and I think I might want to swallow her. *The heat.* Her tongue searches the inside of my mouth, and I know she hungers for me, too. I kiss her so hard I'm inebriated. She in turn oohs, and I know we are vibing. I lick the side of her face and again smell her making a vacuuming sound with my nose. *The heat.* I nibble her earlobe and hold it between my teeth, and she pushes her hips into me as she ahhs and moans my name.

Roughly I tuck my hands under her denim shorts and into her panties where I find her wet and waiting. Her breathing is now urgent; she is panting. She spreads her legs apart ushering me to go into her, and I do. I slip my middle finger inside of her and move in and out before I change the tempo; massaging her clitoris. She pulls me by my hair until I'm leveling with her, and she sips me with her succulent lips. She moans against my mouth when I flip my finger over to the wall of her warm pudenda, and I speed the motion of my fingers until I feel her crumble in my arms, until I am left with all of her weight, and I pillar her between myself and the fridge.

My breathing is frantic, and I am solid and in need to release. She opens those big chocolate eyes, and they are ignited with want, with need, with lust. I can't stand to be teased right now, not by those eyes nor by that mouth, so I pull her face close but instead of kissing her, I stick my middle finger in my mouth then in hers, and she sucks my finger keeping her eyes on me and my breath quickens again and she slides down holding on to my steady yet flaccid legs. She unzips my trousers and frees me from my confinement.

She imitates the same action, yet this time not on my fingers but on my length: my excited and agitated muscle. The inside of her mouth is warm and wet and smooth, so smooth.

"Oh, fuck," I hear myself grunt.

I spread my legs and put my hands against the fridge as if I am being frisked by a cop. At this moment, there is no me without this girl and only, only this moment matters, more than a cold beer, a cool breeze or ice-cubes on my tongue. Her tongue snakes and gyrates around the head of my erection before she completely envelopes it with her sweet wet mouth.

My body vibrates before I deposit the evidence of this glorious experience into her gorgeous mouth, and she rises up to meet me, and when our eyes meet, she swallows and makes the most beautiful sound; the sound of someone eating something delicious and exotic. This excites me all over again.

I smile a devious smile and my barbaric instinct returns. It turns me on that we both got off and yet we both are still fully dressed. I gently and playfully push her against the fridge and kiss her, tasting myself on her mouth. I push my tongue to the roof of her mouth and sweep it until I am sure I know the exact taste of me in her mouth. I pick her up and place her on the countertop, and I slowly, very slowly unzip the denim, keeping my smile and my eyes on her, and then pull on the waist of her shorts. She lifts her hips, so I can easily slide them off, and she does it again when I pull down her white underwear, arching her body into a C. I take it in my hand and sniff it,

"You're so fuckin' hot," I growl.

I put my head through the leg of her underwear and wear it around my neck. I rub my hand over her bare pubis and watch her as she anticipates my next move. I, one by one, spread her legs wide and bring my head to the center of her and just take her in, the smell of her need, her craving for me is intoxicating. I drink her and suck her into my mouth as I take in the taste of her, the smell of her. She buckles her legs around my head until I have to hold them apart and when I insert my tongue in and out of her, she pulls me by my hair and then pushes me down to her, so she's in control of the rhythm and the speed. I place my hand on her belly and stop when I feel her slightly begin quiver.

She all but begs when I pause for a second to undress myself. I am ready to bury myself inside of her, to be in her warm and wet center where I know I am welcomed, so I scoot her to the edge of the counter and let out a sharp breath as I effortlessly inch into her, and she lets out a sound that lets me know she is relieved that I am tightly and securely inside of her, she closes her eyes, throwing her head back and lets me fill her as I begin to thrust into her in slow shallow movements. When I pick up the speed and dive deep into the core of her, she bubbles from within and eats my name.

"Yesss," I seethe behind grunted teeth.

I am not ready to let go yet, so I tease her a little. I pull out of her and rub my length on the outside of her now sensitive labia and penetrate her again, and she compresses to me from the inside as if capturing me with no intent of ever freeing me. I *aah* and give an *ooh*, I am but merely a molecule that slowly dissolves. She seizures and loses herself in me. I, in turn, only let her be, let her do what comes naturally at such a circumstance.

I release myself and give into the heat, the overwhelming intensity that is in her, outside of her and around her as she moans a long note before she un-clamps around my muscle. I ease myself out of her and climb on top of the cool black marble beside her and on my left is the ketchup, honey and mustard, and we both lay naked facing the ceiling, breathing unevenly.

I wake, and my back is stiff and am blissfully sore. I find that July is dressed in my trousers and tie and nothing else. She is propped up on her elbow with her face real close to mine, and she is rubbing her fingers through my hair and staring lovingly at me.

"Hello you," I say to her as softly as I have ever spoken without whispering.

"Hi," she coos.

"What are you doing?"

"Just counting your hair," she concedes as she raises her eyes to my head.

I lift myself up, so I am sitting with my legs folded on the counter, and she puts her head on my naked lap and elongates her legs to the opposite di-rection, so they dangle at the knees.

I grab the honey from my left and stick the small tube in my mouth. I ad-just my weight and take July's curls out of her tight ponytail. I take the bottle and squeeze the small tube into her hair. I brush it with my right hand as I squeeze the content with my left. Pretty soon, her hair is sticky and drenched in honey, and it feels so good and smooth, giving her hair a solid weight.

She sits up and stares at me, lifting her arms to her head and coming back with sticky hands. I dab a little on her nose and lick it off.

"Do that again," I plead.

"What?"

"Put your hands up to your head again."

She lifts her hands up to her head and the skin on her chest extends, making her breasts look rounder, softer and more delicate.

"Hold it right there."

Her breasts morph into perfection, the shape of a teardrop, and I want to catch it in my hands before it trickles down. She smiles shyly and turns her head to the side, revealing her perfect neck and, ah, I want to kiss her and keep her in my mouth till kingdom come.

I stare at those beautiful teardrops with my tie between them, and for seconds, I'm immobile. Her features soften as she licks her wrist where a small bead of honey has landed.

Slowly, I pull her by the tie around her neck, fixing my eyes on her, leading us both off the counter and onto the floor. She kneels down on the cherry wood floor between the island and the fridge, and I kneel beside her. I take her in starting from her hungry belly to her teardrop breasts and then her long neck that is now soaked with honey. I spread her on the floor, hovering above her as I prop her head with my free hand and gently lay her head down on the hardwood. I pick up the bottle of honey and draw a circle around her navel, another one around her left breast and another one around her right breast. Instead of licking it off of her, I lower to her and slowly rub myself up and down her body with my chest, breathing in through my nose, using our breathing as the music; the intoxicating sweet smell of honey, intensifying our foreplay. The silence is loud, but we only hear what we see in each other's eyes.

She giggles softly and slips her head into the other leg of her underwear that is still around my neck. This restricts me from moving up and down, so she takes the honey out of my hand and pours it down my back as she plants small wet kisses along the outside of my mouth while rubbing it all over me. I move from side to side so that the honey spreads between us. The smell of sex, the stickiness, and the humidity created by our breaths and heat from the unconditioned room makes me feel dirty and nasty, and somehow that makes me feel liberated, carefree. I am outside of my body and floating with the beautiful aching that transforms to ecstasy.

July, my drug, unhooks from the underwear and sits me up, so I am facing away from her. She rubs her breasts on my back, and I feel myself increase as I listen to her breathe behind me, making the nerves on the back of my neck come alive. I close my eyes and deny myself any other feeling, any other thought.

She starts kissing me, and every touch, every sound ignites a craving that burrows deep within, and I am afraid I have a thirst for her that cannot be quenched. Against her, I am a breathing paradox; I am hungry but not for food, yearning but full to maximum capacity. I am arrested by a wild eruption of sensation but free and insatiable. I am spent, but won't slow down. When she nibbles my ear, when she whispers into it, I lose all of me, I succumb wholly under her power. My being is liquefied, and I pour myself into her as she remains suspended in the air breathing me in and out.

I turn and face her, looking, no, staring at her, into her, through her and her terracotta eyes hold me captive as she bewitches me. We both bow ourselves from within, acknowledging our vulnerability without speaking a word, but the look we exchange says what we both can never say with words. My heart strings are pulled, and I ignore the tugging, refusing to consider the meaning. Right now, I am merely a flame dancing on the candle that liquesces below me. I scoot myself up and lay down, holding her, so she is sitting above and on top of me.

She detaches from me, and I watch her as she rises and towers over me. Her cocoa eyes melt right in front of me as she holds me in place with them. I watch her unzip my trousers, and she removes herself from them. Her body is tall and athletic as I look at her from a low angle where I lay. She simply holds me with her eyes, denying me the opportunity to stare at her body.

My tie now drenched in honey remains between her beautiful teardrop breasts as the tip of it stretches all the way down and halts as if pointing to her upside-down heart of a pudenda; pointing to the warmest and sweetest of all of July.

She slowly kneels back down next to me, and she stares into me as she searches for me with her hand and finds me. She inhales and holds her breath as she closes her eyes and eases me into her, keeping her eyes closed as she moves up and down, back and forth. The honey holding her soppy curls in place but drips behind her ears, making its way down her neck, and I just continue staring at her, in control and utterly out of my senses.

We make love on the kitchen floor as if that is the only way that it should be done. Forgetting and forgiving all and everything of the past up till this point. Just us and the now, Dorian and July and the now; fucking, sucking, and pollenating.

The rest of the day, we enjoy swimming in the lake and exchanging our stories about the best and worst relationships, never once visiting the topic of family and childhood memories. She convinces me to sleep inside this time, and I cave in, comforted by the thought of making new memories and shutting out the old ones.

July lays peacefully beside me. I imagine she got hot and moved to her side of the bed like she always does. I love it though, that she lies next to me and tucks her feet under me until she is warm. I look at the alarm clock, and the alarm is about to go off in three minutes. I turn it off and tiptoe to the bathroom, making certain I don't awake the now sleeping beauty.

I walk into the bathroom and crank the door shut, hoping to drown out the noise of the running water. I splash my hot face with ice cold water. My muscles awake, and I look at my face in the mirror in front of me realizing that my five o'clock shadow is actually at six.

The door suddenly opens, and July stands by it and looks at me sheepishly, her hair in a disarray of curls.

"Good morning."

"Morning," I reply, mirroring her look.

She walks past me, touching me just barely and sits on the edge of the bathtub while watching me. I pretend to pay no attention to her as I squeeze toothpaste onto my toothbrush. She walks past me again, lightly brushing against me, and horripilation becomes my skin. This bathroom, the space surrounding us is big enough for me and her and another pair of us, but I find it erotic that she feels the need to touch me.

Her pretense encourages me to play along, and I decide to be the villain and let her work for what she wants.

She brushes against me with her butt, and she mutters teasingly, "Oh, ah, excuse me."

I watch her in the mirror as she walks to the back to the tub and brushes her perky breasts on the lower part of my back, and I am well aware that she is touching me, with what she is touching me, and where she is touching me. She sits down at the edge of the tub and immediately lifts herself up again. She walks to me, and we are both framed by the cooper mirror with lights above us, and she looks at me in the mirror and again she uses her seductive words of the day:

"Excuse me."

She picks up the toothpaste from my toiletry bag and squeezes out a large amount of its contents into her mouth. I watch with a nonchalant look on my face pretending not to be affected, but a very south part of me pursues her game with no shame.

She inserts her toothbrush into her already full mouth and pushes it in and out but not in a way that the rest of us mere mortals brush our teeth. She spits out a big glob of blue form and washes it down the drain while I am still holding my brush in my mouth rubbing my gums raw as I pretend to be concentrating and failing terribly at it.

Teasingly and seductively, she walks past me again and brushes my butt with her hand while hers lightly rubs past the back of my thighs,

"Oops," she mutters.

Like gravity, I have no choice but to go where it pulls me. I turn myself around and face her, all pretending aside. I am at awe and very impressed with the look she gives me. Longingly and hungrily, I lower my face to hers and scold that teasing mouth of hers with mine. I taste her minty tongue, and she bites hard as if to say, *Finally.*

Both our minty-fresh mouths match each other while our crisp breaths combat as though each is fighting to swallow the other. I place my hands on each side of her waist, lifting her up and placing her on the marble sink beside the floss and hand soap, and she whines against me as though edging me to do to her what Samson might do to Delilah.

I pull her close to me, thrusting her pelvis against mine until the only space that's left between us is that that is occupied by our clothes. She sighs into my ear, and her breathing deepens as mine shallows. I swallow her breath as she dispels it, tasting it as I do so. I pull her as close as I can have her without entering her. I feel the heat pierce her satin shorts, burning me, causing me to fever.

"Dorian!" she whispers in my ear. "I want you to do to me what sun does to night." She sucks in her breath before she finishes, "Make me disappear, Dorian."

To watch her sheer desire for me, to hear her wanting me and not be afraid to show it is such a turn on. I kiss her hair, her eyes, her nose, and finally her neck before I whisper, "I don't want you to disappear. I want you here with me." So I can stroke her, and rub her, and fill her with myself.

I can see her, feel her, I can smell her, and I can taste her as my tongue pollutes her mouth, and I hear her pleading with me with her moans and her sighs as she soughs against me, tightening herself around me.

I kiss her shoulders, and through the dark blue silk, I see her nipples slowly harden as her need for me grows, and her temperature rises. I nestle on her nipples through the fabric, leaving two wet circles before slightly lifting it up and slowly kissing her stomach.

I push her strap to the fall of her shoulder, and she squeezes her legs around me while I suck on her nipples, all the while teasing them with my teeth, biting hard enough to create a sweet and painful sensation. I repeat with the other side and watch the blue silk drop to her belly, and I withdraw from her and take a moment to look at her while she is undone and completely under my spell. She lets out a long breath that leaves her empty, but then she parts her lips and lets it in again, taking some of mine away.

I free myself from the tangle of her legs and impatiently remove myself out of my boxers, keeping my eyes firmly on her, and she doesn't skip a beat. She modestly bites her bottom lip mentally pulling me to her, and I don't resist her.

I remove her from the marble and pull her close to me. When she stands against me, I haunch down and remove her silk shorts and caress her legs while I help them down. She rubs my head until my ears start to tingle, and I am, I am the salt that dilutes with the sea, that loses its saltiness, I am absorbed into her.

I lift her back on to the sink, pulling her legs apart until I am in them and steady myself as I find my way home. She pushes forward to meet me, and I am engulfed, confined in her. The warmth in my chest that eats me, I am not sure belongs to me. From the inside out, from head to toe, I feel myself waste into a burning liquid, and I hold on to the warmth for as long as I can.

She tangles me with her arms and legs, and for an eternal moment, we stay in place, not allowing anything to unglue us, not even the back and forth thrusting that necessitates our pleasure, or the need to release the heat that is so sensational when we do separate. I am not sure which is me and which is her. We are one, a vessel separated only by a fragment of space, the space that we disqualify every chance we get.

I lay my head against her neck and just breathe; I let what happens happen and just remind myself to breathe. I just breathe, and everything else my body does naturally.

"Dorian, ah, ah, ahh…"

A warm July, undoing me, extricating me, and multiplying me into a million pieces with her vocal expression of satiation. Hearing her crystalize, completely combusting around me does me the way sun does to snow, I just dissolve and precipitate. I expand and collapse,

"Ah, ah, oh fuck," I sing, I grunt, I speak in tongues.

She loses her breath; she misses a beat and forgets how to breathe, and in my own heavenly bliss, I detonate and wholly erupt from the inside out. Then we give ourselves to each other again, caring about nothing else but breathing. We just breathe.

July's thighs encircled tightly around me. I look at her, and she is wearing her blue camisole around her waist like a belt, and while we both catch our breath, I see her smile materialize. I lift her from the sink and kiss her less urgently and she releases me.

"You're a remora," I tease.

"And you are so easily seduced."

She turns away and walks into the shower. Deliberately, she bends so that her cheeks are perfect half-moons and I want nothing more than to burry my mouth between them.

She pulls her shirt over her head and stretches her whole body as she lifts her arms, not having had enough. I marvel at her naked body drenched in the afterglow of our fucking. She is beautiful: her youth, her vitality, her jubilant personality; she is so vibrant and so energetic, I feel untouchable. Immortal. I have satisfied a sex goddess.

Not only is she sexy and irresistible, she is perfectly flawed and flawlessly capable of breaking down my defenses. She tucks her unruly curls behind her ears, and I am putty in her hands. She has pretty fingers, pretty hands, and a mouth meant for kisses. She smells of nectarine and other exotic fruit. Her skin is soft and delicate, smooth with intentional indentations: a paintbrush's fantasy.

I follow her into the shower and stop behind her, watching her naked skin anointed with water. If I could, I would cover her the way this water does: from head to toe.

I step closer to her and extend my hand as if to touch her but dance it past her and grab the shampoo. I take my time to lather my hair with the fruity liquid. I know she is watching with expectation, but I relish at the look she gives. Her eyes stop at my ignored erection, and I let her look, letting her know that I know she is watching, and I don't mind, and I am not shy. I close my eyes and seductively hang my arms above my head, deliberately tightening my stomach, so the ridges on it are solid and hard.

I am sure that I have her full attention, and before I know it, my erection is inside something warm and wet and deliciously smooth, I open my eyes and find July on her knees, praying me like a god. I want to sneeze, I want to cough, I just feel so good. When I can't take it anymore, when I feel my stitches loosen, I take her face in my hands and kneel down in front of her.

I kiss her mouth, tasting myself in it. I push her wet curls away from her face, away from her neck. I gently lower her down until she is lying on the wet tile, under the cascading water.

I spread her legs apart with mine, while kissing her wet breasts, her wet navel, and then…then bury myself in the center of her and she invites me in with the sounds that only a sex goddess knows how to utter. At this time, at this moment, I would rather be nowhere else.

I sit up and pull her to my lap, so we are pelvis glued, face-to-face, mouth to mouth, heartbeat to heartbeat. I steady myself and swallow my surprise thoroughly impressed with my own inveiglement and July's boldness. Her failure to control herself, her need for me gives me a deeper fondness for our chemistry and physical attraction.

I draw in some air between my tongue and teeth, making a sucking sound, and the now all-too familiar sensation of pleasure under water is an added advantage as I try to keep myself in the now.

I feel like a man, like a sex god to have this beautiful creature want me the way that she does. Her insatiable appetite for me, her uncontrollable hands on me make me feel wanted and sexy, and it makes me feel good as a man to have someone have no control for the desire she has for me. It boosts my ego, heightens my confidence to be the subject of her desire, her lust, and her long-

ing, and I plan on nothing short of satisfying every one of her desires; for her…
and for myself as well.

When our hour-long shower is over, primal instinct number two comes
in: Hunger. I walk out to the veranda, and the sun is shining, and the birds are
singing (like my insides).

I walk back through the bedroom and into the living room and am immediately accosted by the heat. Somehow we had slept through it and forgot that
we are in the cabin with no air-conditioner.

I pack the car as July fixes something to eat, and we eat in silence. Eventually she breaks the silence.

"Are your parents still together?"

"No."

"Are they both still alive."

"Yes."

"Are you guys close?"

"No."

"Can I ask you one more question? This one is open-ended."

My jaw instinctively flexes, and my shoulders tense up.

"Ask away."

"Why are all of the pictures of your mom and dad facing down?"

I stop chewing and just stare at my salad. I shake my head and close
my eyes, unable to respond. I just remain immobile until I hear July's
chair shriek.

"Okay."

She clears the table, and speaks no more of it. In the car, we are both quiet
and listen to the radio until the soft lull of the rain contributes to the silence
between us.

The drive back home is a reminder that reality is slowly setting in. What
does it mean that I took July on a mini camping trip? To simply justify it as
me delivering my promise of having her do something that she has never done
before just doesn't seem reason enough. I look over at July, and she seems preoccupied with her own thoughts. She looks at me, serious, and then as if suddenly renewed, she has a devious smile on her face.

"You should pull over," she commands.

"Why?" I ask, suddenly worried that something is wrong.

She gets that all too familiar look on her face, the one where two or more things are happening at once; as if she is deliberating with someone else in her head. Her happy self wins because she now wears a smile.

"Because I desperately need to pee."

I'm not convinced, but I oblige. I turn left at a slight trail that is worn out with tire tracks, and the trees stand aside kowtowing as if welcoming an honored guest deep into the woods. The trees stand tall and green, and I continue to follow the road between them and stop where the track splits into two.

In front of us is a river and a small waterfall on the edge of it, and the water is green surrounded by rocks and trees and nothing else but nature and us. My shiny car seems alien and out of place, it is apparent that we are intruding on nature. We both sit in silence and marvel at the beauty that environs us when suddenly July looks at me and smiles.

"Take off your clothes," July demands without looking at me while simultaneously kicking off her shoes and socks. She removes her sweater and tank tops and throws them in the backseat. She looks at me waiting for me to mirror her actions, and my brain instructs me that anything that involves nudity couldn't be harmful. I obediently remove my long sleeve V-neck. She takes everything off, and when she is completely naked, she opens the car door. I remain firmly in my seat.

"What are you doing?" I yell behind her.

She ignores me as she makes her way to the front of the car. She sits on the hood of the car, looks up at the sky and lets the rain anoint her. With her back toward me, I admire her soft curves, her spine extended in ridges in the center of her smooth brown back, and her hair in a pointed pony like a wet paint brush. She has a magnificent black dot, right below her left scapula, as if a sculptor has put a mark to his finished art, a period. Full stop. End of perfection and no question mark.

"You're going to make yourself sick." For the second time since I've known her, I feel like her father.

She continues to ignore me, and I watch her from the inside of the car waiting for her to come to her senses or for me to lose mine, so at least one of us can join the other. I finally decide that I am the one who has to give in and walk out to get her, still in my jeans and nothing else.

"I've always wanted to do this," she exclaims when she hears me slam the car door.

I cringe and open the door again, making sure that we haven't locked ourselves out with hardly any clothes on, or in July's case, none. I stand by the door and let it close again, internally kicking myself for being so mundane. I decide that I am going to follow Enoch's mantra: *Close your eyes. Breathe. Jump.*

I turn and walk over to July and decide to take her in instead of the beautiful scenery that stretches in front of us. She is protracted on the hood of the car, but she doesn't turn to look at me, and she has let down her hair which is now soaked and cascading down her back along with the rain. The rain, like dancing pixies, shimmers on her skin and hair, and she doesn't blink it away or shake it off; she just lets it evaporate into her pores and gather on her eyelashes. I walk over to her and halt in front of her.

"You are stunning," I say, meaning it.

Her eyelashes are wet and heavy with rain, shielding her eyes from the wetness. She sucks on her top lip and assesses me as I graze her lissome body with a hungry look. I follow a single drop as it makes its way from her neck, between her breasts, and all the way down and rests on her belly-button. I refocus my attention and marvel at her hard, wet nipples and start aching for the texture of them on my tongue. I place my hands behind both her knees and in one swift movement pull her hard to me until I am between her legs, inclined and face to face with her. I am pleased when I see that she is surprised.

I firmly kiss her and don't come up for air until I feel a tense sensation in my throat. I suck hard and vacuum her lips into mine, and I let out a groan when she returns the tight suction as she pinches my lips with hers. I bite her shoulder. I hear her breathing accelerate and her body positioning itself around me, and the ache nomadically deepens through my body. The rain beats hard on my shoulders, but I imagine there is steam emanating from my back, my shoulders and my chest. The cool rain and our body heat cause a tornado of emotions between us, and the sensation has my scalp in prickles. I unbutton my jeans and pull my briefs down with them instantaneously and make my way home inside of July. Her skin is covered with rain and goose pimples, and I am covered in her.

I am a whole but two different entities. I concurrently experience two different temperatures; the cold and wet rain outside the openness of nature, and the warm and moist insides of July. The amalgamation has a glorious and orgasmic effect. She rakes her fingernails along the bottom of my ass, and the pain is sensational. I am inflicted with bliss and swallow every moment of it.

"Slap me," I startlingly demand.

She lightly swats the side of my cheek, and I feel the blood staining my face. "Harder." I command.

Instead of slapping me she bites hard at my bottom lip until it stings. The stinging, oh the stinging is pleasurable, gratifying, explosive. She pulls back and smiles, her wet face diluted with passion for me. She pulls back further to the top of the car, and I am left stranded and homeless, and my now cold erection is pounded by the rain. I step out of the pool of clothes around my ankles and a rush of blood currents through me and straight to my already inflamed phallus.

"Don't toy with me," I groan as I feel my veins expand from under my skin.

My yearning is amplified, blown up and made into a billboard. At this point, synesthesia is my only vice. I am what I should feel, taste what I should see, and I smell what I should hear.

She spreads her legs and in my mind a door opens inviting me home. I hurry to the hood of the car where she teasingly waits for me. I scoot my feet off the ground as if cleaning my feet on the mat outside the door before respectfully coming in. She lets me in, and just as I close my eyes and revel at being home, she pulls away, and I am outside again, and she climbs to the very roof of the car. I am throbbing, I am wanting, and the back of her crawling away from me sends my body into new tremors and breathing doesn't seem to be enough. My chest starts hurting in anticipation, and a raw desire takes over me as I hurry to wait for her to take me inside of her and control me, to hold me into her and absorb me with her other mouth. I am fraught; I follow her to the top of the car, leaving the worry about denting it for later. I don't even care.

Let me in, my muscle begs, and I am madly wanting to be engulfed by her. I think, I know I will be at peace once inside her and one with her.

I kneel with my legs slightly open and motion for her to come to me, and she does. She slides me into her as she lowers herself and sits on my thighs, facing me, staring into me and then slowly, she moves up and down, picking up the speed until we both can't breathe, her eyes boring into me and ravaging me to the core. The rain massages and slices, not deciding on whether to soothe or flagellate our bodies. Immense relief overpowers me, and July is the catalyst. Her skin, her breathing; I can't think of greater pleasure to be surrounded by nature and exalted by her wet body, and to be in both her mouths.

She presses into me as if wanting to swallow me with her other mouth, and I am filled to the brim. She inebriates, domesticates, orgasmicates me as she irradiates me body and soul. I topple over as I feel a burn start at my head and spread to my neck, my shoulders, and stay at the muscles on my stomach. The heat subsides, steaming from the inside of me, and she takes it and holds it inside of her before she pushes it out while she curls her toes and flexes her pelvic muscles, her pelvis glued to mine and her hair full of me. I close my eyes and let her complete me, and when I open them, she is staring intensely at me, overpowering me with her tenderness, her sensuality, her big, beautiful eyes.

My groans match her moans while the rain continues as if celebrating our love making, mudding the Earth. I feel a movement inside me, and I stop listening to it while I catch my heart in my throat and swallow it, forbidding the need to cry. The hum of the rain brings my body to a soft purr, and July unravels like a ball of yarn right in front of my eyes. My body tenses and then explodes into tiny fragments of me, and I grunt as if something that needed to be let out finally escapes, taking with it everything that doesn't belong inside of me. I feel an overwhelming sensation of a relaxation that takes over my body, leaving only the beauty that my eyes now behold.

We lay there, side by side, watching the warm summer rain climbing down the sky. No other noise, no other sound but the rain and our breathing. The rain drumming on the car, on us, and on the ground; the trees watching us is hush silence as if enjoying the show.

Finally, after letting the rain wash me, I jump up, retrieving my soaked jeans and putting them on commando. The weight of the rain drenching them, makes me move slowly. July runs to the backseat of the car and uses one of her tank tops to dry off and wears the rest of her dry clothes. I walk over to the car, and she tosses me my dry shirt. We drive in silence, listening to Pandora on the Enya station.

Surrounded by nature and my nose bathed in Petrichor, I feel complete. Back from the roof of my car, self-realization returns, and July, this creature beside me, this wet creature sitting beside me looking out the window, is the source of all these feelings. I reach over and rake my fingers through her wet hair. I quickly retrieve my hand when I am reminded of the last thought of her that I had, just moments ago. She sits up and looks at me, unexpectedly shy. Suddenly, I am afraid.

Chapter Eleven

Once at home and alone with my thoughts, reality sets in. That cabin, that tiny space is haunted with my childhood memories. How perfect my family was until my mother ruined it all. I hate her, and I have always made that known. She turned my father, a great man, into a pathetic fool of Shakespeare, who believes in nothing more than his memories' shadows. I shake my head to rid myself of those thoughts that I've buried, and somehow have been brought back by my visit to the one place that I have avoided for the longest time. I'm not really sure what I was hoping to accomplish by taking July over there. July; another complication; or at least it's starting to feel like she is.

I walk over to the art room and pull out a sketch pad that I hang up to the easel. I pick up a glass full of clean but old paintbrushes. I take a plastic cup and half fill it with water. I line up all the things I need to work with but have no clue what I am about to paint.

Hours later, I look up, and in front of me is the image of July. She wears her hair in a ponytail and her curls peek ceremoniously behind her slender neck. She is looking at me for answers. She is not mad; she is not smiling either. Come to think of it, I've never seen her mad or sad. She is wearing her favorite attire: two tank tops. One is orange and the one underneath it is pink and she is wearing the same necklace as the one that I gave Sky on her sixth birthday.

I pick up the picture and walk over to the bathroom to the right. I throw it in the tub and set it on fire. I rub my chest and internally warn myself: *Skylar is the only girl allowed in here. No one else.* I sit on my haunches and watch the image slowly burn, leaving a black film around the bleach white tub.

I call Skylar, and she, Jane, and Brady are still in Venus. I make a mental note to hug her more and tell her I love her more often. The cabin brought back the memory of when I thought I might lose her, reminding me of my promise to love her intentionally every day.

I lay in bed and toss and turn for most of the night. I keep moving from one end of the bed to the other, trying to find a cool spot on the mattress and doing the same with my pillows. I am distracted by my confusion. I sit up as the source of my confusion makes itself known.

I don't love her. How could I? She is like any woman that I've been with. Except she is July. Funny, carefree July who not only has an amazing body, but she has an incredible spirit and the softest hands and smoothest skin and the brownest eyes and…

I shake my head and lean my head to the left as if to empty out all those thoughts.

This is merely someone that I enjoy sleeping with, and I think it's clear to both of us that that's all it is: a simple convenience of two people who are not in a relationship, two people who are consenting to provide each other with what the other needs without imposing any commitment. No complication there.

What was that feeling, though? I almost wept. That must have been one amazing orgasm. That's all it was. It had nothing to do with emotions but the physicality and the rain. I've never made love out in the open like that; and the rain and the roof of my car. My car. I distract myself by making a mental note to check the roof and the hood of my car for dents later.

When I am not working, I find myself spending a lot of time with July. It irks me, but it soothes me, too. I go a few days either hanging out with Enoch, visiting Llarel or just in my art studio finishing up Madame Lefèvre's portrait. I have started jogging again and working out in the basement. I always have to remember the time difference because I have screwed up on that a few times. Jane has made it a rule that I don't call them and that they call me, unless it's an emergency. Every time I talk to my sweet girl, I remember the most recent dream I have had of her, and it makes me want her home with me. Here, where I can protect her. Lately, this fear of losing her consumes me so much so that I am afraid of my own thoughts. I don't like spending too much time alone. Every weekend, I find myself at *Blue Baby* and living the bachelor life with Enoch.

Since Skylar isn't here, July is working at a local restaurant and has a lot more time. I take advantage of that because every time I call her to hang out, she comes over. We don't date, we don't go out, we just hook up. Of course, I would never admit this out loud, especially to Enoch, but I've turned into him. I don't want to commit, but I am not hooking up randomly with anyone else.

July wears a pair of my boxers, folding them at the waist and puts on one of her tank tops. I look at her surprised at how well she wears them but say nothing. I put on a clean pair and a button-down shirt, leaving it unbuttoned.

"Come," she instructs. "I want to show you something."

She takes my hand before opening the French doors that lead out to the balcony outside my bedroom. I obediently follow behind, noticing some weeds that need to be pulled out as we make our way to the outdoor sitting area overlooking the pool. She sits down and pats the cushioned wood embroidered by wild vines, and I oblige.

"You can think whatever you want but you can't say anything." She looks up and not at me as she lays out the rules and I wonder why. "Before it starts, do you have any questions?"

I shake my head from side to side even though I am wondering what *what* starts and why I can't talk. Her eyes leave me, and she makes herself comfortable by folding her feet under her and sitting back on her chair before she looks back at the sky. I do the same and find I have no need and no reason to speak at all.

The dark grey sky gradually blackens closing any gaps of light between the clouds, and I imagine a congregation that collects and sits in silence as the preacher makes his way to the pulpit.

The cabalistic dark clouds dominate and move slowly above us. If the world was turned upside down and the sky was our Earth, I imagine that there would be no such thing as murder, or depression, or misery, only joy and serenity and beautiful things. Not even turning to look at me, July's eyes twinkle to the sky, and I take that as testimony.

"This is so much better than fireworks," she whispers without looking me.

Like a volcanic eruption, a mad rumbling train, the sky begins to crack and a clapping electrical charge ignites. The air dances and circles around us, leaving my body blanketed in goosebumps. July's curls fall to her eyes, and she brushes them away with both her hands. For a second, I wonder what Skylar is doing this very moment; I know she's afraid of bad storms. The ground starts shaking, making my body vibrate. July quickly grabs hold of my hand with a huge smile on her face.

I am aware of my breathing in and out, and July's hand still resting on my arm, and she squeezes it with every thunder, and her face is so full of pure and childlike excitement. She looks like a kid in Sunday school who is promised a trip to Jerusalem. I turn to her and open my mouth to speak, but she removes her hand from my arm and puts her finger on her lips, shushing me.

Something majestic and spiritual begins. The tumultuous thundering continues as a veiny silver crack fissures the Earth's roof. As though we are contained in a box, it rattles. The ceiling of the sky cracks, and for a brief second, I get the feeling that we are given a spy's glance to something beyond our reach. As though the sky is our shelter against whatever fight is going on between the gods beyond it.

The monstrous Cumulonimbus cloud opens its mouth and spits out another lightning bolt, letting out a guttural roar that chills me to the bone. I sit and watch the magnificence of it all. I enjoy the beauty that nature presents to me, and for a while, I sit beside July and make myself believe that there is more beauty in this world than I give it credit for. I get lost in the exquisiteness of everything I see as I stare up into the dark and angry sky. I, for only a second, think about how no other artist can do what I see justice: not in song or poetry, or sculpture or painting.

Aside from and more than easily described, I feel the wind, and July next to me. How can such a loud and violent roar create such a harmony within me? Such an oxymoron, what a vicious splendor. My heart fails to make my brain understand, but I find it doesn't need to, I'm quite content where I am; right here, right now, I find I have no reason to want anything more. I don't want, I just be.

I train myself to see and listen, but pleasantly and surprisingly feeling takes precedence. Like a zebra, I am striped with heat and cold, agitation and tranquility. I don't know what to do with myself. Excitement crawls under my skin, and I itch and shake, but I sit still and contain it all. I am, for the first time in a long time, aware of myself: the rhythm of my heartbeat, the depth of my breathing, the temperature of my body, and the texture of my eyelashes. I am aware of the length of my legs and my arms. I can feel the weight of my hair and the excitement in my toes. I relish this feeling; I am outside of time and utterly undefined. Synesthesia deliciously steals me from reality and everything inside of me rejects all that takes me out of this moment. I defy it.

July and I both remain silent and simply marvel at the glorious beauty that possesses our sight. My sense of smell and hearing has been heightened. I inhale and keep the petrichous smell in my nostrils hoping to remember everything exactly the way that I am experiencing it right now.

We listen to the beastly roar of the heavens and watch the skies as though we are inside a world where the rain curtains us from all that is ugly and non-magical.

I feel a lump invade my throat and my skin tingle as tiny spikes enter it, and I'm sure, I know that beauty hurts. I feel my heart palpitate and wonder how I've never done this before. I think I may just have found something as superior as religion, more soothing than a spa treatment, and a purifying piety to my inner wounds. I regret that it has taken me so long to experience it.

I feel electricity running through me as I make sure that I take in this God-filled sight, this pure and untainted smell and sound. I forget myself as a physical being but travel with the wind: Wild and free and intangible; I leave the home that is my body and simply soar. My spirit is cleansed and my soul revived.

The sky begins to break and then precipitation invades the dry ground starting small as if testing and then pouring down in a loud and strong shower. I smell the Earth as the heavens stain it with complete wetness. The wind violently pushes its way across the full space in emptiness, going through, over and under the invisible things unseen but evidently there. The trees stand their ground, wholly trusting in their roots for stability. They sway in the same direction as if adhering to a suction that pulls them to one side and then the other.

The rain blows away from us, and I forget where I am. I return to my body and find I am warm and quite content. I smile. I am happy but sad, something deep within my soul stings and a sudden drag returns; Skylar is afraid of storms.

The rumbling continues, and the thunder feels close by and only a little distance away. It's as though if I ran far enough, I would be able to find the source of the noise; the thing or person that is responsible for this sound. In the far distance the trees sway, and everything around me is lit in such a way that I have never seen before. Green is greener, and blue is bluer, too.

Suddenly, too soon and without warning, as if to hide the rest of its secrets, nature curtains us, closing the distance of our vision. The wild rain, as though tiny soldiers ascending in millions of numbers to do what they have been called to do, pushes us to the inside of the house. The rain changes its course and attacks us, so we have no choice but to run inside.

July runs inside screaming and giggling, soaking wet in a matter of seconds. She shivers and holds out her hands for me to see, and through the wet fabric that covers her chest, I can see her excitement. We close the French doors and glue ourselves to the glass like little kids, the night before Christmas trying to catch Santa Clause.

We stand there for the longest time in silence catching the rain with our eyes as it meets the glass. Eventually I turn to look at her with the intent to thank her for introducing me to a brand-new world, for giving me one more thing to love. She is shivering, from excitement or from the cold; I don't know. I smile at her. I take her hand and lead her through the bedroom to the bathroom. She silently follows me with expectation, curiosity replacing excitement in her eyes.

"It's days like these that make me feel so alive," she exhales, and I agree but say nothing.

I am quiet and decide not to respond. I decide that the only way I can thank her is not by words but by my actions. I let go of her hand, and I stop in front of the bathtub.

I put the stopper in its place and run the water and periodically check the temperature all the while pouring the slick liquid with a pleasant smell, creating bubbles in the tub. While the tub fills up, I turn to her, with a serious look on my face, keeping the serenity that overwhelms me in my demeanor, so she can reciprocate.

I look her straight in her eyes as I lift her elbows, and she obliges and lifts her arms over her head, I tuck my fingers on the fold of her tank top and slowly lift it above her head and leisurely and with no rush, I lay it on the commode. I keep my eyes planted on hers as I lower myself and discard her of my boxers.

She now has a hopeful expression on her face, one that shows a tranquil trust to me. I swallow and listen intently at every sound that we make between us; the fabric against her skin, her breathing, the water multiplying the bubbles. I remove the last unnatural object from her body; the rubber band in her hair and watch her wet curls fall all over her face and shoulders.

I peel out of my wet and already unbuttoned shirt and shed out of my underwear. I climb over the bathtub and then take her hand and lead her in after me. I sit down and spread her in front of me. She sits between my legs and leans her head against my chest and we both listen to each other's rhythms as we watch the tub fill up with warm water and bubbles.

I turn the faucet off using my toes and cup my hands between July's legs and scoop some water and deposit it onto her hair, and I repeat until her head is soapy. I reach up for the shampoo behind me, squeezing a good size onto my palm and lather it into her hair. She leans to the side and closes her eyes as she lets out a long sigh.

I massage my fingers into her scalp and remove the excessive foam as I continue doing so. I knead her hair with my fingers until I am sure that it's clean and then cup some water between her legs again and rinse off the soapiness in her hair, taking longer this time getting the task done.

Her body softens, and she leans against my chest again and relaxes as she matches my heartbeat with her breathing. I give her a moment before I gently push her away from my body, and she takes her warmth with her, leaving a cold area on my chest. I reach up again and come back with a loofah and some body wash.

I spread the silky thick liquid onto the loofah and begin brushing her back with it. I twist to make room and make her turn around as I continue to ensure that the loofah touches every inch of her neck, her chest, her shoulders, her breasts, and her navel.

Her body stiffens in anticipation of my touch the lower I go. I watch her watch me as I govern such a pure act of cleansing, yet it feels more than pure and, in some ways, profoundly sensual. I halt below her bellybutton and motion for her to stand. She reluctantly erects herself, and I watch the bubbles stick to her and slip down her hips to her legs as if clinging on and adamant on staying attached to her. I lift up and kneel in front of her.

The lights flicker and then die. The storm continues groaning outside of our walls but even that doesn't stop me. I let the warm feel of the water, the sound of the liquid against skin, the smell of lavender and jasmine, and the taste of my contentment dwell around us in this room. I feel July breathing above me as she runs her fingers through my damp hair, and I close my eyes for a second and let her caress relax me.

I lightly open her legs, careful not to disturb her sweet pudenda. I run the loofah on her left thigh and then slide it all the way around and down her leg. I do the same with her right leg and feel her anticipate the direction of my hands.

Like the disciples of Jesus, I wash her feet with warm water and clean between her toes, and if it wasn't so ridiculous, I think I may have even anointed her feet with oil.

Gently and soothingly, without sight, I enjoy her soapy skin as I drop the loofah in the water and let my hands caress her so genuinely as though she is a treasure, my one and only Desideratum.

I repeat the work of the loofah, but this time solely with my hands. With my palms, I mop her neck, her shoulders, her breasts; with my bare hands, I polish her navel, her back and slowly caress the center of her and move on to her back where I firmly graze her butt and find contentment in the sharp sound she makes through her teeth before I release her and continue with my hands along the length of her legs.

Lightning strikes, and I see July staring at me. I rise above her and feel her breath on my chest as I hold her shoulder with my left hand and brush her wet hair away from them with my right. I step out of the tub and prudently feel my way around for the towel rack, making sure that I keep one hand on her, so she knows that I have not left her.

I hear her smile endearingly when I place the large fluffy towel around her and scoop her into my arms. I feel the breeze as I walk nakedly from the bathroom to my bedroom with her in my arms and my eyes somewhat adjusted to the darkness so that I see shapes and can make out where everything is.

Lightning offers a glimmer of light, and I see July with her eyes closed. I place her on the bed. Take another towel and dry off her hair, keeping my face close to her as though this is our only form of communication. I thoroughly enjoy the silence of July as she lets me stay silent beside her. I comb my fingers through her curls and take the towel I just used to dry her hair to towel myself off. Still naked, I feel my way to the bathroom and around the counter until I make contact with some lotion I saw earlier.

I return back to July and sit beside her. I lotion her neck, her back, her shoulders, her breasts, and her navel with the lightning making shadows and lighting the room. I cover every inch of her with lotion, and when I hear her yawning. I grab both her feet and tuck her in my sheets and lay down beside her, spooning her.

Although we both know that neither of us is asleep, we simply listen to the storm and let the rain lull us to sleep.

Before she falls asleep, she whispers, "This was a perfect way to end the day. Thank you."

"No; thank you." I kiss her neck as my prayer before I fall asleep.

CHAPTER TWELVE

Ever since Jane and Skylar have come back from Europe, Jane has been hinting on them possibly moving over there for good. Brady never did come back with them. Jane will not tell me the full story, but I think he received a permanent position over there, and they are thinking about transplanting to Spain. I will not have it, and I have been avoiding talking to her because I know she is looking for a way to talk me into letting Skylar go with them. For weeks now, I have not been returning her calls, and that only makes her mad because every time she sees me, when she drops off or picks up Skylar, I pretend I'm in a hurry and refuse to sit down with her.

I agree to let her take Skylar for Christmas, and they committed to coming to my art banquet the weekend before Thanksgiving. We have planned since last year that we will be celebrating Thanksgiving at Llarel's this year. My parents, as soon as we were adults, would go off somewhere tropical and avoid all the family drama. Both with whomever they are dating at the time. It's sort of become our tradition.

The night of the art banquet is finally here and the crowd is impressive. All the guests are dressed up, and the quartet is in the main room playing softly while people walk around looking at the assembled art. The ice sculpture on the side garden in the front entrance is amazingly keeping its shape. In celebration of international art, there are people dressed in their native clothing representing their countries and artists that they support. I meet and greet some key sponsors, which makes Prudence Rose and I incredibly happy.

"Great turn out, isn't it?" Prudence Rose comes from nowhere holding a clipboard.

"We did it."

She smiles her small but weighty smile and scans the crowd proudly.

"Duty calls." She walks off, disappearing behind a young Brazilian artist's gigantic painting of a Eucalyptus deglupta. I take some time to admire the art around me and silently thank Jane for her PR skills.

"Young Dorian. You've outdone yourself." A familiar voice beckons causing me to slowly turn around, monitoring my reaction.

"Jacquiline."

"Ah yes, how are you darling?" She kisses both my cheeks barely touching me, and that all too familiar smell envelops my nostrils, flooding my eyes with the memory of the last time I saw her. I clear my throat. "Beautiful showing. I have my eye on a few pieces already."

"Always an art enthusiast, aren't you, ma'am?"

"But of course, darling. I leave first thing in the morning. Find me later, yes?" She kisses both my cheeks before she disappears into the crowd, her gold jewelry taking some of the light with her.

I greet a few people and shake some hands as I make my way around the gallery. I catch a glimpse of Jane and walk the opposite direction, trying to avoid her. I see Enoch and Llarel and decide to steer clear off that direction; for two people who dislike each other, I can only imagine why they would be outside by themselves with no one around them, not even Burr.

I walk over to a life-size bronze sculpture of half a face with an emphasis on a long veiny neck. It fascinates me, and I find myself getting lost in its presence trying to study all the veins' contours and every protrusion. I'm captivated. I don't know how much time I spend studying it before Jane finds me, shifting my mood.

"So Dorian, did you make a decision?"

"Not now, Jane. Can we wait for a better time to talk about this?"

"No. Now Dorian." She grabs me by my arm.

"Then, no! My decision is no. You don't take my child away from me for the whole summer and then decide you want to move with her to another continent without me. I'm not okay with it."

"Brady and I have already made plans, and we're not changing them for you."

"I don't give two shits about what you and Brady do, but you are not taking my daughter away." I look around as I realize that I may have raised my voice a bit too loud.

"You are being unreasonable, Dorian. You—"

"I'm not. I don't care. The answer is still no!"

"I don't really need your permission you know."

"Yes, you do. I know for a fact that you cannot take a minor out of the country without both parents' signatures. So, yes, Jane, you do, and you are not getting my permission."

She starts digging into her purse and mutters things to herself, and I don't have the time or the patience to wait and see what she is digging for. I start to walk away, and she pulls me by my arm again, and I am ready to throw her to the other direction and walk away, but I compose myself and face her, clenching and unclenching my jaw and balling my hands into fists.

"I knew it would come to this, Dorian." She thrusts a piece of paper into my chest. "It's not up to you. I was trying to be sensitive to your feelings by prolonging the inevitable."

"You call this sensitive?" I smack as I unscramble the piece of paper.

The first thing I see is Brady and my daughter's name on an official piece of paper. My initial thought is that she is insanely handing me adoption papers until I realize it's genealogical DNA test results. My head right away starts buzzing and my palms sweat profusely. I continue reading until I get to the important part. SKYLAR IS NOT MINE, BUT BRADY'S DAUGHTER.

"That's right. Skylar is not your daughter, Dorian." Her words pierce through me like a burning spear.

An inferno starts up at the bottom of my feet, skips my knees and goes straight to my chest. I reread the papers three times before I realize the typed words are not going to change. I feel my brain shake loose from its anchor and my veins begin to burn through my skin. My ears start ringing, and my tongue sours.

I look up at Jane; this woman who stands in front of me; the mother of my child, a child who never was mine, and I am damaged, completely decimated to no avail. This woman who at one point in my life, I thought I loved;

the same woman who used to whisper sweet nothings to me while we made love, the exact woman that I've known most of my life. I notice I've never looked at her the way that I am now; I've never seen in her what I see now.

I am infuriated and so full of hate. I want to hurt her; I want to push her against the wall and out of my breathing space. I want to manifest a disease in my mouth, cough in my hands, and contaminate her with it. I hate her for giving me the best thing in my life and then taking it away. I hate that she's had that power over me, that she is my total downfall.

I open my mouth and try to speak but words escape me. As if a teargas environs me, I feel a burning coal at the back of my throat that melts my esophagus, ashing out my voice box and making my eyes water. My nostrils sting and my eyes tighten and dry. I rapidly blink, trying to moisten my cornea but to no avail.

I toss the piece of paper at her and storm past her, rushing through the crowd keeping my eyes on the target: the bathroom door. I hear Enoch calling me, but I ignore him. The faces I walk past all become a blur, and the music turns into ice cracking, and I ignore everything and everyone, and just concentrate on my breathing as I march myself out of sight. I reach the bathroom door and go through it, shutting it behind me, and punch the wall three times without feeling any pain.

I catch sight of the man in the mirror who stares back at me, and he looks violently mad. The vein in the middle of my forehead bulging to a dangerous extreme and my hands balled into fists in testimony to my rage. I want to rumble, I want to beat something and kick it until it breaks. I pace back and forth in the one stall bathroom and feel trapped in the tiny room. I clench and unclench my jaw still keeping my hands balled up into fists. Purposely, I walk over to the sink and pour cold water on my face but that does not help. All I am now is wet and furious.

I walk back out of the restrooms, turn right and through the red door. I scan the crowd, and the first person I see is July carrying a tray full of *Smoked Salmon Stuffed Eggs* and setting it down on the table full of Jane's friends. As she walks away, I widen my stride to catch up to her. I take her hand and lead her to the next room where we are alone. She looks at me, waiting for me to explain, but I do not have an explanation; I'm surrounded by people but feel lonelier the fuller the room gets. I lead her to the restroom upstairs and lock the door behind us.

I pugnaciously kiss her; squeezing my eyes tight in attempt to erase every feeling in my body.

"Are you okay?"

I kiss her again.

"Dorian, is everything alright?"

I kiss her more urgently this time, pushing her against the sink. I stop and stare at her for a moment, listening to her breathe. I stare into her eyes as I slowly lift her skirt to her waist and knead her butt as I watch her watch me. She doesn't resist me; she doesn't say anything. She shapes her mouth to speak, but I kiss her quickly and seal her lips from saying anything. I unbutton her shirt and put my hot, mad hands on her breasts, and she holds her breath and watches me. I place my hand on her lower back and draw her closer to me, my erection pressing against her stomach. I squeeze her butt firmly as I suck on her tongue.

She puts her cold hands on either side of my face, and I feel a fever sub-siding in one part of my body and arising in another area. Slowly she lifts her-self up and sits on the sink, scooting so her legs are apart, and I am between them. I stare her up and down, not really seeing her. I place both my hands on either side of her waist and lift her off the sink. I turn her around and spread her legs as though I am about to frisk her. I drown myself in her curls and kiss my way down her back before pulling her up from her belly, so she is in posi-tion for me to enter her from behind.

I sit on my haunches and gently pull her stockings and panties down. I kiss her cheeks watching the silk of her skin morph into goosebumps. I control my breathing by inhaling through my nose and exhaling through my mouth while I listen to her panting. I kiss her ass and the back of her thighs until I finally bury my face in between her sweet round cheeks. I run my tongue in the crevice of her and blink hard trying to drown out the voices in my head. She steadies herself by gripping hold of the sink, and I lift myself up, unbuckle my belt, unzip my pants, and drop them to my ankles while clenching and unclenching my jaw.

I grip her hips and slide into her, and she makes a small "ah" sound while she arches her back. I thrust rhythmically behind her and start trouncing from behind staring at myself in the mirror above the sink; my nostrils flared, my veins violently protruding and my skin over one hundred degrees. My eyes are dangerously mad. I feel The Hulk trying to break free from within.

I finally let everything sink in and a tear makes its way down my cheek unbidden, and I swallow the rest of them as I fight the invisible hand that clamps at my throat. I subtract my right hand from her hip to wipe the tear away.

She locks eyes with me in the mirror above her, and I am the first to break eye contact. Not only does that infuriate me even more, it embarrasses me, and I feel emasculated. I pull myself out of her, and she turns around and faces me.

"Dorian?"

"Get out!" I spit at her through clenched teeth as my jaws tighten, my anger heightening.

She pulls her stockings and underwear up and pulls her skirt down. She moves forward with her hand up as if to touch my face. I step back as if shielding my face from someone who is about to inflict harm to it. I open the door and stand beside it,

"Leave!" I command.

She walks out without saying anything else.

I feel my veins enraged, steaming with lava and my right hand piercingly throbbing. I violently kick the toilet and let out a loud roar.

"FUCK!" I yell to no one in particular.

And then I know. I just know there is regret to be had.

Chapter Thirteen

It's been three days since the party, and that was the last time I saw Skylar or spoke to Jane or July. I can't remember how I even got home, but I do remember the wine. I am desolate. I am absolutely devastated about Skylar.

Shit! I saw July sometime after. I know I did. I follow the direction of the pain and halt at the sight of my bruised hand that now looks blue and disfigured. I open and close my hand, sending sharp throbs throughout my whole arm.

What the hell have I done? I am then reminded of everything that took place in the last three days, and no wonder I've been in bed all this time. I know I have a lot of apologizing to do, to July specifically. I dread having to grovel, but I know it's the only thing to do if I want to see her again. I must see her again; not as Skylar's nanny but as simply July.

I look around my room, and there are broken plates and food all over the floor, there is a bloody towel and reflexively I touch my nose. There is an empty bottle of vodka on my nightstand, and my phone lies next to it, turned off. I pick up my phone and hit four on my speed-dial and it goes straight to her voicemail. I hang up and listen to my messages. I have two messages from Jane threatening to call the police if I don't stop harassing them.

I stretch my neck and my other unbroken body parts while I assess my mood.

I have a voicemail from Enoch reminding me about the meeting with the new investor tonight, and the other two are from him as well, panicking about me not calling him back and him threatening to beat me to a pulp if I don't show up to the meeting. None from July.

I call Enoch, and he picks up after the two rings.

"Fuck! Dude. Where the hell have you been?"

"Hell."

"Good, cause that's exactly where I was planning on sending you. You have five hours to get yourself together cause I'm personally picking you up at 7:00 sharp."

Why is he picking me up at 7:00 when the meeting is at 9:00? I don't have the energy to protest.

"Eight o'clock."

"Be there at 7:45." He hangs up.

I walk over to the TV and turn it on obnoxiously loud, avoiding the stillness that creates an emptiness about the house. I take my toothbrush and phone and head to the art room. It's the one place that does not remind me of anything in particular. I avoid the big mirror on the left wall; I can't stand myself. I walk in and lock the door behind me. The room has stale air and smells like a hotel.

We get to *Blue Baby*, and the music is loud, the crowd is raw and the lights are blinding. It's 8:50 when we make our way across the bar to the backrooms where there is a soundproof conference room with a large board table and chairs. Everything is dark with rich wood, and the walls are exposed brick painted black.

"Next week's meeting has got to go well. That location is so money." Enoch's eyes are dancing with excitement. "Can you imagine?"

"There is an element of surprise to this. This location may work for a club, but there is no telling if a restaurant would do just as well." It is a little ambitious, but Enoch and I are looking at another location for a night club and dance classes slash restaurant during the day. The idea is to bring back the concept of the 1935-1946 swing era.

"Dude, have some faith. We already have a big parking lot. We already have a crowd. People have dinner at *Baby Blue* and then come to *Blue Baby* for some boozing and dancing, I mean, why can't this work? It's genius."

"Granted, this is still a big investment, and therefore, a huge risk."

"You are such a buzz kill."

"No, I'm exploring all possibilities." Unlike Enoch, spontaneity doesn't come effortlessly, and I don't gamble.

Since most of the negotiations are done and everything is on paper, I let Enoch do most of the talking but keep my presence known. In the middle of *terms and conditions*, I see July with three of her girlfriends, and she is wearing a tight black dress with her hair up in a bun with a big loose curl, dangling down her back. I turn my body so that she is behind me, and I cannot see her. I face Enoch and Monroe.

"It looks like this might work then, if you agree to the terms," Monroe formally asserts.

"Everything is in terms except we're still waiting for our liquor license. We already have our own suppliers, and we have our own bartenders for the weekends," Enoch adds.

"I also would like to add that the contractor hasn't come back to us with the blue-prints for upstairs, and we can't finalize anything until we have met with him and the inspection is complete."

"That's going to take at least another month," Monroe declares, exasperated.

"And we are in no hurry," I affirm with a solid voice.

Enoch looks at me as though he disagrees but holds his tongue.

"Well then, gentlemen. I'll be in touch."

All three of us stand and shake hands.

"Stay. Enjoy yourselves. Drinks are on the house, and we have a VIP section reserved for you," Enoch invites Monroe.

"Thank you, sir, but I'm still on the clock. I have to run."

And with that Monroe is ushered out of view by a mob of suits that surround him. Raven, a tall dark-haired girl with cat eyes and dark make-up brings in some drinks.

"Are you trying to lose us this deal?" Enoch asks in frustration.

I look over my shoulder, making sure that I can spot July, who is now at the bar, ordering drinks with her friends.

"Not at all." I wonder if I am.

"You know these guys are in a hurry for us to take this place out of their hands, and if we waste any more time, we might piss them off."

"I know, but what we are asking for is not too absurd. This is a big investment; I'm just making sure that we are not left with any of their liabilities. Besides you said so yourself the other day: we need to make sure our asses are covered, first and foremost."

"Your server will be right with you." Raven walks off and disappears into the crowd.

"We already did our research, and our investors agree that this is a good move, so why are you so hesitant? It's like you are doing everything in your power to slow down the whole process."

I turn to face him, giving him full view of my face, making sure he understands what I am about to say.

"Listen, we are not sure that this place is up to code. The location is ideal, but what about our neighbors? We need to wait for the final verdict from the private investigator. We are not about to jump into this blind."

"Fuck it. I know you're right. I just have a good feeling about this place, and I'd hate to leave it to chance for things to come together." Enoch declares.

Enoch starts looking around and drapes his blazer on the empty seat beside him. I discreetly look around, hoping to spot July at the bar but to no avail.

"What good is having a VIP section if you have no women to share it with?" Enoch focuses his attention to a far horizon as the platform rotates, and we have a 360 degrees view of the area.

Raven comes back with an older looking man, who looks to be in his late forties. He stands behind her and makes no effort to speak or make himself known until he's been introduced.

"Gentleman, this is Ralph, and he will be taking care of you tonight." Raven acquaints us.

Ralph nods and takes out a long narrow menu from his back pocket. He hands it to Enoch and impressively reiterates the words on it verbatim.

"Now what the menu does not have is The Ink and The Zero. Those are our strongest drinks. The Ink is three different vodkas, AKA The millionaire's vinegar. It comes in any color of your choice."

I zoom in to my search of July, shutting off my surroundings. As the platform slowly spins, I scan each corner thoroughly until I find her talking to some guy, who looks to be standing a little bit too close, acting a little bit too aggressive; nothing like her type at all. Not that I know what her type is.

"And you, sir?" Ralph asks.

"What he's having," I absent-mindedly declare. Either I go home and wallow or drown myself in alcohol. Tonight, I choose the latter.

"Right away, sir." Ralph retreats, and Enoch says nothing.

I turn to him, curious to see what's occupying his attention. He is pressing away at his phone and when he sees me looking at him, he mutters, "Time to get this party started. I have some people coming to join us and we are going to light this joint up."

I smile and shake my head. I'm not in the right mind space to be around people, but the promise of alcohol keeps me in my seat. Ralph returns with a tray full of blue drinks in tall glasses and another tray full of shots in tall, skinny shot glasses. My eyes widen. There's enough alcohol here for a small crowd, and Enoch starts smacking his lips and rubbing his hands.

"Set them down and keep 'em coming."

I know I should have known better than to order the same thing as him without first checking, but tonight I don't feel like letting good alcohol go to waste. Enoch picks up a shot glass, hands it to me and picks up another one and holds it up to me.

"To sipping and signing."

"Here. Here."

"And to closing deals and getting some ass," Enoch cheers.

I clink my tiny glass to his and watch him take a gulp, shaking his head with a sour face. I swallow the venom and make the same face, I imagine. Out of my right, I hear a familiar giggle; July. I ignore the happy laugh and take another shot surprising Enoch. I get wasted and resolve that I have every right to be.

"Looks like I'll be the one playing catch-up tonight." He nods, giving me a look of approval.

I ignore his grin and take another Ink or is it Zero as Enoch takes his second.

"Remember, Ralph said to drink slowly. You are drinking pure vodka, and we all know that you can't hold your alcohol.

I ignore him and take the tall glass with a blue drink. The velocity in which the platform is now spinning seems to be a little too fast for my liking, why did they change the speed? I clumsily stand up and climb off the platform and start in search of July, waving to Enoch that I would be right back. He waves back, his attention now occupied by his new guests.

I look around, and it only takes me a second to find her. I see the back of her and recognize her by her square shoulders and her incredible posture. Her bun now has a few curls separating behind her in the most familiar way, and it is such a comforting sight. The closer I walk up to her the more I notice a guy amongst her circle talking only to her.

I get closer, and he looks up at me as if waiting for me to walk past or realize that I am joining the wrong crowd. July turns and sees me and then her face drops, and I know that she is not the least bit happy to see me.

"Hello, Dorian, hi?" She seems surprised to see me.

"I saw you from across the room, and I just wanted to say hello to an old friend," I instate with dry sarcasm.

"Well, hello." She turns back around, not at all amused. Her company, including the guy next to her, continue staring at me.

"You've got to be kidding me. This guy? Really? This guy?" Jerk face guy that is with her points at me.

"Why the sudden need to be jealous? It's not like I owe you any explanations." She continues to ignore me but retaliates to "jerk face."

"You are such a social climber. Now you are fucking rich white boys?" he screams in her face.

"You're white, too. I'm guessing you're not rich," I smirk despite my fury.

July turns to me and pushes me out of the circle.

"Dorian, please leave. You have no business being here."

"Funny you should say that. Business is what brings me here," I say as I loosen my tie.

Jerk face comes back and grabs July by the shoulder. He turns her around, so she is facing him. "I need to talk to you."

She yanks her arm away from him and steps away from both of us and starts to walk away, followed by her girlfriends. He steps forward as if to follow her, but I grab him by the arm to stop him from following her. He turns around and punches me, and I hear a chorus of gasps from July's entourage. I stagger, and I let out a warm long breath from the unexpected assault, and when I look up, July is trying to free herself from him and he is trying to pull her away.

I stumble to my feet and try to walk over to them, and out of peripheral I notice a crowd shifting.

"If you don't get your filthy paws off her in two seconds—"

"You'll what? Pay the bouncer to kick me out."

"I'll fuckin' kick your ass." I rub my accosted jaw.

He swings again and lands a punch behind my ear. I swing my right arm and land a punch on his face which angers him, and he launches toward me and knocks me to the ground. I spin around, so I am sitting on top of him and punch him on his neck and then across the face, feeling like I've broken my hand this time.

Someone grabs my arm mid-swing, and I violently turn around in attempts to accost the culprit. Enoch grabs me and pulls me away before I punch him again.

Raven and Ralph follow behind two big bouncers.

"You okay, sir?" Ralph asks me.

"Yes. Escort him out, and make sure he never comes here again."

They take him away. I turn back just in time to see July look at me in disgust and walk away with her posse following behind.

"Dammit, Dorian. You are ruining this for us," Enoch scolds me.

We sit at the bar and order Nitrogens.

"Okay. Enough work. Let's play." He turns his chair over and scans the crowd.

We drink shots and speak no more of the incident. I don't mention anything about Skylar. I am afraid that if I say it out loud then it becomes true and official. I just drown my sorrows in vodka and Nitrogen. Someone taps me on the shoulder, and I turn around but she whispers on my opposite ear.

"You never called."

I look at her with a blank expression, I imagine. I wait for her to offer an explanation but she simply takes my hand and puts it on her hip.

"Dance with me."

I register the face to someone I've met, but I can't place who she is or where I've seen her before. She must recognize my confusion because she introduces herself, bringing her mouth so close to my ear; it's practically in her mouth.

"Bedson. Speed dating. Greer. Ring a bell?"

"Oh yes. Greer. Hi."

"Ding ding ding!"

She takes my hand and leads me to the middle of the dance floor. I glance back at Enoch, who is still talking to the bartender about the specialty drink, just so he could impress the girls at the bar next to him.

"Let me refresh your memory." She takes a pen from her cleavage, writes her number on my hand and kisses it. "Déjà vu?"

What else does she keep in there? I smile at her, trying hard not to stare at her very exposed cleavage where she now replaces her pen.

"Don't leave me hanging again," she declares.

She is oblivious to my mental distance as I look around and continue downing Nitrogens. I grab two colorful test-tubes from the hostess' tray and hand her one. She sits close with her legs crossed towards me and every so often touches my arm when she laughs even though we can barely hear each other. After a while, she invites me over to her place and whoever I am at the moment agrees.

We leave as Blue Baby's staple scene takes place: The whole place turns pitch black, and there is only a pulsing beat while neon blue figures with night goggles pass around glow sticks.

We arrive at her place and waste no time. We pick up where we left off. Once inside her apartment, she kicks off her shoes and heads to the refrigerator. She looks inside and then closes it without retrieving anything. This gives me time to permit my eyes to wonder around. Her apartment is very spacious, very feminine. It is furnished with soft pinks and purples, and her white kitchen is highlighted with pops of pink here and there. Even her paper towel has pink trimmings on each end.

She walks over to the right and very deliberately bends over and retrieves an almost full bottle of brandy. In her other hand she holds a fine Amarula bottle. She walks over to me with both her hands full, holding up her right hand with the Amarula.

"Do you want this with milk or on the rocks?"

"The stronger, the better," I mutter.

"Rocks it is, then."

She sets the two bottles on the kitchen counter and grabs ice from the freezer. Even her ice-cube tray is pink. I down the first glass in a matter of seconds, and she takes a sip of hers and sets it down. She sets a tray of ice on the table, grabs one and starts chewing on it, making a grating sound as she chews, I permit my eyes to wonder around her pink infested place. She gulps hers down quickly after the second sip, arming herself with liquid courage. She walks over toward me and helps me out of my blazer and tie, hangs it on the couch and unbuttons my shirt.

"This is going to feel amazing later."

My eyes follow her as she deposits my black button-down into the freezer.

"You're going to need some cooling off when I'm done with you."

Her name, what's her name? Greer! I note to myself how I have to keep trying to bring my focus back to her. I focus on her pale skin and her soft, full breasts. She is tall and has straight red hair. She is the total opposite of July. I kiss her swiftly, trying to rid myself of the thought of July.

She gently runs her red fingernails across my naked chest, down my stomach and stops at my belt. Hurriedly, she takes my hand and leads me out the kitchen, and I retrieve the bottle of brandy before exiting the room. Down her white hallway and into the second door on the right, she leads me to her room. Everything is nauseatingly pink: her walls, her bedding, her picture frames. She turns off the harsh bright light, and switches on the lamp by her nightstand, with a softer and dimmer light.

I walk over to her and share my liquor with her and kiss her before she swallows it.

I light her like she is a candle and set her aflame. She catches fire under my touch and blazes everywhere my tongue grazes her. My scalp tingles when she moans my name.

I take a sip of whiskey straight from the bottle and empty it into her mouth.

"Don't swallow. I want to taste you in my alcohol," I slur my words slightly.

I deposit another sip into her mouth and continue to drink from the bottle with my eyes closed, while she stores it under her tongue. When I open my eyes and turn to kiss her, she pours the warm liquid from her mouth to mine. It drips from her lip down her chin,

"Let me do it," I volunteer.

I lick her from her chin up and stop at her mouth and then I gently suck her bottom lip. Just as I suspected, the warm alcohol is sharper, tangy from her mouth. I taste her in it, and my throat is ablaze as it luxuriously makes its way down.

I pour some more in her mouth and then drink from her. I do it again and find that I like warm whiskey from a woman's mouth. At the moment, hers in particular.

"Yesss," I hiss emphasizing the S as I watch her red lips open for more.

She takes off her dress and her pink bra and her pink thong. July hates pink, and she hardly ever wears thongs. I shake my head and drain the bottle in my mouth. She climbs on top of the bed with all fours and tilts her body to the side so she is looking back at me.

"How do you want me?" she chants playfully.

"Sunny side up," I sing as I walk over to her.

I place the empty bottle on her nightstand and unbutton my trousers with my healthy hand. I walk over to her. When I get to her, I take a handful of her hair and inhale it. It smells clean; too clean and fruity, none of her in it. She smiles at me with her eyes closed, and I close my own eyes trying hard not to resent her, not to blame her for being her and not July. I kiss her violently and pull on her bottom lip as I retreat. I repeat, and she moans and giggles, and this aggravates me. I push her to the bed and make a choking gesture with my sore hand as I mold her left breast and bite her shoulder.

"Ah yes. I like it rough," she exclaims.

I stare at her not sure what reaction I'm trying to raise out of her. I kiss her again and cover her face with my hand as I kiss her neck and her chest and shoulders and again, I am repulsed by her smell. My lust rapidly mutating into misdirected anger. She smells of perfume and all things nice but nothing natural. Her smell is nauseating. I close my eyes tightly and feel my head getting lighter.

"Bruise me. I don't mind," she moans in my ear.

I kiss her harder and she moans under me. Her voice, her scent, even with my eyes shut I cannot tune my distaste for her out. The harder I kiss her, the more I want to spit her out. I remove myself from on top of her and sit on the side of the bed with my back turned toward her. I put my head in my hands, clenching and unclenching my jaw and will myself to disappear.

She sits up from behind me and starts kissing the back of my neck. Even from behind me, my body rejects her.

"Relax. I'll take care of everything," she whispers.

I stand up to rid my body of her hands. Without turning around to look at her, I shake my head no.

"I shouldn't be here." I whisper to myself, "I don't want this." I declare this to myself, more so than to her.

I turn around and look at her.

"I shouldn't be here. I'm sorry."

I gather my clothes and my keys and head for the door with my jeans unbuttoned and my shoes and socks in my hand. I remember that my shirt is in her freezer and decide to let her keep it as a souvenir.

"I'm sorry," I say again before I close the door and leave a naked woman staring after me. I retrieve my tie and blazer on my way out.

I pay the cab driver and let myself out of the car. My house; it doesn't feel the same. As I walk over through the landscape and the flowers that Skylar and I planted together, it doesn't feel like home anymore. I ignore the feeling as I turn the key and walk inside. I drop my tie and blazer in the mudroom before I turn the kitchen lights on and stand looking into the living room. The house feels big, too big and empty, too empty. Even though it's furnished and resembles no change from last week or even yesterday. It's too big for one person, lonelier with me just standing there assessing it. Neo lays on the couch, waiting for Skylar, and I am sad for him, for me, for both of us. Jane will probably want to take him, and I don't blame her; Skylar will surely want him with her. Skylar, my beautiful little girl, is not mine. Eight years.

I walk over to her room and stand outside her door. Neo waits beside me. I worry that if I walk in, I will desensitize the room of her smell, that I will take away her presence by introducing mine, but I ache for her so much; I want to be or do anything that will bring her closer to me. My brain cannot wrap around the fact that something so precious in my life, someone so dependent on me can no longer be. I have to find another reason for my being; the reason why I keep food in the fridge, look forward to life being about something else other than myself. I cannot fathom navigating away from my way of thinking about life which utterly revolved around Skylar. My throbbing hand reminds me.

I was there when she was born, when she started walking, on her first day of school. I took her to have her first haircut, I taught her how to ride a bike, and I am the one who was her father when she was happy and when she was sick; all those years, all those memories were a lie, a sadistic game of house that Jane was playing without mine and Skylar's consent and knowledge. What will become of our relationship? Is Brady going to try to keep her away from me? Can I survive life without her? It hurts too much. I feel my insides constrict, and I know I'm going to love her; I'm going to miss her till kingdom comes.

I walk in and turn on the light. It smells like her. I pick up her hairbrush on her nightstand and smell it. The soft greens and blues in her room, the pictures of us at the lake. I look around, and I ache. I smell her pillow, and my chest shrinks, squeezing my heart into confinement. I walk over to her bathroom and put her toothbrush in my mouth, tasting the residue of her toothpaste and her, wishing I could keep some of her in a bottle, so I could spritz her on me every time I miss her. Her vanity mirror is trimmed with dancing ballerinas and my sad face is trapped amidst them with the stem of her toothbrush poking out of my mouth, creating a paradox of emotions. I smile a little at the thought of her seeing me like this.

I walk back to her room, wrapping my naked chest with her tiny robe. I sit on her bed, curl my feet under me, put my head in my hands and I miss her.

How can I be the best of me when the most amazing thing about me is taken away from me? Being a father, Skylar's father, is how I defined myself. Her presence still lingers on it, and I brush my hair with it, filling myself with her and cry and cry and cry.

Chapter Fourteen

Morning creeps up through the blinds, and I am accosted by the blinding light. I think about how I don't have to pick up Skylar and decide I have no reason to ever get out of bed. My hand starts throbbing, imitating my heart while last night's events play themselves to me in slow motion.

My head is clouded with grief, sorrow, guilt. I decide I don't want to think about Skylar. I don't want to feel about her, so instead I figure I'll just concentrate on something that probably will not affect my life as well as my internal organs, such as my head and my heart. Worrying about July forgiving me is easier than concentrating on my real ailments. If I don't worry about Skylar, if I avoid the problem, then the problem does not exist. Nothing is official.

I avoid answering Jane's calls and calling her back. If I don't talk to her, then she has no choice but to carry on as if nothing's changed. I imagined reading any papers about my daughter, I drank too much and hallucinated the whole thing, and if I don't talk to Jane, nothing can be confirmed. I concentrate on July forgiving me instead.

I finally call July's house phone when she doesn't answer her phone for the umpteenth time, and her roommate informs me that she is at the track at the university. I drive to two different grounds before I find her.

She is a ballad, saccharine poetry at its finest. She breathes through her nose and concentrates hard on an invisible point as she holds and lets go of her breath. Her ponytail sways daringly back and forth as her whole body moves to her command. The muscles in her thighs stretch and contract as her feet make contact with the ground she leaves behind with each step. She looks at ease and in her element, no thought, no worry as she has now spiritually disappeared, connected with her own world. Her world, I wish I would know but imagine I would never be allowed in. She balls her hands into fists and quickly becomes a blur as she sprints passed me.

I know that she is, and I wish I was too: passionate and obedient to something that chose her, something that she had no choice but to abide to, something so pure that she cannot part with even if she tried. This is what passion sounds like, what contentment and atonement looks like. I've felt like this before on two occasions, I have felt myself ignited with electrolytes that make my whole body sing and my skin light up underneath. I watch her back and even from behind I can tell that this is something that she loves, something that she excels in. How I envy that she has found that something, or that something has found her. In my head, I make certain that I acknowledge that she is superior to me in this way.

She comes running to me with a frown on her face. She has already run a lap in the moment that she zoomed past me. She gracefully saunters over to me breathing heavily as if she has just finished making love with a sex god. She is not at all amused that I am here to see her. I embrace her in my arms, at awe with her. Instead, she stiffens, and my hug is not returned.

"What are you doing here, Dorian?" She demands.

"I came to talk to you. Look, I'm sorry I hurt you."

"You didn't."

"I called you several times. I was worried about you."

"I'm not yours to worry about. I'm fine."

"Can you let the walls down and talk to me please." I plead.

"Like you did?"

Her breathing is now sound, but her heart beats wildly inside her chest. The base, the rhythm is so familiar to me, and my eyes dance with excitement as I imagine holding her closer and listening to her sweet palpitations. I feel her shift like she is about to move, to walk away. I didn't imagine it would be this hard for me to earn her forgiveness.

"I'm sorry about Skylar." She searches my eyes and then looks around nervously but continues to keep a distance between our bodies; as though we've not once known each other intimately. The mention of Skylar's name is like someone peeling off the skin of my heart. I hold my composure and confiscate the thought of falling apart at the sound of Sky's name. I look away for a second before turning back to her. I step closer to her, wanting her to stop talking about my life and forgive me.

A faint smell of her cologne mixed with the sweat on her neck makes me want to fold her body into mine, right here and now. I want to take her hand and have my way with her in this open air, on this soft green grass.

"I've gotta go." She shifts, and I know I'm about to lose her.

"Wait. Stop!"

"Why?" she asks but doesn't turn around for me to see her face.

"July, I know I hurt you. I didn't mean to." I swallow my disappointment.

"You didn't hurt me. You just confirmed what I feared all along," she spits these words at me as she faces me, so I recognize her hurt.

I'm annoyed that she would be so hard at forgiving me. I was hoping I would only apologize once and take her with me, somewhere where nothing else exists. I had expected her to forgive me and then we don't talk but wind and grind each other all day and all night until the pain is grated away from me, until I've sweated all my worries away.

"What have I confirmed?" I wonder more to myself than to her.

"Me to you: I was merely a form of release for you. Nothing but your deposit toy."

Her words take me by surprise because this is something that I have always thought but never would dare say out loud, but somewhere along the way, things changed, lines blurred, and I realize it now as I try to fashion an argument to defend myself. I shape my mouth and start to say something but she holds her hand out.

"It's okay. I've already made peace with it. You got what you wanted, and so did I. I got to satisfy my every curiosity of you, and you actually are not worth all the exalting that I was giving you." She looks like she has already cried about this and got over it.

Ouch! Why does frustration now replace my annoyance? I was quite happy being annoyed. How is it fair; to be removed from a pedestal that I never even knew I was on? I would have fought to keep my place there...had I known. I realize at this point, at this moment that we meant more to each other than we both let on. I took advantage of the fact that she may not always be there when I wanted her to be, that someday I may need her and she may not be there.

I want to tell her that. I want to tell her that I cannot lose Skylar and her, too. I cannot take the heartache, and this is selfish right now but I hope she lets me be selfish. I want to make up for all the times that I was blind. I look up and open my mouth to speak, but she does what I did to her the night at the party. She protects herself from my touch as if my hand on her would cause her body to rigor mortis.

"You think too little of yourself, July."

"No, I don't. You do. When you first mentioned the party, I was so excited. I thought to myself: wow, my first public appearance with Dorian. I would be by his side, as his date, among his friends."

Her eyes glisten and mine widen as I come to the realization of what I have done.

"My naiveté got the best of me, huh? That night though, I realized but tried to suppress the truth about what I really was to you: just an employee. Then you sealed the deal and made it official. You fucked me in the bathroom and threw me out like a whore."

Her tears are running down her face now, and I know I should hold her, but my fear of being rejected, being pushed away, plants me where I stand. How could I have thought that a simple apology would suffice?

"July, I had no idea. I thought...I..." I stutter like a fool trying to compartmentalize my own confusion.

"Of course, you didn't. How could you?"

She takes off running before I even have a chance to say anything else, her perfect posture in a straight line. I huddle over with my hands on my thighs and suck in a long breath as if someone just kicked me in the stomach; in fact, it feels like someone did, right after pouring acid on my heart.

I have ruined her. I have taken beautiful carefree July and turned her into an angry person. It's all too familiar. I have turned her into me...

What have I done?

I go home, feeling defeated. I sit in the garage for a long time, fearing to go inside. I cannot stand the emptiness. I call Enoch, but he doesn't answer. I call Llarel, and she doesn't answer. I decide to go inside and take a shower. I avoid anything that reminds me of Skylar; I refuse to look at Neo, even though he follows me around, vying for my attention. I decide that pursuing July gives me something to do and helps sway my thoughts from the root of my heart-ache. I decide to make things right, starting with July.

I get in the shower and just stand there until I have formulated a plan. I am going to make her listen. I wake up on the couch. I guess I didn't make it upstairs. I replay everything in my head and block out the part about Skylar, and when Jane's words and the words on the paper try to surface, I push them down. I concentrate on my missing July 'cause it doesn't hurt as much as what's going on with Skylar.

I start the engine and my wiper blades start swooshing and the radio comes alive. Ironically the song playing is "I'm Not the Man You Think I Am" by Bryan Adams, and I concentrate on the words and testify internally about the truth they possess for me. At Aker Boulevard, I sit at the light as Bryan Adam closes, *I'm not the man you think I am but I'm the man for you.*

As I turn left at Crossroads Drive, I become self-aware. I am dejected, un-shaven, and my hair is a tangled, wet mess. My eyes give away the little amount of sleep I've acquired, and I bite my lips and try to loosen them, so I am able to smile again.

I park on the side street and decide to leave my sunglasses on as I step out of my dark car. Even with the sunglasses, I shield my eyes from the sun as soon as I step out of the car. The sun burns insultingly bright. I walk slowly to the door marked 58 and knock twice.

She opens the door, and the first thing I notice is her hair. She has her hair down and not in a ponytail like she always has it. She wears her signature tanks, and I internally smile as I become to the familiarity of her presence. She is not really welcoming, or smiling, or inviting me in. She stands in the middle of the door, blocking me from entering. I glance behind her for a second and get a glimpse of her living room. It's small but cozy. She walks out and closes the door behind her.

I follow her as she walks past me and catch a whiff of her cologne. I don't suppose that's something she'll ever change, but then again, I wonder why I think she would change things about herself now that she is not in my life. Not that we ever were together.

"What do you want, Dorian?"

"How have you been, July? Good? Good." I pinch my eyes at the sun as I adjust my Ray Bans.

"I've been alright. Were you expecting me to fall apart?"

"No. No. I was just asking."

"Why are you here? I said what I wanted to say earlier."

"I didn't."

"What do you want, Dorian?"

She stops in front of me as if challenging me to a fight. Out of nowhere and without reason, I just hug her. I don't care that we are on the sidewalk of a busy street, I don't care who's looking or if she rejects me the second I touch her. I hug her tight and inhale her hair into my lungs, I squeeze her as if measuring how long it would take before she breaks. When I realize that she is not pushing me away, I hold her tighter for as long as she'll let me. I will her to dissolve into me. I keep her in my arms as though she belongs there, as though she's all I've been missing. Sadly, time rebels, and she has to push herself out of my arms, and I reluctantly release her, with an aching doubt that I would never be able to do this again.

"Dorian, don't do this," she whispers, keeping her head down.

I place my hand under her chin and motion her head up, so she is looking at me. I step closer, and she takes a step back. I take another step toward her, and she takes another step back. I realize there is glass in her eyes, and it shatters into teardrops, and she shakes her head and wipes them away with the back of her hands.

"Look, July, I was an asshole, I'm sorry I made you cry."

"You didn't make me cry," she stubbornly asserts.

I look at her with a sad smile as I take note about how guarded she is. She seems so adamant on not letting anyone make her feel any real emotion, whether it's love or sadness. We are a lot more similar than I thought.

"I'm not crying because of you, you know."

"Okay. Okay," I say slowly, careful not to trigger any more anger.

"I'm crying because of me. I am so mad at myself for letting myself become what I was to you."

"How could you possibly know what you were…er…are to me?" I choose my words carefully.

"Dorian, I know I was just a number to you."

My jaw automatically clenches and unclenches. I rake my hand through my hair, wanting to pull it out.

"I am relieved that it's over between us; whatever it was. It always felt temporary. All the time we were what we were, I was holding my breath, waiting for something to go wrong. It feels good to be able to breathe and just not worry about the moment when it finally happens."

"July, you're wrong."

"You wouldn't be here if I was." Her tone is harsh "You know, the thing I resent you the most for is that you confirmed the worst things I feared about myself. You proved to me that I am just as I feared: nothing special. Just ordinary old me."

"You are wrong. You are so much more than that."

She rolls her eyes and looks disinterested.

"You are dynamite, beautiful, sagacious. You are extraordinary."

"Damn right I am. Not to you maybe, but I'm gonna make certain that I am all of those things and more to myself. This is why I am ridding myself of everything and everyone that's not worthy of me."

"I shouldn't have treated you the way that I did. I didn't mean to break your self—"

"Go home, Dorian. Don't ever call me again." She walks inside, and I follow her, but before closing the door she mutters, "Please go away."

I make my way slowly to her with my arms open, and she shakes her head "no." I ignore her gesture and hold her to me. She lets me for a second and then all of a sudden pulls away and starts slapping and pushing me away. I hold her to me, trying to help her cry it out and also to shield myself from being hit. She struggles, and finally I let her hands go and just try to block her blows from reaching my face.

I push her against the wall, knocking a vase full of colorful glass pebbles all over the floor. I hold her hands above her head, against the wall and anchor her by pressing the bottom half of her body with my hips. She looks at me with hurt in her eyes through her tears.

"I'm not weak, Dorian, and I hate you for thinking that I am."

"I never said you were. I don't think that."

Her breathing is racing, but she seems to calm down, and so I let go her hands to try to hold her face and comfort her, but she starts swinging again.

"I hate you! I hate you! Don't touch me!"

I push her against the wall again, holding her by the neck, and without thinking, I kiss her hard. I utterly take her between my lips and vacuum her mouth until it swells. She bites me, and I feel my lip bleed but cannot command myself to release her. She tastes like copper and wine and the taste is bitter but sweet. I pin her body to the wall with mine, and I am fire itself as I let go of her and pull her signature tank tops off with little struggle and restrain her hands above her again.

"Say stop if you don't want me to," I don't just whisper but grunt in short of breath.

I look at her and she says nothing but folds her mouth inside her teeth. I slowly let go of her hands, but she keeps her arms above her and against the wall. She reaches for me, finding my mouth and when I deepen the kiss, she whispers, "Stop."

I pause, feeling my breath vibrate through me. She reaches for me and pulls me by my belt and I extend my neck to kiss her again but she whispers, "Stop."

"Do you want me to leave?"

Her answer is opposite of verbose for she simply shakes her head and watches me unfold as she lifts my arms and takes off my V-neck. She rubs her hands on my chin and then my cheek and then my hair. I urgently reach down to kiss her again, and she molds against the wall and softly whispers, "Stop."

She ushers me around, so I'm the one whose back is against the cold wall. She kisses me forcefully, plowing my hair with his fingers, and pulls away when I start to take control. She pins me against the wall with her hands and stretches her arms, so I see the confusion on her face.

I pull her close to me, "Please don't say stop. We both want this."

I watch her as I quickly untie the string of her sweats anticipating her to stop me, and when she doesn't, I pull her closer, keeping my body pressed against the wall.

A tear freely stains her cheek, and I feel her about to turn around, and I pull her against me. She tries to push me away, but I hold her closer to me, forcing her to look into my eyes and hoping that they will relay the message to her that I can't say in words. When I feel her soften, I kiss her again, softly this time, and she pushes me back, biting me with passion, with hate or with revenge. The stinging only intensifies my need to ravage her.

She slaps me hard across the face and then kisses me just as hard before I can react. When she raises her hand to do it again, I grab her wrists and twist my body. I flip her around so she is against the wall and pin her against it and staple her with my lower body and finish undoing her sweats. She lets them drop, and I kiss her hard while I detangle her legs from them, with mine.

I grab her left leg and lift the top of her thigh thrusting myself against her until I am agitated by the clothes that stand between us. I lift her body and anchor her between myself and the wall, and she makes a pinching sound with her nose as she searches my mouth for my tongue until she finds it and uncontrollably kneads it with hers. As though suspended in the air, I hold her with one hand while undoing my zipper with my other. This aggression is something new to me, but everything else feels familiar, normal even. July is my normal... I am pleasantly surprised.

On a floor full of glass pebbles, we don't tease, we don't please, we fuck like animals, making nothing nice about it. She bites and scratches, and I don't care, I just want July in my arms winding and grinding around me, and I push and gyrate inside of her as I hold her against the floor.

I tune in to all the sounds she makes, the faces she contorts. I ease her leg lower and go as deep as I can, letting her swallow me, letting her hate me, love me, do me however and whatever she chooses to me. I place my hands on either side of her and let my face fall to the other side of her neck and just breathe her, hoping and wishing that she's forgiven me.

I shudder and push into her one final time pouring myself into her, finally feeling like I'm home again. Relieved and finally ready with whatever feeling comes with the deed done between the two of us in this moment.

She opens her eyes and looks at me, the tenderness leaving her eyes. She pulls away from me leaving me stranded. She picks up my clothes from the ground and shoves them into my arms and puts on her sweatpants.

She walks to the door and opens it and stands to the side.

"Goodbye, Dorian."

As I gather myself, I know I've lost her for good. There is nothing I can do or say. July gives no second chances; I know that now. I walk slowly towards the door keeping my eyes on her and hoping she'll change her mind before I reach the door.

"Goodbye, July."

She gives me one last sad smile before closing the door. I walk away but can't command my body to turn around and look for her at the door. I stop fighting it and look back one last time before climbing into my car. I sit there and wait for my breath to finally let out. I'm closing this chapter of July. I am done. If only I knew that it would be easy to just move on to another part of my life and stop obsessing over someone who never really was mine to begin with. I slowly put my shirt back on.

I try to convince myself that she is not the reason why my heart aches. I try to make myself believe that it is not her that I want, that it is wanting to want her that gives me a sense of urgency. I realize that deep down I know it's not that simple, and so my mission is to keep from what's really ailing me; something I can't do anything about, and that is scraping all of Brady's DNA out of Skylar's genes and replacing them with mine.

How though? How do you tell yourself that you are making the right decision by walking away when you know you haven't had enough? But that's the thing; it never was my decision to make. It is not I who walked away; July had her part in it, too. She gave up on us first. When there are two people involved, you have no choice but to hope that the other person choses what you chose. It has to be unanimous.

In the car, Bryan Adams ironically sings "Please Forgive Me." I drive off thinking maybe this is what was meant to happen all along and the lesson I was supposed to have learned; I was right all along: the more people you let in, the more you are susceptible to heartache. I'm glad I protected myself from loving her; it would hurt 10 times as much if I hadn't.

Chapter Fifteen

Monday rolls around, and I have not talked to Skylar, but I know she is due to be dropped off after school. I have a busy day at the office trying to connect buyers with the artists and get checks and addresses synced and dated with the gallery's account and letterhead. The day goes by fast, which is welcomed since I have so much that I would much rather not think about.

I get home early and prepare spaghetti and meatballs, Sky's favorite, and by the time I'm done, I notice that Jane is two hours late dropping her off. I wait another hour before I call her, but it goes straight to voicemail, and I call her again and again, but she doesn't answer. I finally call Brady who answers and asserts that we meet tomorrow after work so we can talk. I kept the schedule as is. I didn't think things would change so abruptly. Even after that, I refuse to believe that they can just take Skylar away from me just like that. I agree to meet with him tomorrow with the hope of setting things straight.

Brady has agreed to meet me at *Baby Blue*, and I'm so anxious for this conversation to happen, I get to our table 20 minutes early. He strolls in 10 minutes late, and he's on the phone. He holds his finger up signaling for me to wait, and it angers me even more, and for the first time, I realize how pissed off I am at him.

I wait patiently and look at my watch. I relax as I sit back in my seat and look out wondering about how this situation can be resolved. A big part of me feels like a fool: all along they've been playing mum about his paternity, and I am expected to cooperate. How are there no laws against something like this?

I have yet to see Jane since she told me the news, and I have no desire to talk to her or see her, if at all. If I could, I would work this out without ever having to be in the same room with her. How can someone so maternal be so cruel? How do you keep such a secret? For so long?

I look back at Brady, and he is still on the phone. I look at my wrist again, and five minutes have passed. I stand up and grab the phone from his hand and hang up before returning to my seat.

He looks at me perplexed.

"What the hell do you think you are doing? This is an important business call."

"We agreed to meet at 3:00. It's now 3:20."

"And I have a business call that I was finishing."

I breathe in and out before I calmly assert, "My time is just as valuable."

"So, you thought hanging up my phone call would drive your point?"

"No. I thought hanging up would get me your attention."

He looks at the phone in my hand and sits down across from me.

"I thought we could handle this in a civilized manner," he asserts, keeping calm.

"And we will. As soon as we establish a mutual respect. We agreed on a time, you show up late, still—you keep me waiting. Would that appear as a mutual respect to you, if the tables were turned?"

"I suppose not."

"That's what it boils down to then. See where I'm coming from, and I will return the favor."

He flares his nostrils but cooperates. I am surprised that he is being so reasonable. I came with my game face, ready to face whatever he throws at me, and yet so far, it feels like I am dealing with a moderately levelheaded guy. I bow my head in his response to his subtle apology, never for once letting my guard down.

"Man to man: why?" I get straight to the point.

The first thing I ask him is why? For all the times I've pictured this conversation, I didn't think that Brady would be the one to answer the why. The *when*, maybe but the why, I had saved for Jane.

"Why? You know why." He exaggerates his tone.

"No, I don't."

"If you don't know why, then you are more ignorant than I thought."

"Let's say that I am ignorant. Why?" I say through gritted teeth.

"I blame you. I BLAME YOU!" Brady stares me down. I clench and unclench my jaw, a bit confused. Then it hits me.

"And you think taking my family from me is going to solve everything? After all these years?"

"Yes. Everything and everyone you love is up for grabs. Even after all these years."

"So, you use your own daughter to get to me?" I give him a disgusted look camouflaging the pain that comes with admitting my daughter's tie to him.

Attaching Skylar to Brady for the first time and saying the words feels like a sword slicing at my heart. I wait for the pain to subside as I listen to his reasoning.

"I didn't know. For the longest time, I didn't know about Skylar until she was five. That time she hit her head and almost drowned, remember? We all thought that she might need a blood transfusion. Well, she did. You just didn't know about it."

I think back to the most horrible time of my life when Skylar almost died. She miraculously recovered without needing a blood transfusion. She had one; Brady matched her blood type. I ball my fists so tight that my skin feels like it's going to break. I start to boil, but hold my composure and try to nail myself to my seat.

I tighten and loosen my jaw, "Three years! Three years? You've known about this for three years, and you felt compelled to hide it from me. You vindictive son-of-a-bitch!" I rise from my seat, and he does the same, readying himself to retaliate if needed.

"I was waiting for the right time to hurt you. I wanted to see you tear your hair out and cry at the top of your lungs like I did. I wanted your heart to be eaten by sorrow, for sorrow to chew on you and spit you out like it did me. I hope it hurts."

"What kind of man lets another man raise his daughter? Do you not care about hurting Skylar?" I'm so angry, I want to punch a wall—or better yet, his face. I can't help but feel furious that my child is a pawn to his seeking revenge. I pick up my chair about ready to throw it at him when I hear a few gasps from our audience. I violently drop the chair and master all that I can to walk out of there without giving Brady a fat lip.

"I am going to make sure you never see her again."

Those words halt me without my consent. I march myself right back to where he sits and pull him by his shirt. I lift him till he is level with me.

"Listen here, you fucker. You are not going anywhere with my daughter. Do you hear me? Over my dead body!"

"No; over Marcy's!" He detangles himself from my fists and walks out, leaving me in a room full of people staring at me. My demons have now been awakened.

I walk out, slamming the door behind me. I drive straight to Jane and Brady's house and ring the doorbell rigorously. I call for Skylar and Jane, and nobody comes to the door. I yell and kick the door; it seems no one is home. I peek through the window and see shadows; I go around the back and find Jane and July's car outside the garage.

"I know you can see me. I want to see my daughter." I am yelling. "Skylar!"

I just walk around the house and keep yelling my daughter's name until Brady shows up with the cops, and I am escorted off their premises with a warning.

I don't even remember the drive home. I just get there and collect all the alcohol that I can find in the house and drink till I pass out.

There is a knock on the door that mimics the pounding in my head. I wake up from a pool of drool, and I am laying in Skylar's room which as soon as I open my eyes, the memory of earlier's tremor with Brady plays itself in severing stitches that make my head hurt, and the aftershock of the pain travels all the way down to my chest.

I decide to ignore the knocking and the dinging of the bell. I know that today's Sunday because Selena's not here to answer the door. I sit up and touch my feet to the ground, and there is a half empty bottle of Svedka vodka on the ground. I pick it up and hold it tight as if it's my only solace.

My head is spinning, and the knocking is not going away. I'm not sure if it's all in my head or if there really is someone at the door. I stumble over to the bedroom door, almost stepping over Neo who is looking at me like I am a stranger.

I make it to my bathroom and vomit my guts out; for a second, I am scared that the amount of bile coming out of me may not be normal. I sit against the toilet without flushing it and fold my knees in front of me and rest my elbows on them as I rest my head in my palms. I take the vodka bottle and place it on the side of my forehead, as if to let its cold texture suck the heat out of throbbing cranium.

The knocking and the dinging continue, but I am in no state of mind to care. The noise stops, and I am irritated more than I am because right after I hear keys rattling and the door opening.

July's voice calls my name. *Fuck! What does she want?* I have no desire to talk to anyone; I don't want to be comforted; I want to feel the pain as evidence for my love for Skylar. I don't want to be consoled, and most importantly, I refuse to be pitied.

I ignore her calls in hopes that she will leave, but the proximity of her footsteps and voice lets me know that she is not going anywhere.

"Dorian! I know you are home."

She walks into my bedroom and stills for a second before approaching the open bathroom door finding me sitting on the floor all pathetic and dejected, in my worst possible state.

"Dorian!" she runs and kneels next to me and removes my buried face from my hands.

"Oh, Dorian, I am so sorry. Jane told me about Skylar."

I ignore her and don't even bother to care about my state of appearance. She gets up and flushes the toilet and takes the bottle of vodka and empties it out in the sink. She turns on the shower and helps me out of my clothes.

I get in and almost yelp when the ice-cold water assaults me. But the numbness inside of me turns itself inside out, and I don't even care enough to register the uncomfortable gelidity. I just stand under the algid waterfall and concentrate solely on that sensation, bricking out any other aching or thought.

"I know it's cold, but it's good for you," July yells from the other side of the shower door.

I ignore her and hope that she is gone by the time I am ready to get out. I stay under the water with my eyes closed and just spread my arms over to the wall anchoring myself as everything else spins around me. Eventually she opens the door, holding out a towel.

"You probably should get out before you get hypothermia."

I ignore her until I start shivering and feel my lips trembling. She opens the door and slowly adjusts the temperature to warm. I just listen to my body's pain and its adjustment to temperature change. A vacuuming sound of the door opening is accompanied by my agitation and then July's face looking at me with pity in her eyes. I yank the towel from her and wrap it around my waist without drying off. She ignores my rudeness and prudently walks over to the shower and turns it off, avoiding getting wet.

I walk over to the bed, toss the covers to the side, get in bed and bury my wet self under there as if to create another world outside of the real one which sucks at the moment.

"You should at least dry off."

July pulls the covers away from my head, pulling me back into the sordid world that I am trying to escape from. I pull the covers over my head once more with an exaggerated force and hold on to them in case she tries again.

"Oh no you don't. We should go take a walk. You will feel so much better afterwards."

My head is buzzing, and it feels like my skull is cracked. I don't want to deal with anything, especially a giggling playful someone who is trying to make me feel when I am so determined to stay numb. After a while, I notice the silence, and to my relief I release my grip on the covers above me, thinking she is gone, when all of a sudden a light lifts, and my head is exposed again.

"It's not the end of the world you know."

"How would you know?" I spit at her as I sit up, a big part of me wanting to kick her off the bed, "How the fuck would you know?" I annunciate each word.

"I—I—I know that things get better with time. I just think—"

"I don't care what you think. I just want to be left the fuck alone. Why are you here anyway?"

"I thought you could use a—a friend."

"And you thought you would be that friend? What makes you think you're my friend?"

She stands up from the side of the bed and walks over to the door.

"I'm going to make you something to eat. I know you are upset, I know it feels like—"

"You don't know shit! If you did you would know that I don't want you here right now or ever!"

She walks out the door, and I am relieved that she is leaving. I take the towel wrapped around me and dry off my hair and wear a pair of boxers and climb back to bed on the side where it's dry.

I cover myself up and shut off the world, and just when my breathing is level, my wall against doom is yanked away again, and July is smiling at me.

"I made you something to eat."

I throw the tray of food on the ground, and the noise startles her. I am so mad, so furious, I feel my eyes growing big as the seething from within me tries to escape. The noise, the clicking and clanking of the breaking dishes only fuels my anger. I walk around and throw things and walk over to the baseboard and punch it multiple times; the throbbing from my hand is magnified. I am sent into a destroying anger, a vigorous rage. She has a frightened look on her face as she watches me try to control my breathing, and I imagine the face that stares back at her has something to do with it.

"I don't want your food; I don't want your pity. Stop breathing on me!" I yell as I run my hand through my hair, wanting to tear it out.

My skin crawls, and I want to beat my chest like King Kong until I'm so exhausted that I fall into a coma. A chemical ball of toxic vapor explodes above me and fills my head with a cloud of adrenaline, of chaotic madness moistening my face with rage.

"Dorian!" She is looking at me like she is about to cry and this only angers me even more. I can't deal with her or whatever problems she has about me, I am dealing with my own mess right now.

She runs to the bathroom and comes back with a towel.

"Dorian your nose is bleeding."

I violently yank the towel from her.

"Stop trying to take care of me. I don't need your pity."

She looks at me and shakes her head as if I am some injured animal stuck in a trap. I see pity in her eyes, bewilderment, and pure clemency, which only infuriates me to the core.

"Are you getting your satisfaction right now?" I speak through the towel pressed up against my nose, "To see me vulnerable and pathetic."

"Stop! I am only trying to help."

"Well, don't. If you want to feel needed go somewhere else. I don't need you!"

I am inconsolable and petrified at the intensity, the anger that courses through me, and I want nothing more than to be left alone in case I turn into the green Hulk himself. I don't know if I can be held responsible for what happens thereafter.

"Let me help you." She approaches me with a tender voice and outstretched arms as though I am a wounded animal, and she is trying to show me that she is not a threat.

"Let's get one thing straight," I reproach, trying to keep my voice calm. "You are nothing to me. You don't owe me anything, and I you. I don't need your help, I don't need your pity, I don't need your suffocating scent," I spit at her in a rage.

Her face changes, and I don't really bother to register the emotion it portrays because I am now outside of myself watching everything unfold with no power or control to do anything about it.

"It's going to be okay," she tries to console me.

"You were just an easy lay. That's all you were, so don't kid yourself into thinking you were anything more. Now that Skylar's gone, we never have to speak. So, thank you for a good fuck, now leave me the hell alone," I am shouting until my lungs hurt and my nose bleeds heavily.

She starts crying, but whoever I am, at the moment, doesn't care.

"Why are you still here? Take your shit and go!" I am yelling at her, and I throw the bloody towel at her, pushing her out.

She takes the towel that's just assaulted her and throws it back at me.

"Fuck you, Dorian. Fuck you," she fires back before she turns on her heels and leaves the room.

"LEAVE YOUR KEY ON THE COUNTER!"

A few seconds later, I hear the door slam, and she is gone. July is gone, Skylar's gone; I don't ever have to feel again. I crawl back to bed and bury myself under the covers.

Sky, you may fall now.

CHAPTER SIXTEEN

The sheets smell clean, but the smell nauseates me. Selena must have changed the detergent. My nostrils sting as they bathe in floral powdery. I kick the duvet to my feet, untucking and ripping the sheets off the mattress. I lie back down on the bare mattress and sulk at the realization that my pillows hold the smell as well. I violently jolt up and throw them to the right, next to the armchair by the door. I lay back facing the ceiling with my arms stretched out and my hands under my head.

My muscles are aching, my throat is raw, and my stomach is coiled into one big knot that won't release. I smack my lips as I attempt to moisten my dry tongue, trying to listen but fail at sorting through my convoluted thoughts. Does anything have to change? So what if Skylar is not biologically mine? I'm still her father. As for Jane, everything I shared with her was a lie, my past with her, she was with Brady when we were together. How long has she known and how can she be so cruel? I decide I'm going to fight for Skylar, I promise myself to call my lawyer first thing Monday morning. Yes, that's what I'll do. I close my eyes nodding, thinking I can finally go to sleep with my resolution, but my wary eyes refuse to remain bolted.

The thought of never seeing those eyes or hearing that little voice call me by my favorite name in the whole world is enough to…

Her little fingers, the sun that lives in her eyes. Her name: I gave her that name. She is so innocent; she didn't ask to be put in this situation. She cannot be asked to choose.

I go back and forth between Skylar and July as I float in and out of sleep.

I stay in bed all day and don't bother to call the office. In the morning, I am woken up by Selena's gasps and her poking me, making sure I'm still breathing. For the fifth time, she asks me if I want anything to eat. I wake up, and without bothering to shower, I grab a pair of jeans and a grey V-neck and rush out of the house before she has a chance to assess me. I drive to Llarel's.

"Just because you are blind and beautiful, doesn't mean you are amazing... even though you are." Enoch seems to be talking to my sister.

She cocks her head to the side and takes a moment to take in the unexpected compliment from her old-time nemesis. She touches her lips, her cheeks and straightens herself as her face becomes morbid.

"What? Have I upset you with my comment?"

"Would that worry you if you did?"

"I doubt it."

"Then don't worry about my being blind or beautiful or amazing or upset."

"I'm not."

"Leave then, Enoch, and don't you dare slam my door."

"I'm sorry, what?"

He slams the door behind him as she starts to say something, finding me hanging my head with a confused look on my face.

"Did I just hear you compliment my sister?"

"No." He fidgets with his pockets as if looking for his keys. "Where have you been? I've been trying to get hold of you for the last week?" Enoch demands.

I ignore him and stride past him, walking into the room and find Llarel looking away from me. Her body shifts to my direction although her eyes remain vacant.

"Dorian?"

"Yes, Llarel, it's me."

"Tell your friend Enoch that he should leave his loser tendencies outside my door and stop being so loud. I'm blind, not deaf," she says it loud enough for him to hear it.

He sticks his head through the door and loudly yells, "I am sticking my tongue out at you right now," in a sing-songy tone and slams the door again. I don't even wonder what he's doing here.

"How childish," she mutters to me.

I walk over to her and kiss her, letting her feel my face with her fingers, and she pulls me in and finally kisses my forehead.

"Why are you so sad, Dorian?"

For a second, I have one of those rare moments when I am happy that Llarel cannot see me. I take advantage of that, letting my bottom lip quiver and the veins on the side of my head swell to the max, making my ears hurt.

"Why are you so hot? What's wrong, Dorian?" her eyes moving about as worry crosses her face.

"Do you hate me?" I blurt out.

"What did you do?" She is starting to panic.

"I killed her, didn't I?"

She moves her head as if to turn her right ear to my direction, so she can hear me properly, but she doesn't ask me to repeat the question, she holds herself close as if to make herself smaller.

"Dorian. You are scaring me. Killed who? What are you talking about?"

"Marcy! I killed Marcy."

It takes her a second to register what I'm saying but she reaches for the air until she finds me.

"Marcy Lux?"

I am quiet for a second as I replay the cold memory in vivid imagery with no audio.

"You don't still blame yourself for that accident, do you?"

"Maybe I should. Brady still does."

She holds my face in her hands, gently massaging my earlobes.

I hold her hands away from my face and squeeze a little but more for her sake than mine.

"Dorian, what is it?"

She squeezes back and holds on to my hand for dear life. I decide that prolonging the silence only tortures her, and so I brace myself and state my source of sadness.

"It's not good Llarel. It's really bad."

I'm beside myself. I swallow a jagged lump in my throat and press the base of my nose with my free hand. She scoots closer to me taking both my hands in hers.

"Tell me. My heart can't stand it."

Her soft, warm hands offer comfort, but nothing is of solace; nothing and no one except a brand-new piece of paper that assures me that the last piece of paper I read was inaccurate, one which states that what I read before was a lie.

"It's Sky. Llarel, Skylar is not my child." I'm sobbing and crying like a baby.

Her eyes blink behind me as if they see something, a thought bubble that explains everything else that I haven't said. She smiles briefly before her face becomes gravely pale.

"If this is some sort of joke, Dorian, it's cruel and unnecessary." She moves her hands to my face to find it saturated with tears. She attempts to dry them with her fingers and palms. "It's not…it's not true. We can fix this."

I shake my head. I vigorously shake my head until it hurts.

"It's true. Absolutely and indubitably," I state, my voice finally catching up with my emotions.

"We'll find a lawyer. We'll do a paternity test."

I stand up and start pacing the room.

"It's no use. I've exhausted all the possibilities."

"What do you mean? You spoke to a lawyer already? How long have you known about this?"

"He's going to take her away. He threatened to take her away from me."

"Who? Who's going to take her away?"

"Brady. Brady's Skylar's biological father," I admit through clenched teeth.

"No!" Her face contorts to a deep thought, and I know she is calculating the years and weighing the evidence. "And they have kept this from you all these years? How barbaric!" She stands up and moves towards me as if sensing the heat radiating from my body even from such a distance. "How did you find out?"

"Jane told me."

"Why now? Why is she telling you this now?"

"Because they want to move to Europe. They are taking her with."

She catches her breath simultaneously clutching her chest as if forbidding her heart from leaping out of her chest.

"He still blames me for Marcy's death."

"I don't know, Dorian; I don't think he is punishing you for something that happened so long ago. You two have been in each other's lives far too long for him to still be holding on to the past."

"You would think," I say as I try to replay all the times that I've spent with Brady in the past several years: the birthdays, the holiday dinners.

"He looked me straight in the eye and told me he still blames me for her death."

"No, all this time he's hated you, and he was using his own daughter to get back to you? And Jane? What is her role in all of this?"

She paces faster this time minding the chair as if she sees it and then she stands by the window placing her hand on it.

"She didn't know. They both didn't know until about three years ago when Skylar had that accident at the cabin, remember? We thought she would need to get a blood transfusion."

"Yes. But she never did."

"She did. And Brady was the donor."

Llarel and I go back and forth about the timing, the motive, and most importantly how this is going to affect Skylar. We talk about involving attorneys and opening the case to the courts but nothing I haven't already exhausted. Llarel, always being the optimist, believes there is a way that we can work it out to share custody.

I think about Skylar as my little girl. I see us dancing to Louis Armstrong's "What a Wonderful World" and how happy she was when she had the lead in the recital. I think about the time that she was sick and the first thing she said when she woke up. I think about how empty my life would be without her, and I decide I need more proof; I need to see her birth certificate.

I realize, for the first time, that I am not the only one losing Skylar when Llarel starts crying. I just hold her, and like me when I found out a few nights ago, I just let her cry.

"Leave me alone, please, Dorian. I am feeling too much right now," she finally says.

So, I stand up and walk out, finally realizing that I've said it out loud; it's really true. Brady is my daughter's biological father. Brady also hates me and still blames me for the death of his sister.

Chapter Seventeen

I decide on an impromptu trip to Europe. I decide to run away from my feelings, from anyone who knows about them. I decide to go to Europe, alone and explore this continent, this country that will be housing my Skylar. I don't tell anyone but Llarel and Prudence Rose. I just disappear for the whole majority of December.

I have a meeting with Madame Lefèvre scheduled early in January, and so I just have Prudence Rose move it, and since I was ahead with her portrait, I just justify some of my irrational and rash behavior by peppering in the fact that I will be doing some work there. I am at least being responsible.

My first week in Europe, I spend it in Paris. Most of it in my hotel room, numbing myself with my work and alcohol and spending a lot of time at the hotel gym. Some nights are worse than others, but I concentrate on finishing Madame Lefèvre's painting. I bury myself in perfecting this woman's face, so much so that I start to hate the sight of her. I seriously think about burning the painting and starting over but decide against it out of sheer laziness. I finally meet with Jacquiline on my second week in Paris.

I can't help but think that the last time I was here, it was raining, and now the snow-covered streets match my heart. I cannot and do not even appreciate the beauty. I am a different person than I was back then. So much has happened. The same girl, Marjorie, opens the door and lets me in, as before. We walk down the hallway and up the stairs. The house still looks and smells the same, but I am different. I can't help but dwell on how I'm the one who has changed while a lot of other things remain timeless.

I am ushered to a different room this time, on the opposite hall from the one that I was in, the last time I was here. There is not much of a difference between them, even the size except for the contents. I look at the different portraits of Jacquiline Lefèvre, in some of them she looks much younger. There are even a few of them where she is nude. It's as if I am looking at a timeline, and my portrait of her as the most recent. Jacquiline does not make me wait for too long.

Jacquiline walks in and sashays to me, wearing a baby blue tunic that's oversized but looks comfortable.

"Hello, my love. How was your flight?" She kisses me on both cheeks, barely touching me.

"Well, thank you."

"You little devil you, you left without saying goodbye at the showing last."

I shyly bow my head realizing that the last time I saw her was at the art banquet where I made a scene and left my guest without so much as a goodbye or an explanation.

"Something came up. I'm sorry about my rude exit."

"No problem, love. I still had a great time."

We always have these amazing conversations, and she is an amazing philosopher. She asks me questions that I have never been asked before, questions I wouldn't even think to ask myself or anyone else. We talk about the portrait and about some of the art in the room. She is happy with my work and likes that I *see* her.

Within minutes, her mood changes, and the conversation takes a left turn.

"Dorian, what do you wish to discover about yourself?"

It's not out of the blue when she asks me that, but it takes me by surprise.

"I don't know." I think as an adult I have a pretty good grasp of who I am, or at least I thought I did, up until a few weeks ago. "I pretty much know who I am," I answer her, utterly insecure with my answer.

"Have you ever been in love?"

"Yes. All kinds of love," I bask in sarcasm.

She is not very impressed with my egocentricity or the airy way I joke around a question which she so obviously takes seriously.

"Real love, Dorian." She looks me straight in the eye and makes sure that I can read between any lines and understand anything that may be subliminal in what she is about to say.

"Have you ever had anyone burn a hole inside of you? One that leaves you empty and wanting nothing else? Have you ever thought the stars were ugly simply because you were jealous that someone you wished loved you thought they were beautiful?"

She beats on her chest with a closed hand as she continues, "Have you ever had something reside in this part of you that you feel with your every fiber, even though you are so sure that you couldn't coexist with it, and you thought if you had to choose, you would choose for its existence over yours because you know that yours wouldn't be possible without it?"

I am stunned and empty of words. I think about Skylar.

"No. I can't say that I have."

Her accent is so thick at times, I am replaying what she has just said to make sure that I understand or that such analogies would even be a probability.

"Then; how can you say you know yourself?"

I take a second to examine her loaded question. She lets the silence haunt the room as I think to myself.

She takes off her tunic and walks to me.

"You can have me now." She directs as she lets down her hair.

I'm not sure that's what I want. I'm not sure I can even refuse her, but most importantly, I'm not sure why she asked me all those questions before she decides to have meaningless sex with me. I obey. I don't think; I just do.

I lay next to her with my arms over my head and her next to me. Done with our passion session. The most refreshing thing about her is her calmness, her air. She is so strong and confident, and she is a force that cannot be shaken, at least not without her permission.

She shifts, facing me, and then she props herself up by her elbow. She pushes the sheet from my waist and exposes me.

"So beautiful and so youthful. You are like a Greek god. Like Hercules."

I smile and find myself feeling shy. I grab the white sheet and try to cover myself, but she pushes it down again.

"Don't be shy. You have nothing to be ashamed of."

I feel myself heat up but make no other attempt to cover myself. She looks me up and down hungrily but says nothing.

"If only you would see what I see when I look at you. You would be so vain."

I look at my exposed body and feel unnatural in such a state. I, in turn, pull the sheet from her, revealing her big breasts that hang low on her chest and just admire the sharpness of her nipples, how significant they look on the center of her large, pale areolae.

"Do you like poetry, Dorian?"

I nod slowly as I make my way to them and kiss them slowly and softly.

"Read to me then."

I level my head to hers and smile at her, ready to protest. She points to the wall facing us on the far end of the room as if eliminating any negotiations.

"Do you have a favorite?"

"I love them all. Why choose when you don't have to, no?"

"Yes. Why indeed."

I stand up and hold the top sheet close to me but she gently pushes my hand away from it, so I have no choice but to stand up without it. I stand well aware of my nakedness, and I am not entirely uncomfortable, but I feel her eyes on my skin, like the sheet that is supposed to cover me, her eyes do its job. I walk over to the wall she initially pointed to and scan the shelf that's level with my eyes. I scan with my index finger: Rumi, Merwin, T.S. Elliot... They are not in any alphabetical order.

"I ordered them by brilliance," she states as a matter of fact. "No one can ever figure out my system because it is a matter of preference."

"Uhm, that would explain why you have Foucault right next to Freud."

"Yes, are you familiar with his work?"

"Only a little bit."

"Only a little bit? You should be ashamed, Dorian."

I pull out a thick book with red and gold bindings and textured patterns on the cover but has no words or title. I open it and there are hundreds of pages but no words, only small bumps that make intricate patterns and some sort of drawings.

"What is this?" I ask, marveling at a book without words, "It's empty."

"Oh, but it's not."

I gather that it's a book for the blind, but how does a person with an untrained eye recognize the fullness of such a book, it's full of pages, yes, but none of them have words that one can read.

She comes from behind me and stands close without touching me, so I can feel her heat radiating in the vicinity that allows our bodies' temperature to interact.

"You are so innocent, so blind," she whispers in my ear, and she pastes herself to me and runs her hand down my arm.

The hairs on the back of my neck stand, and I allow myself to relax as she takes my hand and lightly runs my fingers on the texture of the first page of the woodless book.

"Close your eyes." She whispers, "Now: Don't think, don't listen, don't smell, just feel, just touch."

She directs my hand from the right of the page and moves it to the left. It's an odd way to attempt to read any type of book; unless, of course, it was Chinese.

"These are direct verses from the Torah…"

She switches our hands so that mine is on top of hers and she is running the thin skin of the tip of her finger on the words

"Can you read Hebrew?"

"When I was in college, I spent some time in a Kibbutz."

She licks me behind my ear and breathes into it. I am so warm and so close to her as we stand there, naked, and she runs her fingers over the perforated paper, and her breathing gets louder and louder, and I can't help but get turned on.

How is this not a sin? We are finding lustrous pleasure while reading the Torah.

"I can purr in Hebrew, too," she whispers into my ear, and all the tiny hairs in my body spark.

"Have you ever cummed without someone touching you?"

I shake my head no with the faith that she may attempt to make that into a possibility.

"Close your eyes, Dorian."

She moves her hand away from under mine, and I inch my head to the direction that I feel her move towards, as I now am at a disadvantage without my sight.

"No matter how much you want to, don't open your eyes."

I bite my lip and pinch one eye shut as I open the other in nervous curiosity.

"Cheating only puts you at a disadvantage in this game, Dorian."

The way she whispers in her soft French accent is all the more ammo for my excitement. I pinch both my eyes shut.

Back in my hotel room, I think about that hole that Jacquiline was talking about. It's a different kind of love, but it's love nonetheless. I love Skylar with my whole being, and I do feel a hole without her. I am utterly incomplete and irrevocably damaged. I feel suffocated; I can't be here any longer, I feel like the room is spinning and the air is stale. I just pack my duffel and leave the hotel without checking out. I get in my rental and drive straight to Amsterdam. Bad weather and all, I make it there late that night. I go to two different hotels before I find one that's not sold out for some Christmas parade.

I drop off my bags in my room and walk out, avoiding being alone in a still room. I walk around aimlessly, my head, a big cloud of turmoil; every sound around me, a buzz, every face, a blur. My insides feel like one big rubber band that gets strummed and vibrates with every breath I take. I put my hands in my pockets and head south of downtown, passing happy crowds and passing streetlights.

I turn left at the corner of Bass and Broadway, noticing for the first time the bakery that has been one of Llarel's favorite dessert places. I keep heading south and away from the highway and the restaurants, not really having a specific destination.

I wander away from the crowd and eventually get to the quieter side of the long street where there are a few restaurants and more night clubs and bars. I envy the young people sitting around in groups, talking carelessly as though they have no worries in the world.

I don't look back or around. I move my head in small motions to keep my hoodie in place. My mind is in conflict, my heart: black with metal constraints. Doom washes over me like acid rain and the bright lights scold me.

I finally look up to see where I am, and a bright red light blinds me. Next to it is a woman's silhouette in neon lights that read: *JUDGMENTS ASIDE!* Once through the door, there is a long hallway, which it appears that I am still outdoors, and there are green doors on each side of the hallway leading up to big black double doors with a sign at the top that reads: SIRS' BOROUGHS.

I walk in, and the whole place is dark with soft seductive music with a woman moaning in the background. I walk through the doors, and right away,

I am in a different world. There are people kissing, touching, sucking, fucking in groups, by themselves, same sex, different sexes, white, black, Asian, all kinds of assortments.

Women look at me with their arms lingering on me; men, too. An older woman who looks to be in her fifties stops me and kisses me with her mouth open, leaving a wet kiss as she walks away slowly and seductively. She turns around and looks at me as if expecting me to follow, but I continue on in my initial direction. There is a tiger in a cage, and a woman in the cage next to it dancing around, and a whip that screams every time it makes contact with the metal.

I keep moving towards the end of the room, and the deeper I walk into it, the kinkier and wilder things get. I keep myself tucked into my hoodie, and I avoid eye contact although there really is no reason to because everyone is preoccupied.

Reaching the back, I see the two large double doors like the one I encountered when entering, but these are a sinful red with huge hinges and two guys on each side of them wearing only bowties and a pair of speedos. I feel invisible, so a part of me feels like I am. I ignore the two bouncers and reach for the knob to turn it.

"Members only," guy on the right of me asserts.

"How much?"

He ignores me and continues to look straight ahead although he positions his body is such a way that lets me know that there is no way he's going to let me in.

"How do you know I am not a member?"

Silence. Both guys ignore me. I decide to launch myself forward and rudely insist on walking in, but the guy on the right grabs me by the neck and slams me hard in the floor. Before I know it, I am pinned to the ground with a knee in my neck, cutting off my air supply.

"I am going to release you. You are going to get up. You are going to turn around, and you are going to leave," he declares.

I close my eyes in response without being able to utter a single word or move my body. Clumsily, I rise upon his release and stumble over to the direction I just came. After a few steps and with the crowd now curtaining me from the men in bowties, I make my way to the left and end up at the bar sitting next to a woman.

"Strongest you've got," I demand to the waiter.

The woman in a gold sequence dress turns around.

"Next time wear a blazer and a button-down shirt. You'll have better luck making it past that door."

The woman is, in fact, a man. His thick voice warns me, and upon close inspection, I can make out his Adam's apple and a hint of hair on his knuckles.

"Have you been past it?"

"Are you kidding? Look at me."

I look at him in his short gold dress and his red stockings and matching gold platforms. His demeanor or the way he carries himself gives him away.

"What's behind that door anyway?"

He looks at me from top to bottom, sizing me up. He shakes his head in amusement as if he is in disbelief of my ignorance.

"Bigger and better things, honey. This…" he scans the whole room with his eyes, "…but bigger and better and richer and sweeter; the forbidden fruit on steroids."

He grabs his glass short of gracefully and drinks it like a man, his Adam's apple bobbing as he swallows.

I finish my own drink and look around as my curiosity peaks. I take another curious look at the big red doors. The woman in the cage next to the tiger gestures with her hands and a gentleman is let into the cage with her. I watch the show as she strips him down to his underwear and whips him repeatedly until his back is beet red. People stand around and cheer, men and women alike.

I get another drink and let the alcohol travel, so the scene in front of me is tolerable. My acquaintance beside me clears his throat and vies for my attention by blowing in my ear.

I jump and turn to face him, my expression seeking an explanation.

"What the fuck?" I yelp.

"Relax, honey. This place is judgment free, all of us have faces and genitals, but we don't have names. *Welcome to the hotel California, you can check out anytime you like but you can never leave.*" He sings. "Oh, honey, you are so innocent. You should leave, you should forget about those doors, and never come back. Trust me; ignorance *is* bliss."

I remove myself from my seat and decide to walk over to the opposite side of the room to a less crowded bar. I can feel my insides soaking in alcohol, I am inebriated and there is not a single thought in my head even though I am constantly accosted by shocking and disturbing images, blurry but vivid.

A magnetic pull steels me before my eyes even catch sight of two half naked women making out. They both stop and look at me as I stand there gawking at them, the blonde one whispers something to the tall brunette, and they look at me all smiles and continue making out until I have no choice but to join them.

They don't reject me; they pull me between them, and we are immediately enveloped by a cloud of breath and arms and hair. Long blonde retreats and sticks her tongue out revealing a round white pill and then she draws me in for a kiss where she deposits it in my mouth.

I play with my tongue until the tiny round object evaporates into my taste buds, and the two women kiss me, not minding the sharing. I kiss one mouth and move on to the next without any sort of difference in the taste or texture and decide I have no need to feel bad or guilty, for this is all taking place in my head.

I decide that this is some twisted fantasy where everything feels and tastes real, although not really. I hear laughter, and blurs of light zoom past me as I glide to the direction where four hands are pulling me.

I realize I am an object with weight and temperature and breath within me, but that's all I am. I don't know who I am or what I am doing, I follow what feels good: warm skin, sweet lips, perfume, soft breasts, long hair. I black out.

January

FEBRUARY

MARCH

APRIL

CHAPTER EIGHTEEN

No differently than the last few months, I reluctantly exist in a daze and complete my responsibilities as best as I can. I head to the mall to buy a wedding gift for Cornelia's wedding. I go to Von Maur and find there are still items on her bridal registry. It turns out that I waited till the last minute and whatever is left on the registry will have to be ordered and shipped directly to the couple. I overcompensate and get two items. I walk out of the store in my normal daze, my thoughts keeping me company.

The only people who can stand me at this moment are Enoch and my sister, out of obligation. Work is work, and everything is a big blur. Jane and Brady have cut off all my communication with Skylar, and since they moved to Europe, Llarel has been communicating with them and filling me in on how she is doing. For a long time, I was mad at Llarel for forgiving them and not hating them the way that I do. I'm just glad she can show me pictures and tell me new stories about Skylar. As I walk out of the store, another shopper runs into me and almost knocks me over, bringing me back to the now. We both apologize, and as I look up and look around, I see her. July.

She is talking on her cellphone. She is smiling, laughing, and unmistakably happy. I've seen her like that. With me, she's been that way with me. Happiness looks beautiful on her. I can see her exquisite dimples 20 feet from where I stand. I want to march right over to her and demand that she forgive me. I want her in my arms and in the same air that I breathe. I take a step toward her direction and stop dead in my tracks. What would I possibly say now that will make her listen, that will make her forgive me? I inch diagonally from her and hide behind a cellphone kiosk, keeping my eyes on her. I went too far; I realize she may never forgive me.

She turns around as someone calls her name, and it's a male's voice. My fingers tingle, my skin tightens as I follow her eyes to see its owner. It's a tall blond male, about my height, my size, and my throat starts hurting as it is now full of my heart. She walks over to him and hugs him, still smiling.

I want to run over to them and yank his arms off her. His nose buried in her hair, his pelvis so close to hers, it makes me sick. Who is he, and why does he look so familiar? Is this her type, now that she is done with me, she's found another me? My ego is bruised to learn that I can be so easily replaced.

I watch to see if they hold hands as they walk off, but they don't. Good. He does not know her well enough yet. This, for some unfathomable reason, gives me hope.

"Excuse me, sir. Did you want to buy something? You are scaring our customers away," the cellphone salesman at the kiosk disturbs my stalking.

I walk away, for the first time being aware of how ludicrous I seem to everyone who sees me. I follow them from a distance as they enter 32°, Sky's favorite dessert place. My heart constricts at the association. This must be a date. I get a sickening ache at the pit of my stomach when I think about him knowing her. Of course, he will fall in love with her; she is beautiful and smart and funny and perceptive, and she smells good, and she's worldly and a sex goddess... Why didn't I see those things when I had a chance to make her mine? This thought sits like a tangible burden on my shoulders, making me a foot shorter.

I must sabotage this date, or I will lose her forever to *Don Juan* over there, and I can't have that. I am standing in front of Bath and Body Works right across from them, and I can't stand how close his knees are to hers. He is deliberately looking for a way to touch her, and of course, he talks close to her ear, and she laughs with her whole body, bobbing her curls behind her.

My stomach churns. I cannot stand to be on the outside looking into the life that I should be having with her. He should be the one standing here, envying me. I don't want his hands on her, caressing her, heating her skin and making her wet. I can't have him kissing those lips of hers, touching her body. Only I know how to do that, I don't want him to have the chance to try.

I close my eyes and stabilize myself as I see him in my mind's eye kissing her hair, kissing her neck, licking, brushing her hair out of her face. I ball my hands into fists and breathe deeply as I clench and unclench my jaw. She won't let him; she still has me coursing through her veins. My taste is still in her mouth. I hope.

He won't know how to hold her the way she needs to be held, the way that she deserves to be held. He doesn't know her warm spots, her sweet and soft spots. I walk over to the water fountain and sit on the edge keeping my eyes on them. She laughs again, slapping him lightly on his arm. *Oh no*, my eyes widen; she is reciprocating his stated affection. I need to do something.

I anchor myself for a brief moment, breathing into my lungs before I violently stand up and march myself over to the frozen yogurt store. I open the door and head over to the wall picking up a cup and pouring the first flavor closest to the cups. I set it on the scale and just put a $10 bill on scale as I lift my cup and walk towards them.

"July? Wow, fancy running into you here," I exaggerate my pseudo surprise.

Her jaw drops, and she goes from flirty and smiley to shocked and skeptical as she narrows her eyes. I don't wait for her to reject me or her date to compose himself. I walk over and join them pulling a seat from behind Don Juan.

"Hope you don't mind if I join you. You wouldn't refuse an old friend, now would you?" I smile at her, crinkling my nose. She looks at me about ready to explode. She shapes her mouth to speak, but I interrupt her by ignoring her and talk to her date. "I'm sorry, where are my manners. I'm Dorian, an old friend of July's, and you are?"

"I'm Vonn Swann. I'm—"

"Vonn. What kind of a name is Vonn? Are you guys also old friends?" I deliberately embarrass her.

"I'm her date," Vonn is starting to air his frustration with me.

July grabs me by my wrist and pulls me to the side, and I rise and follow her.

"Excuse me, Don," I say deliberately, and she smiles an apologetic smile as she scoops me away.

"Leave! Now, Dorian."

"No." I throw my two-year-old tantrum, and I rejoin Don Juan leaving her standing helpless with her arms crossed.

She walks back to the table and joins us kicking me under the table. Just by looking at him, the way he talks, I can tell that he is a lover of love. She deserves that. I should step back and give her a chance at happiness, but I want to be selfish. I can be that for her. Can't I? I can love love and her in it, I can be in it with her. Surely, I can try.

It's uncanny, though, how we are so similar, physically, but not in any other way. He is more talkative and somewhat flamboyant, while I am more reserved. He is very verbose and seems to lack confidence while I am neither. He has big blue eyes like mine, a strong jaw, a thin nose and a narrow line of a mouth. He has freckles, more visible than mine at the top of his nose. I stare at him as he speaks, trying to see him through July's eyes. They both start laughing in sequence, taking me out of my reverie.

"Well, aren't you such a peach." I sarcastically scrunch my face in dark mockery.

"Anyway, we ended up taking the long way home," he continues, finding a way to take charge by ignoring me.

I find a hint of amusement in July's face. He has impressed her. She likes a man who takes charge.

"What do you do, Don Juan?" I interrupt.

Vonn looks as me as if I'm something bitter in his mouth or a foul smell in his nose.

"The name's Vonn, and I'm a stenographer."

"A stenographer? Aren't you guys extinct?" I jab at him, knowing very well I'm being a jerk.

"Aren't you a jackass?"

I smile wickedly and extend my hand, mocking him, "Yes, hi; nice to meet you." He ignores my hand.

"What's the deal with this guy anyway?" He looks to July, starting to lose his cool which gives me incentive to keep poking.

"This guy? I thought we already established that my name's jackass." I shake my head at July and point at him, "This guy." I smirk.

July in turn holds her breath while scolding me with her eyes.

"What do you do, Dorian?" he challenges, using my proper name.

Alright. I put on my sparring gloves. This guy wants to spar.

"I do whatever it is I want to do, depending on how the wind blows."

"So, is that code for unemployed? Are you gonna tell me you're an artist as well?" He leans forward with his elbows on his thighs.

"Actually, I do call myself an artist, along with a few other people."

He chuckles confidently.

"So what? You make food stamps a year?"

July gets up from her seat and clears her throat.

"We should go, Vonn. Now, please."

"Now hold on a second. I'd like to know how Dorian keeps his fridge stocked." He asserts, very pleased with himself.

"Right now, it's pretty empty. Except for the molded cheese you left after we made love."

I look at Don Juan's eyes widen, and July cringes before composing herself and flaring her nostrils.

"Dorian, you are such an asshole," July shouts at me.

"What an ass," Don Juan reiterates July's agitation.

"Why?" July looks straight at me with daggers in her eyes.

My phone rings, and I rudely hold my finger up, putting her on pause. This infuriates her, and she takes my finger and folds it so far back, I yelp.

"Hello, Dorian Benson," I say my full name in case he decides to look me up later.

"Daddy!" A tiny voice excitedly calls me by the only name that disarms me, the one name I thought I'd never hear again. Everything halts and disappears. My face immediately pales, the cement in my stomach becoming concrete. Her mother hasn't told her the truth.

"Hi Binkie," I whisper as a wave of sobs crowds my throat. I clear my throat and bow down as my eyes threaten to water, and I put my hand on my brow and listen to my little girl and tune out everything else, not caring about the world, about Don Juan, or July. I don't care that I get emotional in front of July, in front of her date. I press on the base of my nose as I try to control my voice, so Skylar does not sense or hear my trepidation. I stifle back my runny nose and listen to her talk to me as though nothing's changed.

"So, you love it there?" I pause and listen. "Venus is your favorite? No, sweetheart, mine is Peru...tomorrow? I ask between tightening and untightening my jaw. "Really?" I close my eyes and picture her smile as she talks to me. "Yes. Yes, she's right here, wanna say hello?"

I hand the phone over to July and look at her through the glass in my eyes and turn to look at Don Juan as it shatters and pools out of my eyes. He looks at me stunned and confused, his attitude vacant from his eyes, like he is genuinely concerned.

I continue staring at him until he looks away and hear July talk to Skylar about the weather and art. I stare at my untouched yogurt which is now a mixture of a shake and juice. July hands me back the phone, and Skylar is still sunrays and butterflies on the phone. I choke all over again.

"Vonn, can I call you later?" July's voice is apologetic and concerned.

He rises from his seat, they hug, and he whispers something to her and leaves.

"I love you, too, my angel. More hugs." I hang up.

I glance over at July and then stare away from her. I feel desolate, unraveled and utterly divisible. I clench and unclench my jaw, emotionally traveling through my body and numbing every bit of myself in my course. July is saying something, but I sit there staring into space for a moment, minutes, shit, probably an hour. I look up eventually, and she is still there caressing my arm, I meet her eyes.

"Fuck!" I eventually breathe out.

"Damn it," she agrees with me in a staid but mocking sensation.

"You know, I almost lost her when she was five. We were at the cabin. She fell off the boat, hitting her head and almost drowned. I remember thinking… I thought, this world would never be right without Skylar in it. I stayed up with her all night at the hospital." I smile as I recall her exact face as she said those words. "The first thing she did when she woke up that morning was ask me if I was okay. She was lying in the hospital bed, but she took my hand and told me to be alright. That's when I knew; I knew right then that I would never be able to love anything or anyone as much as I love her."

July simply brushes my arm and listens to me talk.

We sit there in silence, and when I feel like I am through having her feel sorry for me, I decide to make one final plea before possibly parting ways for good. I speak without looking at her, still staring into my space.

"I'm sorry." I whisper.

The dynamic changes between us right away. I seem to have triggered something that should have been left untouched. I realize right there and then that this wasn't the time or place to bring it up. She releases my arm and sits up so she is no longer close to me.

"For what? What is it exactly that you are sorry for, Dorian? You didn't per se do anything wrong?"

My jaw drops. This must be a trap. If I didn't do anything wrong, then why does she think I did?

"For hurting you," I say slowly, saying what I know she wants to hear and believing that I mean it.

"You should be sorry. For tasting good and being an expert at making me feel special when you've already made up your mind that I am not. I resent you for numbing my fingers and curling my toes, for making love to me but never intending to love me."

I look at her in shock, realizing that this is beyond my control. I can apologize all I want, but I will never find atonement for what I'm accused of.

"July, I just thought that we were both consenting adults succumbing naturally to what is primal to us."

"Of course, you did. At this moment though, right now, you just made me realize that it is you that I should feel sorry for and not myself."

My face morphs into a question mark and I think, *Come again?*

"You don't feel and that's simply because you won't let yourself. Even though I'm the one that's messed up over this, at least I feel instead of being in a state of constant numbness."

Did she not just witness me break down like a fool in front of her? I think to myself.

"Thank God for Skylar. She's the only thing human about you." Her eyes are cold.

The sound of her name infuriates me. I, in turn, defend myself in her honor.

"You are so sanctimonious and judgmental. This is more about you than it is about me."

"Enlighten me." She folds her arms over her chest.

"Like you don't already know."

She presses with her eyes.

"You seem to have all the answers. I'm curious to see what your diagnostic is for me."

I stand up and decide that I am the one that will do the walking away this time. At this point, I've realized that whatever ill feelings July is harboring about me are not about me at all.

"I never promised to love you. We didn't make a pact. It just happened. I admit how I treated you at the party, and the day you came over was fucked up. I messed up, and I apologize for that." I pick up my cup still full of yogurt that is now in liquid form and toss it in the trash by Vonn's vacant seat. "What do you want me to say? I love you? I don't."

She looks at me as if I've just injured her, as if she is someone falling off a bridge and I'm not reaching out to help her.

"...I'm still trying to love myself," I close in a whisper.

"Well then, you do that."

I start to say something, anything that will keep us talking, but soon realize that I've apologized enough. I'm exhausted from coming up with apologies. I walk out without looking back, mentally preparing myself to close the July chapter for good. Although a pang in my chest lets me know that there might be a small tear in my heart.

As I walk out the door, there is nothing that compels me to turn around and look at her one last time. It feels final, and no part of me wishes that she runs after me or calls my name. I have been mentally exhausted, and there is no fight left in me. I am not my father, and so I pull myself together and choose to let every stich that July separated from my seams glue itself together with time.

I am not my father. *It's all irrelevant. None of it matters.* I force myself to be proud for finally walking away and promise to stay away for good.

Chapter Nineteen

How do I describe emptiness? Emptiness is a cancer cell that infects everything else around it. I see it, it's all around me. I smell it, it's under my nails. I sit at the stool in front of my easel covered in an emptiness disguised as a white piece of paper. Emptiness is a picture of Skylar smiling, Neo looking at me with eyes that question when Skylar is coming back. It's my phone ringing, and when I answer, it turns out to be someone else but not the person I want to hear from. It's that hollow feeling that lets itself known within, that keeps screaming I am here to stay.

I wake up in the morning not because I want to or because I have to but because this emptiness has found me even in my sleep, it's got its own weight and its own voice. It's heavy and loud and occupies a space that is literal as well as hypothetical. I hear people laugh, and I envy them. I eventually decide to hide under my sheets where I cradle myself until I can't take it anymore. Short of cold sweats, I'm in withdrawal. My fingers are numb, my toes cold.

I miss her. I miss the arch of her back, her expressive eyebrows and her laughing lips and the dimples that pinch her cheeks. Coffee is not coffee without her. Drugs, nicotine…all the consequences that they produce on one's body would have no effect on me.

I am incandescently alight with yearn; her presence would quench the thirst in my tongue, the burn in my throat. At this point, right now seeing her,

I feel, would swallow up this invisible wound that opens wider with time. I am irreproachably and inconsolably fine missing her, just as long as I have her in some way. July. Skylar. Suddenly I am missing them both.

Somnambulant, I carry myself in small motions that I can master: breathe, blink, swallow, walk, but inside, I am deadened and starved for slumber. I won't pity myself; I won't stay here and wallow. I've given myself time to mourn my tragedy; now it's time to pick myself up and do something about it. Starting with Skylar. I deserve all this misery; somewhere, someday, I must have caused someone some harm, some pain, and the wheel has turned, what went around is now coming around. I never was punished for Marcy's death, maybe this is it.

I don't mind dreaming about her, finding her waiting in my fantasies. If there is some way that I can keep her, some way that I can find her when I look for her. If I can't have her as a tangible being, then…then I can anatomize every memory I have of her, lay her out and make her up to be something permanent or temporary to my need. I am sick with sadness, utterly desolate. I manifest my longing to be Skylar's father into something that I can handle. I think about July. I'm not sure that I miss her as much as I think I do or am just replacing Skylar with her because her absence is easier to compute. I can handle her, but the thought of Skylar is absolute misery. A misery I have no desire to dwell in.

I've missed the way my scalp would prickle when she kissed the back of my neck, or the way that my breath would catch when I see her meeting me halfway for a kiss. I just miss myself the way I was when I was with her.

Her soft skin, her curly hair, her teardrop shaped breasts…I've got to see her again. I must find her and tell her to forgive me. When I see her, I'm going to kiss her and caress her and love her and make love to her…if only I could. If only she'd let me.

I walk to the car and open it and leave the door open. I notice a dent on the roof of the car and am taken back to when and how it happened. Even the dinging of the car agitates me. I close the door and right away feel claustrophobic, as if I am breathing in stale air that has been sitting inside the car overnight.

I start the engine, and the radio starts blasting so loud, I think my ears actually pop. I turn the volume down and leave it at a low setting, so I won't have to listen to the hum of the engine and the friction of the tires as they make contact with the concrete.

I press all four buttons at the same time and all the windows descend in unison. Before the garage door comes to a halt in its hinges, I note how loud and annoying the sound is. I am determined to find an outlet, and I am aware of the rigidness of the cushion of my seat.

I stop at the Thornton's Gas Station and pull up next to a police car. I walk inside and buy a five-hour energy drink and a pack of Camel cigarettes. I walk back to the car and turn around. Before I open the door, I realize that I forgot to buy a lighter. I unlock the car and place everything in the backseat before walking back into the store and find that they only have two choices of lighters. I settle for the pink one and walk back to the car, keeping my eyes to the ground as I avoid a group of fraternity boys.

Jack Johnson sings "Banana Pancakes," and I find an ease in my anxiety, and my skin slowly losing elasticity. The crawling in my head begins and I end up on River Road parked in the parking lot and facing the river.

My obsessive compulsion for cleanliness gets the best of me, and I decide to walk outside and smoke. I avoid getting the smoke inside of my car, and I sit on the hood and light one up. I watch people walk around: a couple chasing each other, an old man on the phone, and an attractive female walking her dog. I cough after the initial inhalation and then inspect the thin little stick between my fingers with smoke coming out at the end.

I take a long drawn-in breath and feel my insides relax as the toxic air fills me, ironing out any stress that resides within me. I feel the screams within silence, the anxiety collect itself as I pinch my eyes and release it. I inspect my conduit to tranquility as I hold it between my fingers wondering how something so thin, so light can make such a difference.

I draw in another breath of the toxic smoke into my lungs, and all I think is how I can willingly pollute my body with a well-known slow death. I let out the smoke, and it's as if the stress leaves me in the form of smoke, and I think, *Maybe it might be worth it.*

I draw in a fourth puff, pinching my eyes as I do so, and the smoke goes straight to my chest, settles there momentarily, and draws out with my exhalation taking any type of hurt or distress inside me. As if everything that's heavy gets emptied out with every smoke puff I let out. Ironically, the smaller the filter burns and dissipates, the emptier I feel of everything I want out of me. I feel lighter, and my mind somehow feels clearer.

The smaller my cigarette gets, the better I feel, and I wonder if I could just smoke three more and quit, would that solve the guilt that accompanies such pleasure? Maybe I won't even have to throw the box away, I could keep it somewhere and take it out for emergencies, for times when I feel like this; that qualifies as an emergency, doesn't it? If not, it definitely should.

As I take in the last puff, everything that I thought I emptied out comes back tenfold, and with a new type of guilt. I have now polluted the being of me, and my core remains unbalanced. I feel filthy and guilty and bloated with smoke. I want to vomit.

I try to cough, as though that would cleanse me, and I feel my teeth rot with the smell of nicotine that now pollutes my nostrils. I feel my lungs shrink and my throat swelling. The release, the relief that was so apparent only a few moments ago is now a worry, an ulcer that grows and grows.

I walk over to the trash can and throw out the whole box. I take the remaining filter of my cigarette and throw it to the ground and ash it out with the bottom of my shoe. I pick it up and throw it in the trash alongside its original box. Disgusting; I am completely and utterly disgusted with myself. I have stooped to a new low.

I end up at Blue Baby with a table full of Inks and Zeros. Since Europe, it seems my alcohol tolerance has heightened. I drown myself in the alcohol and my own company until I pass out and am suddenly woken up by Enoch. I try to recall how I ended up here, but it sends an agonizing jolt to my head and spine.

"You need to cut out this behavior and pull yourself together."

"For what? Why should I?'

"For Skylar, for one." Enoch tries to reason with me.

"Skylar is no more; therefore, I am no more."

"You talk about her like she is dead." I lift myself up and pat myself for my wallet. "You wouldn't understand."

"Maybe not. But it doesn't excuse your behavior."

"You would be in worse shape if you were in my shoes. Believe me."

"Stop fucking up and get your shit together man. Skylar is not dead, just not biologically yours. Get your ducks in a row, and fight for her."

Life lessons from Enoch. I'm intrigued.

"Wait. How do you know about Skylar?"

"Llarel told me."

We are now in his car driving down a deserted downtown.

"When did you talk to her?"

He is quiet for a long time and the traffic light turns green. I turn to look at him.

"Now is not a good time. Let's get you home and sobered up."

I wonder what's so complicated about him just telling me when he talked to her, and since when do Enoch and my sister talk?

We pull up to my neighborhood, and this question just does not process in my head.

"Since when do you and my sister talk?"

He is quiet again.

I optimistically check my voicemail and find I have one from my mother. I spit to the ground subconsciously. Suddenly I realize...I have fought so hard not to be like my father, I didn't see myself turning into my mother. My skin starts to crawl as I feel her coursing in my blood. I would never be able to escape her: she is around me and inside me, and that is why I avoid her so much...I don't want her bleeding into any other part of me or mine.

CHAPTER TWENTY

Just when I'm ready to move on; I had decided that from now on I should do what I should have done a long time ago, and that is to guard this muscle of mine they call a heart. Forbid it from loving and keep it from breaking.

It's the start of a new day, and I wake with every hope of starting this day as a new man. I've promised myself to swallow my pride and apologize to Brady. One thing that I haven't changed my mind on is maintaining a relationship with Skylar. However, I am, whenever I can, going to be her father, and I've decided that no one can stop me from making that happen.

I sit up on my bed and stretch my arms as I assess my digital alarm clock on my left. Today, I am a new man. I repeat in my head. I have completely cleansed myself of my obsession with July. I choose to believe that I've succumbed to what I've been avoiding all along and now that I'm familiar with the seasons of my winter, I plan on turning my winters to summers only. I am not my dad. I am not pathetic and weak, and I do not grovel. I am a successful individual and I don't need a woman who will be what my mother was to my father: a cist that grows and grows until it's all that's left of you, and you become invisible.

The blinds lift up in command to the remote in my hand and rays of sunshine flood in, making me smile as I look forward to letting my face soak in the glorious and abundant marvel that is nature itself.

I take my time in the shower, enjoying the warm spray as my muscles are awakened by the temperature of the water. I brush my teeth to the tune of "Feeling Good" by Michael Bublé. I am invigorated, relaxed, and alert.

I wrap the towel around my waist and walk over to the kitchen and find a pot of coffee already brewing. Selena must already be here. I walk back upstairs with a big mug of coffee in my hand that reads, "NUMBER ONE DAD," a Father's Day gift from Skylar. I walk into my closet and pick out my power suit, power tie, and a pale purple shirt with stiff collars. I forbid the thought of seeing my parents today to even enter my head.

I put on a grey pair of boxer briefs, black socks, and walk over to the bathroom and spritz myself with cologne. I moose my hair and dig my fingers into it while combing through it until I am satisfied, and then I walk back to my closet and stand in front of the full-length mirror behind the door, smile at myself, happy with my physique.

While still humming Michael Bublé, I slip into my trousers and head to my naturally lit bedroom and sit on the all-liquid grey bed and pick up my phone to examine it. It's only 10:00, I'm early.

I have one text message and before I even think about anything else, I open it. A strong gush of ice-cold wind suddenly and sharply passes and lands on my face. It's a message from July.

You were right. I was looking for you to save me from myself.

My summer turns back to winter in a matter of seconds. Michael Bublé is attempting to sing "I Want to Go Home," but I won't let him, I drown him out. My temples start sweating, my scalp itches and my jaw clenches and unclenches without my command.

My initial thought is, *Fuck you, I'm over you.* Who does she think she is? She makes me chase after her like a fiend, and when I am finally done being one, she decides she likes the chase. She is just like a lot of these insecure women; hungry for attention at the cost of someone else's happiness. I delete the text and yell, "Fuck you!" at the phone as I delete it.

Today of all days, she sends me that message; today was the day I had picked to make everything a new beginning. I am angry at her and myself; angry at her for not letting me move on and angry at myself for the brief excitement when I first saw her name, with the realization that she reached out to me.

I stand up from my bed and walk back to my closet changing from my pale purple shirt to a dark purple. I resent her for attempting to turn me into my father. I had made up my mind a long time ago that I would not be one to sit around and wait for a woman to love me, or in July's case, forgive me. I just won't love anybody, so that way no one can ever have the power to hurt me the way my father was hurt by my mother.

I owned up to being wrong and apologized for it, and whether she realizes it now or not, I don't give a fuck. If anything, I learned that she is a piece of work, and right now, I can only afford simple and uncomplicated. Although our fling hadn't expired, and I wasn't ready to give it up, she did; better then than later anyway.

I switch Michael Bublé out and replace him with Buck Cherry. Although something heavy tries to pull me down, without knowing what it is, without waiting for it to surface, to reveal itself, I push it down and fight the urge to fall into my foul mood from the last few months.

I realize I feel a need to glorify what memories I have of July. I deliberately make myself think of reasons why *she was just a number*. I use her own words. But then I think, *Why not let go with no animosity?* I choose not to care what she wants but smile, for my own peace of my mind, to find atonement for my wrongdoing against her.

To prove to myself that I am a man of my word, I decide not to harbor any ill feelings, that I can move on and still be cordial with July. I am sure she would accord me with the same courtesy, she is, after all, making amends, and she doesn't have to. I decide not to hope, not to want anything but to extend the waving of the white flag.

I dial 411. I send her flowers from *Petunia's Petunias* with just my name on the note.

———

A black limo waits outside with Enoch in it. How ostentatious. I reluctantly walk over, and the driver with a black tux and white gloves walks around and holds the door open for me. I nod in thanks and climb in. Enoch is deep inside and pouring us both a drink.

"How modest of you to bring a stretch limo for only two people," I grumble.

"On the contrary my friend. I did find us some dates."

"Oh no. No, Enoch, we are not bringing strange girls to your sister's wedding."

"Who said they were strange?"

"I meant strange as in strangers. Why would any self-respecting woman want to go to a wedding with someone they don't know?"

"Who said they don't know me?" he defends himself.

"But they don't know me."

"Wrong again."

I look at him stunned. Who is he bringing as our dates? And why am I getting an eerie feeling about this? Enoch is so easily manipulated by women; I wouldn't trust him to exercise good judgment where any woman is concerned. The first face that comes into my mind is Simone, our PR at *Baby Blue*, he's been trying to fix me up with her since we've met her.

"Simone?"

He shakes his head no.

"Although that would have been a great idea, had I thought of it earlier." He hands me a scotch neat and clinks his glass to mine. "Salud!"

He takes a sip and then looks at me with a devilish look on his face. I stare back at him waiting for him to reveal who our mystery dates are, but he calls my bluff until I break eye contact and take a sip of my own poison.

"I would rather go solo, so I hope you are ready to entertain both girls."

"Who said they were girls?"

My eyes widen as my stomach churns. I would never put anything past him. His pranks know no bounds. I rub my temples and clench and unclench my jaws.

"Dude, you have three seconds, or I'm gonna sucker-punch your ass."

"Relax. These are women. Not girls."

He smiles and points to the door with a finger that detracts from his perspiring glass while the rest of them cling around it. The car comes to a halt, and I look out the window to a house that I vaguely recognize but can't think of how or where or who might walk out of the now opening door.

I turn to face Enoch with wide eyes and a building anticipation. He simply shrugs, keeping a cocky look on his face. I turn to find out for myself, but now all I see are two pairs of legs and white glove reaching for the door.

I scoot over to the far side of my seat and look to the direction of the gig-gling and the now opening door. My face pales, and I adjust my tie as my throat expands with shock.

Greer ushers herself in and takes her seat next to me, claiming me, and her friend Piper makes her way to Enoch. She is like a boomerang. No matter how hard you throw it, it always comes back.

"I think we are already acquainted."

Enoch pushes himself forward and busies himself at the side bar.

"I know you, and you know me," Greer whispers as she presses her hip to mine and puts her hand on my knee.

I think about the last time I saw her. I never did tell Enoch about how I ran out of her place like paper on fire. Why would she want anything to do with me after that incident? As if my actions weren't clear enough. I let out a nervous laugh as I watch her bright pink nails dig into the top of my knee.

"Are you glad to see me?"

She stretches her legs until I have no choice but to look at them as she folds one over mine. I give Enoch a look full of daggers, and he ignores me and hands a drink to his date and then one to Greer.

"What shall we toast to?"

"I know, I know." Greer raises her hand like a kindergartener. "To new beginnings." She turns to me and whispers in my ear, "And to you and me."

How original, I subconsciously roll my eyes. I feel her hand still on my leg, and my body is well aware that something alien clings to it, and it rejects it as my thigh prickles from the weight. I bring my knees closer to each other, letting her hand drop and pretend it wasn't on purpose as I propel myself and stretch over to the bar to add ice to my scotch neat.

We all raise our glasses and air clink. Greer, though, touches her glass to mine and tries to establish eye contact, but I swallow the content of my glass in one gulp, taking a cube of ice into my mouth.

Enoch stares back at me as if he is on to me, and I know he notices the tension between me and Greer, but she, on the other hand, is ignorant to the iciness radiating from my body.

I look at Enoch's date Piper, and she looks uncomfortable. She is so quiet, which I am surprised at Enoch. She is not the typical girl that he would sort out for a good time, which would explain why he would choose to bring her to his sister's wedding.

She looks out the window, and I follow her eyes to the beautiful spring day outside. The weather decided to corporate for Cornelia's wedding day. The sun is shining, only a few clouds intrude the sky.

Greer's long, pale leg rests on my knee again, and I deny myself the chance to admire it. I will myself not to find anything enticing about her although it is obvious that she is beautiful. I look back out the window and ignore the weight that pushes down on me literally as well as metaphorically.

I don't know why or what it is that causes my subconscious to repel her the way that I do. I feel certain that even if I tried to look past her pink jewelry and her pink nails and her pink smile, under all that pink, there is still another nauseating color.

Tolerate! That's the word. Now that I have her here, I will not be rude; I will tolerate her as I must and then hug her at the end of the evening, and she'll go her way and I, mine. There really is no need for me to torture myself and her by counting the ways which she annoys me, I shall simply make the best out of the worst situation and call it a night first chance I get.

Fuck, I still miss her. I decide not let my mind say her name. Instead I turn to Greer, knowing very well that the last time I tried this, I failed.

"How did Enoch convince you ladies to come?" I state my inquisition as politely as I can, keeping my shallow smile as bright as I can master.

"He just had to say your name, and we were sold!" Greer scoots closer.

I look at Piper.

"What about you Piper?" I am impressed that I find it easier to remember her name.

"I know for a fact that Greer would kill me if I told you the truth." She looks at her friend who shoots her a warning look.

"Ladies, it's okay. You both can admit that my charm and persuasion was without mercy."

Both girls roll their eyes at the same time, but Piper throws in some sarcasm, "Of course. That goes without saying."

She has an easy air about her, a genuine smile and something about her makes me like her right away.

We arrive at our venue: a large golf course decorated with wildflowers of different creams and whites. I fight the urge to look around, to search for *them*, but I can't overcome it. I make an excuse to myself that it is because I need to figure out the corners that I am going to need to avoid. I hope they are tables away from each other, although I am not quite certain that she would even show up.

"I just love weddings. Don't you?" Greer is by my side looking around with a dreamy look on her face.

"Sure," I continue my scoping.

"Me personally, I prefer a church wedding."

I turn to face her, making sure that it is me that she is talking to and not herself. I wouldn't exactly put it past her. I see her, and everything inside sours. For the umpteenth time, I don't just wish she was July; I wish she was anyone else but herself.

Enoch excuses himself, leaving me alone with his date as well as mine. I spend more time talking to Piper than Greer, which she doesn't notice. I find I actually like Piper, although I am not sure if it's because next to Greer, anyone can be intriguing.

The white tables stretched out across the large green lawn are starting to fill up with people. Everyone around is in good spirits, and I hope it's contagious.

"I've never been to such a big wedding. I can't wait to see the bride's dress."

Greer is not aware of her monologues, but I pay no attention to the two girls as they weigh the reasoning behind the color scheme of the wedding. I continue to look around to find either one of *their* faces, and then I spot her first. She came; my mother and her lover, holding hands, giggling as they walk over to their table.

I gather myself and master as much strength in me to look away and don't ever look back. I manage to do that for most of the ceremony but notice that my father came without a date. I choose not to be bothered by it and find things that I can entertain myself with, so I can leave the thought of my parents where it should stay.

After the couple's first dance, I do the most dreaded; I approach my father. We sit and just enjoy the silence while watching people.

"Hey Dad."

"Son. Long time no speak."

"Yeah." I brush the back of my neck.

"How have you been?"

"Good." I lie.

"I see business is doing well."

I just nod. My relationship with my father does not require much maintenance. We talk about business, about the future. Nothing warm or comforting about it. There is silence for a long time, and I find that I am in no rush to fill it.

"Look at your mother. Isn't she beautiful?" He longingly stares at her.

This infuriates me, and at this point, I am in no need for subtleties. I bust out without even thinking.

"Why do you pity yourself? Why do you live in this tedious continuum of being, this state of mind?"

"Because I choose to."

"We all know you choose to, but why? Why do you choose to live in misery?"

"Misery? I am happy with my choices, and I truly find that there is no reason to explain them. TO ANYONE."

"Why do you do this to yourself, Dad? Why haven't you moved on already?" I imagine I have a look of pity and disgust on my face.

"No one can ever understand. Not unless they've experienced it. Dorian, I don't want to have to explain; I don't care if no one ever understands."

"We've all experienced some form of depression at one time or another, we—"

"No, son. I'm not talking about depression. I'm talking about true happiness."

I tilt my head to the side and assess my father, wondering if he's finally become senile.

"What happiness? You've been among the walking dead for the past 10 years. Dad, I feel sorry for you. We all do."

"And I feel sorry for you. All you'll ever know is what you let yourself. What you give permission to."

I look at my father with anger threatening to tear open my chest. How can the wisest person I knew growing up deteriorate like this mentally, all because of a woman, one woman? No one should have that power.

"I hope someday you understand."

"I never will. I don't want to. Understand what? How to live with my existence as simply that? Existing? Breathing but not really living, or laughing, or making love and giving love? How is that happiness?"

"When you have enough love and memories to last you a lifetime, you do nothing but live in them, and in those memories is where you'll find me smiling and laughing and living, and making and giving love." This is the most my dad has said in many years; to me at least.

"So you live in the past?"

"Yes. For now, while I wait."

"Wait for what? For Mom to come back? She's not coming back, Dad, look at her. She moved on a long time ago."

"That's where you are wrong, Dorian. It's only a matter of time." I think he is smirking at me.

"A matter of time till what? Till you die waiting, because it's sure as hell not till she comes back, she never is."

He looks at the direction where my mother sits laughing with her young boy toy. He looks at her with a sad hopeful look before he turns back to me.

"She's going to come back. Just you wait."

"No, she won't Dad, can't you see. She moved on 10 years ago. Why do you not hate her? I DO!" I am desperate for him to see my point.

"No, you don't, Dorian."

"Yes, I do. She is a whore and a—"

"Hey! Hey! Don't talk about your mother like that. Your mother is the most amazing soul in the universe. She is brilliant and wonderful, and she gave me the most precious gifts in the world."

"She also gave you the deepest darkest sadness for the longest time of your life."

"NO, SHE DIDN'T! No, she didn't." he grunts his teeth in attempt to control his voice.

"She tore our family apart. Dad, she ran off with your son's best friend!"

"Everyone makes mistakes. You take people's breaths away by the things that you do from your heart, and the happiness you bring into their world. Not by the mistakes you make."

"That was a big mistake that she made. She almost ruined our lives. She did."

"Your mother is a supernatural force; she is too big of a force to hold on to for one person. She needs to share herself, or her spirit will die, and it's always been understood between her and I. Someone so big can be shared; it would be selfish of us, of me, to keep her only to myself…"

"And what about us? What about Llarel and I, Dad, do we not matter?"

I scoff. He is under her spell, he's deluded. *Someone so big deserves to be shared.* What is he talking about? What man sits around for 10 years, waiting for a woman he loves to come back to him? What man wouldn't fight for what he loves, if he loves someone so much that he stops living his life, waiting for her to come back? I hate her; she is the incarnation of Jezebel herself.

"Do you remember what I used to tell you and your sister when you were kids?" I try to remember one specific thing, something that pertains to the subject at hand, but he continues before I can come up with one scenario. "I used to tell you this over and over again, about money."

I nod my head as I quote my father from his earlier days, "If you hold on to money, it dissolves into your hands and disappears into that greediness. Spend it wisely and freely, and you'll always be free of it."

"Yes. Don't you see? Love is like that, son. If you don't give it space, it takes up space inside your chest and turns your insides into something else in order to fit the room you have inside you. I choose to let my love for your mother be love instead of hate or anything else."

I almost laugh at him. I am certain that the most respected man in the diamond business has finally lost his marbles. I feel sorry for him, more now than I ever did before. Even though I am taller than him, my father was always the tallest person I've ever known; the most powerful person I aspired to be when growing up. It saddens me to see him shrink, to lose respect from his business partners and employees. This is the main reason why I refused to join the family business. I refused to be anything like him.

"Look at your mother, Dorian. Look at her. She lights up the whole place. She is…" He looks at her longingly. "How can one forget about such a bright light? How can I be happy with anything dimmer?" He points to her.

"You've been living in darkness. Dad, she took her light with her when she left with Benz. She left you in a lightless world that you never came out of."

"No. She lit my torch and kept my heart warm. She still does. What we shared is enough to keep me warm for a million years, and I will stay fueled until she returns to me."

I just want to tap my knuckles against his skull and see if there is anyone in there.

"How can you see her flaunt all her lovers at you and still think she'll come back?"

"She loves me. I know she still does."

"Dad, she doesn't love you. She's moved on, and that's what you need to do."

He shakes his head at me as if I'm the one who isn't making any sense, "I promised to love her till Kingdom comes…Kingdom is yet to come. She's my Desideratum."

My eyes widen. That word. That's July's word.

"Your what?"

"Sadness is happiness because it's about her. With her, to me, misery and bliss are synonymous. I hate her, and I love her, she suffocates me yet makes me come alive."

"All the more reason to let her go," I state in desperation.

"And feel what? Nothing?" With the same desperation, he holds glass in his eyes, but it doesn't shatter. "I'd rather die."

He looks away from me, stares at the far horizon as if seeing something that's invisible to me.

"I know someday she'll come back to me. I wake up every morning think-ing today…today might be my someday. Now if I let that hope die then I'd have no reason to get out of bed and that…that, son, is misery."

The glass has become a solid blank in his eyes and walls in his emotion, so you see him but nothing else in those eyes. He looks up at my mother as she laughs at some joke over at her table, and he smiles a sad smile, "If she's happy, then I'm happy."

Through gritted teeth, I ask as I stare at her, "Even if it's with someone else?"

"Even if."

"For how long? You'll die loving someone who doesn't love you back. That is such a waste of your life."

"Do you know that she still dances?" rhetorically, my father states as he stares back at the horizon.

"No." I stare at it, too, seeing nothing but what is really in front of me, although certain that's not what he sees.

"She dances. Every Sunday morning before the sunrises, she drives up to her studio and dances."

"The studio that you built for her." I shake my head and wonder if he's been following her. He still supports her and caters to her every need, while she shares that wealth with her lovers.

"George Bernard Shaw said, *There are two tragedies in life. One is to lose your heart's desire. The other is to gain it.*"

He's still for a moment as if waiting for me to protest or agree.

"He was a wise man. But what he didn't mention was when one has neither."

I look at him baffled by my own realization that I may be the man who has neither. I become defensive right away. What's wrong with that? What's wrong with going through life safely without ever having the danger of being hurt? I would much rather walk around thinking that I am happy without ever knowing about what happiness is. Isn't the whole point of being happy walking around thinking that you are even if you are not? As long as you think you are happy, no one else's definition of happiness should taint that. If what I believe is true, then am I not contradicting my own theory? My father's happiness...why then am I trying to define his happiness with my own personal dictionary? Shouldn't his definition be just that? His.

Someone gently places their hand on my shoulder, and I turn around to find Llarel and Burr behind me. My father smiles and stands up to hug both the women.

"How are you, my darling?"

"Fine, Daddy."

My heart hurts, it cracks in several places, and I am reminded of why I tend to avoid my family, my mother and father specifically. Poor Llarel tries to be the arbitrator between all of us; always looking for a resolution to unite us. I stand up in preparation to leave when out of nowhere another visitor comes to the table.

"Hello family." My mother, all smiles.

"Gloria!" My father offers her a hug.

"Michael." My mother hugs him back.

My day gets from bad to very bad. I kiss Llarel on her cheek and whisper that I will come find her before I leave and walk away before she can protest.

"Dorian, wait!" I hear her call from behind, but I continue walking fearing what my heart might do if I see my mother smile at my father, giving him hope again while she holds the hand of another man. I roll my eyes as I see Greer approach.

"Is that your family? Aren't you going to introduce me?"

"Not now." I shrug her off as I pull Enoch to the side and mouth, *Excuse us*, to Piper who nods politely.

"What, dude? This better be good."

"Gloria is here, and she is sinking her claws into him again."

He turns to look at the direction I just emerged from with a panicked look on his face before he straightens himself up and sobers his expression.

"Don't get involved again. You know it's a lost cause."

I flex my jaw and open my mouth to respond to the same thing that my best friend has been telling me over and over again for years now, but he cuts me off.

"Your parents are both grown. They'll survive their own mistakes."

I wonder for a second if, like my father, I've locked myself into this impenetrable bubble where I cannot let anyone in nor can I get out of. I've lost Skylar, among other things, and like my father I live with what-ifs, and maybe's, and am too afraid to look outside of them.

"But she's taunting him. Look at her," I press.

He turns again to look at my parents with Llarel in between them.

"Or she is only trying to drive the point home to him."

"Not likely. I think she enjoys seeing him suffer."

"Look at them."

I turn to look at my parents,

"Look at how they look at each other. Even after all these years, their love is palpable.

I roll my eyes at his last sentence; does she have all these men under the same spell? Men, young and old admire her, even though she is the succubus. Her lover returns with drinks and takes her hand again.

"And Casanova over there?" I point at him with humor in my voice.

"I don't know what that is, but it's obviously transitory."

"Not you, too. Do years mean nothing to you? Do you not see my father deteriorate under this false hope that she'll return?"

"Why does it have to be false? Maybe their love is timeless, maybe—"

"Get the fuck out of here, man."

I walk away from him, too, and leave him speaking his gibberish to the air. Since when does he believe in all that nonsense?

I sit back at the table, which is now only occupied by Piper. I look at her and she looks back at me from across the table.

"Would you like to dance?"

She nods indifferently, "Sure."

I take her hand and lead her to the dance floor.

Nate King Cole's "Unforgettable" starts and I see my mother and father dance together, and I fight everything in me that compels me to go over there and yank her tainted hands off my father's body. This is why he keeps hoping; she keeps him on the back burner.

"I won't mind if you want to sit this one out," Piper chimes.

I feel bad that my bad mood is so palpable. Even she notices, and she doesn't even know me.

"No. This is okay."

"You are so tense. I hope it's not because of me."

"Not at all."

"Well, whatever it is, I hope it works out."

"I doubt it, but I appreciate your concern." I fight the urge to clench and unclench my jaw.

"It will. It always does."

I smile, a little intrigued by her naïveté but grateful for the effort. We dance in silence till the song comes to a close and when Natalie Cole sings, *I wish you love*, I see my mother release my father's hand, leaving him alone on the dance floor and rejoins her date for a dance. Llarel takes my father's hand and whispers something, and my father nods and keeps his head low, resting on Llarel's shoulder.

"Do you wish it was someone else in your arms right now?"

"Yes. But mostly, I'm wondering why they are playing such a depressing song at a wedding." I am a little shocked at my honesty.

"And I don't suppose it's Greer?"

I don't say anything.

"Your secret's safe with me. It's amazing though… There are so many people in the world, and yet we are all lonely."

"I guess we are all just losers of love then," I say sarcastically as I watch my mother dance in another man's arms while my father watches.

"Better to love a loser than to lose a lover," she states sadly as though speaking from experience. Quoting the quote I am much too familiar with.

I add my own experience, "No. It's better to lose a lover than to love a loser."

"That would certainly make you a loser of love then."

"I guess it would." I think of Skylar for myself, and my mother for my father, more than anyone else.

Chapter Twenty-One

"Okay kids. Break the furniture. Don't break your bones," Enoch calls from the inside of the limo as Greer follows me out.

I am drunk and dreading the headache that I am going to wake up with tomorrow morning. I don't turn around to see if Greer follows me, and I feel no need to be a gentleman. I only wonder why she is climbing out of the limo with me. I decide that if I can't fall asleep, I would much rather experience insomnia with some company than alone.

Greer stumbles out of the car and giggles before shushing the air, as if she doesn't realize that all the noise she is shushing is made by her. I take her hand as I try to hold her from falling, wishing the limo would stop, and everyone would realize that she needs to go home to her own bed. My head is not that clear, and I am not of sound mind myself, and I realize this as I start to entertain the thought of having her overnight and naked in my bed. I laugh with her as we walk to the door, and I fumble around my pockets before finding my keys and waste more time trying to unlock the door.

We walk into the semi-lit house, and Neo barks for a minute and quiets when Greer shushes him. She giggles and makes the shushing sound again, and I dance around trying to keep from falling as I stumble around trying to catch her and balance myself.

I eventually find the light and turn it on, almost blinding us both. Neo barks only a few more times before getting bored and running back to his spot on the couch by Skylar's tent.

I walk Greer to the living room and sit her down on the couch and walk over to the wall to turn those lights on.

"So, this is where Dorian Benson lives?"

"Yes. This is it." I throw myself next to her.

She looks around and giggles again, making Neo bark in agitation.

"Not exactly what I expected."

I fight the urge to burp but do it anyway, simultaneously as I speak, "What did you expect?"

"That."

I shoo my burp away by brushing the air in front of me, "You mean a home of no gentleman?"

"I mean this is more like a family home. You have a poodle; you have toys for it."

"No, those are my daughter's."

"You have a kid?"

This sobers me up right away, "Yes. Maybe. Sort of. Yes!"

"Well, you kind of do or you don't."

"Kind of," I insist firmly, hoping she drops the subject.

I lift myself up realizing that I am a little bit too sober to deal with Greer; the topic of Skylar and explaining it when I haven't even clarified it in my own head agitates me.

"You're not married, are you?"

"Why? Would that make me hotter?" I try to distract her and myself as I take two glasses from the bar and a 1990 scotch.

"No, that would make you a cheating asshole."

"I would taste just as good if I was though, right?"

I lean in closer and kiss her with a lingering taste of scotch in my mouth, careful not to spill the contents. I scoot myself as close to her as I can without touching her and let her breath sink into my pores. I feel her lust for me; her longing radiates from her skin and mouth, and I am dizzied by the strong smell of alcohol in her breath. Only with my mouth, I kiss her, and she kisses me back hungrily with her inebriating tongue.

Somebody else takes over my body even though a small part of me still hangs on to my repulsion for her. Whatever it is about Greer that repulses me seems to be vanishing or hiding away under my furniture or behind the doors and in the alcohol.

I retract from her and place the drinks on the table. I inch really close to her face and barely whisper, "No, I'm not married. Never have been." Although it doesn't seem like it would have made a difference.

She holds my face to hers and does not kiss me but sucks on my lip so hard I'm afraid it will bleed if she doesn't let go soon. I pull myself away from her, my senses momentarily returning. She stands up and grabs her glass of scotch.

"Come on. Give me a tour of your house."

She takes my hand and leads me even though I'm the one who's supposed to be giving the tour.

"What's this room right here?"

I turn on the lights and stand by the door next to her.

"This is the dining room."

"This is a pretty big room with a pretty big table for only you?"

"Yes. Just me," I say as a pang in my chest echoes my sadness. I recall the number of days it's been since used and since I've seen my Skylar. I turn off the lights and lead her to the next room before my heart catches up with my thoughts.

"This is the laundry room." I turn on the lights for a brief second and turn them back off.

"Wait." She turns the lights back on and walks over to the dryer. "There are still clothes in there."

She pushes the knob, rotates it and then pulls on it. The dryer roars to life. She looks at me and grins as she walks with her back to it and places her hands on the machine. She then hoists herself up and spreads her legs, so I have full view of her pink lace underwear.

I catch sight of Skylar's pink tutu and her ballet leotard hanging on the line by the ironing board. I walk over to Greer and take her hand and lead her out of the room, and her smile fades when she realizes I am not walking over to claim what she is offering.

She obediently follows without protest. I show her the whole of the main level turning the lights on then off and announcing the function of each room.

She listens attentively and makes no sound but periodically drinks from her glass which is now dangerously close to empty.

I lead her back to the initial room and sit down on the couch where we started. I have no desire to make my way to the stairs and having to explain Skylar's room.

"Your bedroom. Where's your bedroom?" she persists with liquid courage and no room for modesty.

"Upstairs." I nonchalantly point with my head, ignoring the implication in her voice.

She gets up and runs to the stairs clumsily climbing them two at a time and disappears at the top of them. I take the last sip of my scotch and rise. I go in search for her, calling her name, but she doesn't respond, and the only thing I hear is silence and the sound of my own clumsy footsteps. I head straight to my bedroom and find the light on, but she is not there. I turn the lights back off and start to walk out of the room when I see light under the door to my walk-in.

I tiptoe, making sure not to screech the hardwood floor. I, for a second, feel like I am playing hide and go seek except with Greer and not the last person I played this game with who happened to be July. My heart constricts. I call for her, but my shouts go unanswered, and she is to no avail. The alcohol courses my system, and I enjoy it as it travels through me using my veins as transportation. It agrees with my decision to have selective amnesia because I now have shut off any portal in my brain that leads to any thoughts of July or my baby girl, the source of my despair.

I open the door to my closet and find Greer wearing my grey shirt from the hamper. Even with the alcohol coursing through me I think about her lack of originality. She lifts the breast of my shirt to her nose and inhales it.

"You smell so good. I'm wearing Dorian Benson's shirt, I'm in his closet, and I am about to make love to him. In his bed."

The alcohol finally reaches my head, and her voice is a sexy hymn that heats my groin, and even though I don't hear what she is saying, the way she sings the meaningless words with a voice so seductive, I automatically like what she is wearing and the way that she is wearing it.

I walk over to her and bite her ear.

"You wear that better than I do."

"Oh my gosh, you are so hot when you whisper. Whisper to me again."

"Take off that shirt and slowly walk yourself over to that bed," I command in her ear.

She hurriedly obeys and giggles all the way to the bed, stopping to assess how real her fantasy is.

"Now spread your legs and shut that raw red mouth of yours."

"And what happens if I don't?"

"If you don't, I will fuck you on the foot of that bed and cum in your mouth."

"Do it. Cum in my mouth. Cum all over me." She walks back to me and slaps me right across the face. "Are you mad?" She provokes.

I like her taking command.

"Punish me, Dorian Benson. Hurt me."

This, I take as my opportunity to wear out some frustration.

I feel myself lift out of my comfort zone. I'm not sure whether I like or hate this game that she is playing. I grab her hair and pull her by it. She moans with expectation, determination, anticipation, and it's frightening to see some-one enjoy pain so openly.

I throw her on the bed and violently push her legs apart. I grab a condom on the side of the drawer and dress myself quickly before thrusting myself in-side of her without warning or introduction. I thrust back and forth, harder and harder as if I am beating her up. She moans and yells and scoops her breasts and kisses them while touching herself.

I squeeze my eyes shut as if to concentrate on the task at hand, but I am trying to mentally block her wild and crazy moaning, her teeth framed by her red mouth as she pulls me into her with her eyes, trying to capture a moment, trying connect. I lower myself and let all my, weight rest on my elbows as I allow myself to breathe through my nose on the side of her ear while I fight the nauseatingly sugary smell from her hair. What does her hair smell like? Something pink, I'm sure. I hate that smell; I hate that she is here when July should be.

I am aware of her fingernails digging into my back as she yells for me to go harder. Groaning hard, I squeeze my eyes shut and thrust deeper and faster, although I am not sure that's even possible.

"Pull my hair!" she yells.

I take a handful of her hair and lightly tug on it.

"Pull!" she snarls through gritted teeth.

It frightens me a little how she is so eager for punishment; physical or otherwise. I think about the last time and how badly I treated her, and yet here she is again. How can she be so oblivious? Is this the way she allows men to treat her? I find nothing attractive about that at all.

I go as deep into her as I possibly can, not sure if I am aiming for pleasure or pain; whether I am doing it for her or myself. I am rough and careless, and yet her moans of pleasure are augmented. She is like a wild cat or an animal in a confined area and I wonder if any of my neighbors are accosted with the sounds of her screams.

She pulls her own hair and scratches her chest making a sound that makes me think that I've hurt her, but she continues to sough beneath me and something about the way she wraps herself around me, letting me know that she is thoroughly enjoying herself, minimizes my fear of having hurt her. I pull her close to my chest and roll her over so she is on top of me, and I can see her pale face glow from within. I feel her red fingernails digging into my chest, and I hate that I love this moment, watching her turn into a wild animal right on top of me.

She bends down and hungrily sucks on my bottom lip forcing her tongue into my mouth and then pulls my tongue out of my mouth and sucks on it until I can't breathe. She stretches so her full breasts are brushing up and down my face, the weight of them making me breathe deliciously while she thrusts me in and out of her. She pulls the covers above my head until they are bunched up on top of my head. I squeeze my eyes shut as the thought of July surfaces. Another portal immediately shuts as my mind registers the thought.

Greer's pales skin glitters under the glare of the moonlight through the window. Her beautiful breasts smell of sugar and spice and all things nice, and her nipples extend on their own and taste sweet and firm inside my mouth. She is pushing into my pelvis so hard that the friction and the weight of her makes me chafe and my thighs begin to burn. I forget about anything aesthetic about this tall and pale woman, or the fire that cascades from her head down her shoulders to her back, about this moment and concentrate on my screaming lust that alcohol and Greer bring forth and out of me.

She yells all kinds of profanities and growls and moans and does all of it at once. It's hot, it's scary, it's very alien. I am so turned on by my own surprise and fear of her. I grasp her hips in an effort to control her speed and roughness. She climaxes and finishes with a loud feline growl that makes my ears pop. I follow with my own climax right behind her and feel myself decrease as a liquid part of me spews out.

She climbs off me, and I feel a sense of relief, as if my pelvis has swallowed a mint and now a breeze blows over it. The chafing, the bruising finally stills, and I feel the muscles on my gluts relax. She lays beside me covering my dewy face with her hair, and I brush it off and spit some of it out.

I lay beside her for the longest time and listen to the drumbeat of my heart finally decelerate, and the sweat on my skin turns to a fine power. I also listen to Greer as she paces herself and then finally turning to her side to face me. My first thought is to get up and go shower, but I worry that she will follow and make an intimate memory over the simple act. She smiles and tucks herself into me both our bodies succumbing to each other's heat.

"Outside of this room, beyond the moon and in the sunrise, reality will set in, won't it?" she finally speaks.

I am quiet for a moment and am anxious to find out where she is going with this.

"Once the alcohol clears out of our system, when we leave this bed, life will have no choice but to go on as it should. You will go your way, and I will go mine, and maybe we'll see each other and maybe we won't," she continues.

I shift my weight unwilling to offer a response. The smell of her hair, the sound of her voice, I start to feel nauseous. I detach myself from her hip, and she shifts closer to me, closing the little distance I just tried to create.

"Life always gets in the way when fantasy finally fleets," she continues.

I hear myself swallow and fight the warmth that makes the sleep heavy in my eyes. The reality is that I can't wait for the sun to rise, so I can be clear headed and start over without her and without July. I welcome the sunrise and the new morning.

"I'm spending the night in Dorian Benson's bed," she declares to herself.

I wonder why she keeps calling me by my full name, as if I'm a product she would see on a billboard, but could never afford, and now that I am not just a picture, real and tangible beside her, she has to remind herself that the real thing is so much better than the ten foot billboard on the side of a busy street.

"If you want to." I try to give her the option, in case she felt obligated to stay.

"What do you mean if I want to. I thought it was assumed."

"It was assumed. It wasn't confirmed."

"So, you don't want me to stay?"

"I didn't say that."

"Then you do?"

"I didn't say that either." I hear myself say the words, knowing very well I shouldn't, but I can't stop myself.

"What?"

I knew that my response would piss her off, but sometimes I surprise myself with my own honesty; I've actually considered that I may have a touch of Asperger's, although it has not yet been confirmed. It's so obvious she's been wanting this; I gave her what she wanted. Now I wish she would just leave. What else could she possibly want from me? Not a relationship, 'cause that's something I can't afford to give.

"I knew it. I totally called it. You are him, aren't you? You are the *wham-bam-thank-you-ma'am* kind of guy?"

She sits up and subconsciously wraps the sheet tighter around her as if to protect herself from me. She slaps her hair, so it swoops from her chest and falls behind her.

"Listen." I sit up and take my time constructing a sentence in my head. "I can't...I don't know...I just—"

"You just think you can lead me on and then dispose of me when you are done."

I put my hands in the middle of my face and rub as hard I can. This sounds all too familiar. Not so long ago, July said something similar. I have no time to assess my errors because Greer is now standing up, screaming as she collects her clothes.

"You think you are better than me, don't you? You saw an easy target. You pointed and shot a bull's eye, and now you want to retrieve your arrow?"

Her analogies baffle me, but I remain stoic and try not to say more that could cause much damage than already afflicted.

"Do you go around seducing innocent women, so you can add to your number of conquests?'

This maddens me. I am absolutely in disbelief that I again have to defend myself from what I see as a consensual understanding between two able bodied adults. Now I hear her, but I am not listening.

"Whoa! Whoa! Whoa!" I stop her, holding my hands up, "I didn't seduce you; you seduced me. Let's get that part straight. I didn't invite you in, you invited yourself in, you ran to my bedroom, you wore my clothes and you! You! YOU!" I am at a level of a full-blown scream.

"So, you are the innocent victim then?" She smiles as she pulls her dress over her bare skin with no underwear on, "You are the righteous one who had no choice, who is seduced by me without any control. Poor you, Dorian Benson. Life must be so hard for you."

I wait for her to say her peace, so she can leave; the sooner, the better.

"You have no control on who's heart you break. You flaunt your bright smile, flaunt your muscles, and invite women into your expensive house and whisper sweet nothings to their ear...but you have no choice, no, not you. It's not your fault you have those big blue eyes."

She rubs her eyes and looks at me before declaring, "How protected your heart must be. You keep everyone at arm's length. Shame on you. Shame on me."

She states her last point so calmly, it's unnerving. I begin to consider that silence on my part is not the way to go. I actually think I prefer her screaming over her spine-chilling and controlled voice. I wonder, for a second, if it was a good idea to show her where I live but hope she doesn't remember once she's sober.

"I can't leave right now. It's too late, and I'm too fucked up to get a cab," she lashes out.

"You can stay here. I'll go sleep in the guest room." I realize the irony.

She lays back on the bed and turns her back on me. I close the door behind me as I lead myself to the guest bedroom, remembering the last person it was designated for.

In the morning, I wake up, and Greer is gone. I'm left alone with Neo, and this house has never seemed so big. I'm done. I'm done with everything. I'm done with empty meaningless relationships, with self-pity, with wallowing. I'm done not talking to my daughter and letting Jane and Brady dictate my relationship with her. I'm just tired. I must do something about it. I just know I can't keep going on like this.

HEAL

All week, I walk around like a zombie, not aware of anything except the ringing in my ears. Prudence Rose steers clear of me and only talks to me when it's necessary. I go between *Baby Blue* and the gallery for the whole week and avoid alcohol and *Blue Baby* as much as I can. Brady is in town, tying up loose ends as they've put the house for sale and have extended for six months in the United States before they move to Spain permanently.

I've spoken to Skylar only a handful of times since I found out and Jane has been monitoring our conversations and has decided that we don't see each other until *I* calm down. I make up my mind to try to work things out with Brady first. He agreed to meet with me, the next time he's in town. I realize he doesn't have to, but I decide to beg him to let me co-parent without having to fight him legally. I know it would be a losing battle for me and for Skylar's sake.

The conversation starts off well in the beginning until it twists into something else, somewhere along the way. It seems there are two sides to Brady. I plead with him to let me into Skylar's life.

"Why should I? Why shouldn't I hurt you the way that you hurt me and my family?"

"Because you know I don't deserve it. All these years. We've gotten along so well. You can't want to hurt me after the relationship we've built raising Skylar. If you love her, you wouldn't just yank me out of her life like that. You know she wants me in it. The three of you and I are a family. Brady, there's so much more that bonds us besides us being in Skylar's life. We both lost part of ourselves that night. We lost our childhood."

"It doesn't matter. You don't matter."

"Yes, it does. I love you guys. Whether you like it or not, Skylar now has two fathers. I'm not backing down. I'm not walking away from this little girl."

He bows his head and thinks for a long time. I let the silence linger, careful not to disturb his thinking until he looks up.

"I had let go of all the negative feelings about that night. I had forgiven you. It wasn't until I find out about Skylar that I suddenly had this notion to visit the past. I don't want to. I'm not that person. You've been a good father to her, and I know it's selfish of me to want to deprive her of that."

I am relieved that Brady is the reasonable guy that I know him to be. I pinch my eyes shut and just take in what he is saying.

"I wasn't there for her," he adds quietly. "I never got to say goodbye."

"Brady, you need to heal. You can't blame yourself or me for Marcy's death. You know she had a mental disorder. It wasn't anyone's fault," I tread lightly. "I blamed myself for the longest time. I knew we were at the wrong place at the wrong time, but Marcy that day…something bad was going to happen regardless. I knew it in my bones. I just didn't think it would be that bad."

"But why didn't you stop her? Why did you go with her?"

"I went with her because I couldn't stop her. I thought it would help if I was there."

Brady starts heaving, and I've never seen a grown man cry like that. I feel my own tears as I swallow the growth in my throat.

"You were the last person she saw, and you ran away and left her there all by herself," Brady's sorrow is palpable.

"I stayed with her till she passed. She wasn't alone. I didn't leave her. I swear I only left when she was gone," I assure him.

"But you ran. You ran away and left her there. You left her there and got away with it because of your last name and the influence that your family has. What money can do!"

"I was just a kid. I didn't know what to do. I ran away because I didn't know what to do." I look down and watch the tiny puddle grow between my shoes. "I'm sorry. From the bottom of my heart, I'm sorry."

He is quiet for a while, avoiding eye contact, and now it's his turn to watch me cry as I am now sobbing uncontrollably, reliving a past, I thought I had buried forever.

"For a long time, I couldn't sleep. Every time I was happy, I felt guilty. I blamed myself. I saw a therapist for three years."

"I know. Jane told me that you beat yourself up for a long time, and I just didn't believe her. I thought she was protecting you." His face softens a little bit.

It still lingers in my mind, but I just won't bring it up. I've been wondering if they were seeing each other behind my back. Could Jane have been cheating on me? Does it even matter at this point? I just want my daughter back. I want things to be the way they used to be when life had a purpose.

"And Jane…she loved you…it was only those few months when you absolutely went insane that she came to me for comfort. I just need you to know that she loved you."

"It doesn't matter. We all should just leave the past in the past. I'm ready to move on."

"Me too, man. We have a daughter to raise."

He just pats me in the back and things feel like they have fallen into place.

As I sit at home, later, thinking about this conversation. I think about how it needed to happen a long time ago. I think about other conversations that need to happen. Talking to Brady made me realize how time plays such an important role in mending relationships and one's own mental health. I call my dad and make plans to meet with him.

After the gallery on Wednesday, I meet my dad for supper. As I drive up to the long driveway with perfectly manicured grass, I'm reminded of my childhood. All the good things and all the bad and am assured that doing this is the right decision, and I feel a little foolish that it took me so long to do this.

My dad and I engage in small talk and eat in silence for a while. He still has some of the old staff from when I was a kid, keeping the house together and preparing his meals. I eventually start the much-needed dialogue; the reason why I am here.

"I'm sorry, Dad. I've come to ask for your forgiveness. I know…"

"Son." He holds his hand up as if he doesn't want to hear what I have to say. He comes close and motions for me to sit next to him.

"Son. You have nothing to apologize about. You were true to yourself. To your own truth. I understand why you despised me."

"I don't hate you, Dad. I just couldn't understand why you would let Mom treat you like that."

"I didn't let her do anything. I couldn't do what a lot of people do—what you do—and numb myself. I have to feel."

"But you can do that. You can grieve and move on. You could have closed that chapter of Mom when you signed your divorce papers. Or take a few more years, whatever, but not 10 years. Not 10 years, dad. You have to live."

He shakes his head, and I know that I've lost him. We've had screaming matches about this topic for years before Llarel and I decided to give up and just live our lives.

"You have to live, Dad. Leave her behind. She left you behind years ago."

"I'm alive, son. I'm waiting for her to join me. She's the one that continues to chase empty relationships when all she has to do is love me again. She would be so fulfilled."

Now, it's my turn to shake my head.

"You can't fulfill her. She just doesn't know how to be full."

He listens, but he doesn't understand. He is determined to wait for my mother who is never coming back. Like a functioning alcoholic. He is so addicted to the thought of her, I wonder if she could live up to this pedestal he has set out for her.

"Dad, I'm through trying to define happiness for you. If that's what you choose to believe and you believe that, without a doubt, you are happy, then who am I to contradict you? I love you, Dad, and I don't want to be angry anymore.

"I love you, too, son. I pray that someday you tell me that you've loved so passionately and so unconditionally. Only then, will I believe that you were truly ever happy.

"I understand now what I want. I do. I know what I want."

I stand up and head straight to July.

"Dorian, you can't keep showing up like this. I'm starting to think you're a stalker." July stands firmly at her door, clearly having made up her mind not to let me in.

"I know. Sorry, but I had to come see you," I say with a big smile on my face, sure, more than ever, that what I'm about to say will change everything.

"What do you want?" her voice is so hostile; it deflates my wide smile. I cannot read her stoic expression.

"You! I want you." I smile again, hopeful.

I take out a piece of paper that I've kept in my wallet ever since the time we went to my parent's cabin. In my father's study, I had found one of his poems, titled "Bare." Just as it is, in my father's handwriting, I give it to her. She starts to unfold it, and I close her hand with the paper inside it.

"Just take your time reading it when you're alone. If it touches you; if it, at all, tugs at your heart the way that it does mine, please give me another chance."

She shakes her head and starts to hand me the piece of paper. I carefully push her hands back to her.

"Please."

She just stares as me.

"I'm going home, and I'll be there for the rest of the weekend. Meet me for dinner tomorrow for a fresh start. If you don't show up, I'll know not to ever bother you again. This is me with my heart on my sleeve telling you that I really hope you show up."

She clears her throat and starts to say something, but I kiss her forehand and turn to walk to my car, hopeful that this is not the last time I see her.

I drive home in silence with the windows down. My mother is on my mind the entire drive back. I pull up to the driveway and park the car outside of the garage. I just sit in the car and am determined to make amends. I have been wrong about a lot of things, but I want to make right the things that are in my control. I think about how bitter I've been over my parents' divorce and their relationship ever since. How I need to give them a second chance the way that I've been given a second chance with Skylar. I pull out my phone and go to my Contacts List. I stare at my mother's number for a long time before I dial it. She picks up after a few rings.

"Mom."

"Dorian, is everything okay?" I can tell that she is a little bit panicked. It's been years since I've just called her out of the blue with no agenda.

"Everything is fine." She is silent, surely waiting for me to state my case. "I was just calling to say hello…"

She sighs in relief and I think she starts crying.

"…and to ask you to do something for me."

"Anything. You know I will do anything for you, Dorian."

"You need to let him go, Mom. Set him free."

"I know," she admits, barely audible. "I know."

"I've been so angry with you. I'm just so tired. I need to let it go. I need to forgive you."

"I'm sorry. I'm sorry, Dorian."

"I forgive you, Mom. I'm ready for us to move forward."

"Me, too. I love you, son."

I hang up.

Saturday morning, I wake up feeling monumentally lighter. I feel rejuvenated, like I've slept for days. I decide to drive over to Llarel's. I need to tell her about my long-awaited conversation with our parents. It's about 11:00 in the morning when I get there, and I find Enoch's car in her driveway. This is the second time that I've found him here without me, but because I'm familiar with their dynamic and how much they hate each other, I don't even suspect that I will walk into what I find next.

I knock once and let myself in, and Burr is surprised to see me. "Dorian. Hi… Were we expecting you?"

"Morning, Burr. No. I just wanted to talk to Llarel. Is she here?"

"I don't think she was expecting you. If you wait here, I'll go get her."

She motions for me to stay put, and she seems a little panicked, but I don't pay too much attention to her behavior as I follow her to Llarel's room. Llarel is sitting on her bed, still in her bathrobe, which is unlike her to not be dressed this late in the morning. Before I even say anything, a man walks out of the bathroom in his towel with another one on his head, so I can't immediately tell who he is until he starts talking.

"Babe, your water pressure is amazing."

I recognize the voice. It's Enoch. My eyes widen, and before I even become aware of myself—

"You son-of-a-bitch!" I yell and tackle him to the ground and punch him hard in the face.

There is a chorus of voices yelling, and Llarel and Burr are screaming in the background.

"Dorian, stop! We're married," I finally hear Llarel crying.

"You're what?" I raise up off Enoch.

"Enoch and I are married," she repeats desperately.

"Uhuh, no." I shake my head. My jaw clenching and unclenching, my hands still balled up into fists.

"It's true, man. I love her."

"You shut up. Shut the fuck up." I shove him back in the bathroom and grab Llarel's arm and pull her outside to the courtyard.

"Explain!"

She tells me everything. It seems I was so caught up in my own depression, life was going on without me. Turns out that Llarel and Enoch have been secretly seeing each other, and they had eloped. Llarel had long made amends with our parents, and she has a healthy relationship with both of them, and they even know about Enoch. I've been selfish and pathetic and just assumed that life revolved around me.

My life, in a nutshell, has been compacted into the last several months, and things are suddenly clear to me. I've met with a lot of people in the last few days and all of them have been an integral part to my growth, whether it be as a father, or friend, or a son, or a brother, or a lover. I can't go through life alone without them. I selfishly lived a life of a solipsist, but I realize now that that was a foolish notion. I've been sleep-walking. I couldn't grow, couldn't feel, couldn't love without all these people. I can admit out loud that I need them to be complete.

I congratulate them both and return home feeling like today is the beginning of my new life. I pull up to my driveway and next to the main garage is Jane's car. Brady, Jane, and Skylar all get out, and Skylar runs to me. I lose it. I bend down and pick her up and just hold her. I haven't seen her for so long, her hair is so long, and she has blue braces all over her mouth. I cry like a baby. I hold her so tight, I don't think I'll ever be able to let go. I don't know how long I hold her, but she lets me hold her for as long as I need to. She smells like hope. She smells like home. Right now, at this moment, nothing else matters.

It's the first of September, and I couldn't tell you where I was or what I was doing this time last year or three years ago. I decide to no longer worry about the past. What matters is how I live my life moving forward. In a few hours, I will know whether July chooses me or not. She might not show, but she might. All of me is hopeful that she does. I have chosen; I have decided that I will love like I have a heart that will never break, share like I have an abundance of everything, forgive like I've been forgiven, and to do like I've never done before.

BARE

Drown me.
Baptize me with death.
Hurt me so bad it feels good.
Banish me.
I just want to die,
I want to expire in your arms
and cease to be.
Only you can hurt me,
deep through my muscles and
into my bones.
Bury me.
Burn inside of me until I burst
into flames.
I just want to die,
I want to perish with your arms around me.
Nothing is enough,
breathing digs my grave.
Swallow me.
Hold me inside your mouth until
I dissolve into you and disappear inside of you.

Envelope me with your hair.
I can't live;
I just want to die loving you,
breathing you,
wanting you.
Take hold of my soul and never give
it back.
I bleed you.
I infect myself with you and die with
every breath you take without me.
I'm hypnotized by you,
consumed under your spell.
I hunger for you,
crave your every fiber.
Confine me.
Turn me inside out.
Run through me like a fever,
Don't let me go.
Don't ever let me go.

CPSIA information can be obtained
at www.ICGtesting.com
Printed in the USA
LVHW012119070821
694771LV00010B/796

9 781649 579072